RIDE OR DIE #1

A Devil's Highwaymen MC novel

By *USA Today* Bestselling Author
Claire C. Riley

Ride or Die #1 A Devil's Highwaymen MC Novel

Copyright © 2017

Written by Claire C. Riley
Edited by Amy Jackson ←awesome badass!
Cover Design by Eli Constant of Wilde Book Designs ←also an awesome badass!

This book is licensed for your personal enjoyment only. This book may not be resold or given away to other people. If you would like to share this book with another person, please purchase an additional copy for each reader. If you're reading this book and did not purchase it, or it was not purchased for your use only, then please return and purchase your own copy.

This is a work of fiction. Names, characters, businesses, places, events, and incidents are either the products of the author's imagination or has been used with that person's permission.
Thank you for respecting the hard work of myself and for purchasing this from a reputable place.

About the book

Ride or Die #1
A Devil's Highwaymen MC novel

"We would blow up this world and create something beautiful in its ruins"
Jesse & Laney 1985

We were each survivors of our upbringing: lost, unloved and afraid. Yet like moths to a flame, we couldn't stay apart.
We loved.
We lost.
We fought.
We cried.
And then we shattered each other's hearts.
Jesse was a hard man; a biker outlaw for the Devil's Highwaymen MC Club. I was Laney; the daughter of a dead mother and a father that didn't know or want me.
We were doomed right from the start.
But this was our romance.
And this was our disaster.
And hopefully, this would be our second chance.

BOOKS BY CLAIRE

Odium The Dead Saga Series (zompoc)
Odium Origins Series (zompoc)
Limerence (*The Obsession Series*) (pnr)
Out of the Dark (dystopian)
Twisted Magic (pnr)
Beautiful Victim (dark thriller)
Blood Claim (horror)
Wrath #3 in the Elite Seven Series (NA romance)

Co–Authored Books with Madeline Sheehan:

Thicker than Blood
Beneath Blood & Bone
& Shut Up & Kiss me

MC Romance

Ride or Die a Devil's Highwaymen MC series
Devil's Highwaymen Nomad Series:
Crank #1
Sketch #2
Battle #3
Fighter #4
Cowboy #5

RIDE OR DIE #1

A Devil's Highwaymen MC novel

By *USA Today* Bestselling Author
Claire C. Riley

For those of you who love the *unlovable*.

PROLOGUE

1973

It was different this time.
I didn't know how, or why; I just knew it was.

Even at five years old, I knew the difference between high and dead.

Watching her from my hiding place, I stared silently at her slack jaw and pallid skin. Her chest was rising and falling, quickly at first and then slowly. Her mouth was open, the hue of her pale tongue just showing near her yellow teeth. I wanted to reach over and close her lips, but was too afraid to.

I didn't want to touch her.

I never did—not when she was like this.

She wasn't my mommy when she was like this. She was a monster.

Gone were her loving arms and soft kisses, and instead she was…someone else.

I glanced at the ticking clock above the fireplace, wishing that I could make time speed up. I didn't know what time it was; I couldn't tell the time yet, but Butch had said he would be home by 4 p.m. and he had pointed to where the hands of the clock would be at that time, so I would know. But it seemed so far away now, and I wondered if I should go get help, because this time was different.

I knew it.

I started to crawl out from under the kitchen table. It was a big old wooden thing, with scratches and score marks across the top. Underneath was where Butch had carved both of our names. I almost bumped my head as I was getting out from under it; I was getting bigger now, but I ducked just in time, thankfully. My head still hurt where she'd hit me and I rubbed it tenderly, feeling the large bump below my fingertips.

She would be sorry when she came around—she always was. I was her Jesse, her little gunslinger, and she loved me more than the moon and the stars. She couldn't help the things she did; she was sick. I understood that.

She was lying on the hard linoleum floor, and I crawled to her, my blue eyes blinking slowly as I took in her face, my body drawing closer to her.

Vomit had dribbled out of the corner of her mouth. It smelled bad, like stale cookies and old carrots. The needle was still poked in her arm, and even though Butch had said never ever to touch them, I couldn't help myself. I reached over and I pulled it out of her arm, because I didn't like it still being stuck in her. If I could, I would have taken all of the pain and the poison out of her too, so I could have had my mommy back.

A small drop of blood bubbled to the surface where the needle had been stuck in her skin, and I wiped it away with the sleeve of my dirty gray hoody.

Her skin felt cold—too cold for my mom, because Mommy was always warm and soft. I chewed on the inside of my cheek, wondering what to do. I made my way to the living room and got the blanket from across the back of our brown sofa, and then I dragged it back to her in the kitchen, carefully avoiding the vomit, and I laid it over her, hoping it would warm her enough.

I sat and watched her, not wanting to move in case she needed me. I still had the needle in my hand, so I put it on the table, out of her reach, and I prayed that Butch would come home soon, because he would know what to do.

Her body got even colder, and I curled up against her side and put my arm around her to help keep her warm. I needed to pee but didn't want to leave her alone, and at some point I must have fallen asleep and peed myself, because when I woke up, Butch was picking me up and I was wet and cold.

The fading sunlight shone in through the kitchen window, glinting off the wedding band she still wore. It had a green stone in it that matched her eyes. She used to tell us that that was why Daddy had given it to her.

Butch carried me across the kitchen.

I cried for her then, for my mom.

I reached out with my small hands and clawed at Butch as he continued walking, ignoring my tears and screams.

But Butch continued on, whispering in my ear that we would be okay together, that he wouldn't ever leave me. And that he would always be there for me, no matter what.

We passed my daddy on the way out. He was standing in the doorway with his arms folded over his huge chest, his gaze on Mommy.

I knew he was my daddy because Mommy kept a picture of him by her bed. She told me he was the love of her life. She told me that they were like the modern-day Bonnie and Clyde and that they were meant to be together forever.

But Daddy rarely came to visit, and when he did, he didn't look at Mommy like he did in that picture, even though she still looked at him like that. And he never, never, ever looked at me with anything like that. I was scared of Daddy, even though Mommy said not to be.

Daddy turned away from the kitchen, and put the house phone to his ear, the long green curly cord dangling like spaghetti. He sounded angry-sad, a mixture of the two things. And I could understand that, because I felt the same way. I was angry-sad. Angry because I didn't want to leave. Angry because I wanted my mommy to stop hurting herself like this, and sad because I already missed her.

All three of us left the house—me, my big brother Butch (who was carrying me), and my daddy, and we climbed in daddy's truck. And then we left, and I never saw my mommy or my home again.

Butch said it was going to be okay, and not to cry because it would make Daddy angry. He said Mommy was in a better place now anyway. But I didn't understand.

Because how could my Mommy be in a better place when I wasn't with her?

CHAPTER ONE:
1982
Jesse

"Goddamn it, Jesse, will you stay out of my stuff!" Butch stormed as he came towards me!

I dove off my bed with Butch following me quickly, my hand still clutching the magazine I'd found under his mattress. I threw open our bedroom door and ran down the short hallway to the main part of the clubhouse, taking a good look at the breasts of one of the club skanks as I raced past her.

"Looking good, Bernice!" I called, laughing my ass off. She blew me a kiss and kept on walking, her pert ass swaying hypnotically.

Butch was already tiring, and there was no way he would catch up to me. He may have been big, but I was fast. And he was still hungover from the night before. I slowed down and turned around, finally dropping the magazine and flipping him the bird with both hands while laughing.

And then I was flying through the air and landing on my ass.

I looked up at the ceiling, the wind completely knocked out of me, wondering what the hell had just happened, when Dom's face came into view, his wolf-grey eyes staring down at me. He grinned and then moved out of the way for Butch to grab me.

"Shit!" I swore as he grabbed me by the scruff of the neck and dragged me up to my feet. He was taller than me, but not by much considering our five-year age gap. He was much stronger, though; it would be years before I could catch up to him. That much I was certain of.

Butch was almost six foot already, and built like a machine. So much so that I'd worried for a while that he was using steroids or some shit. But no, it was all just good, honest, home-grown Hardy DNA. His skin was, so far, bare of tattoos and piercings, though I'd seen him flipping through magazines for weeks picking out what he wanted.

Butch slammed me against the wall of the clubhouse and glared at me, and I waited for his fist to hit me. But it never came. Instead he shook his head and started to laugh and dropped me back on my feet. He scrubbed the top of my head and tapped the side of my face with the back of his hand.

"Thought you were gonna piss yourself then for sure, little brother," he laughed and started to walk away. Dom, another member of the club and Butch's best friend, was laughing and followed Butch.

I looked around the clubhouse, noting some of the other members were watching us with annoyance.

This wasn't a school house and it sure as shit wasn't a playground, yet I treated it as such because this place was all I had. The bikers grumbled and cursed when I ran around the place causing havoc. The women, though, they loved this shit.

"Ladies," I said, taking a quick bow, and a couple of the skanks gave me a wink.

I jogged to catch up to Butch, and started following him outside, matching my stride with his. He was my big brother, and despite how annoying I could be—his words, not mine—he didn't mind me hanging around him all the time. He was seventeen, almost eighteen, and prospect for the Devil's Highwaymen, our dad's MC club, and I was proud as shit to be able to call him my big brother.

He'd been looking after me since I was a baby, and had never made me feel like anything I did was any trouble to him—more of a father than my own had ever tried to be. We pretty much lived at the clubhouse, which was normally unheard of, but Dad spent almost all of his time there, so it had made sense to convert one of the wings of the old motel into a home for me and Butch to live in. At first we thought it meant we'd see our dad more, but that wasn't the case at all. We probably saw him less, though neither of us really cared. Hardy, our dad, was not father material. He was a brutal dictator to both of us, though he had a particular dislike for me, for some reason.

Outside the day was hot, and Butch straddled his bike and slipped on his shades and a helmet. Dom did the same and they both started their bikes. Butch rode a custom Harley Davidson Road King, and he smoothed his hand over the dark green body as if it were a woman's body. My brother loved that bike.

He saw me watching him and smiled. "You still saving up?"

I nodded.

"Good, because me and you, little brother, we're going to build you the best damn bike there's ever been."

I smiled broadly. "It'll be ours," I said.

He reached over and scrubbed at my hair, and I darted out from under his grip self-consciously even as he and Dom laughed.

"Where you going?" I asked, wishing I was going with him.

"Club business, little brother," he said with a smile. "Just waiting on Gauge turning up."

"When will you be back?"

"Soon enough," he replied, not even the slightest bit irritated by me.

"I want to come with you," I said. I hated it when he left.

"You'll be prospecting soon enough, little brother, then we'll both get patched in and the real fun will start." He smiled again.

Despite my father being the president of the club, I wasn't really a member of the club. I was too young right then and if I was honest I wasn't even sure if my dad would let me join. The man always seemed to have beef with everything I did. So I got told two things about club business: jack and shit. It pissed me off, but Butch assured me that he was saving a spot on his right-hand side, just for me—no matter what our father said. I just needed to grow up some more was all.

The sound of a bike—and not Dom or Butch's—drew our attention and we all looked over to the main gates of the clubhouse, where one of the prospects was pulling them open. Gauge, the Devil's Highwaymen's sergeant at arms, pulled through the gates and parked his bike, duck-walking it back into position alongside all the others that were lined up. A skinny pair of arms were wrapped around his waist, and Butch pulled his glasses off to get a good look at who it was. Whoever it was, was female, I decided.

Gauge never had a woman with him.
Never.
Club whores were more his thing.

Not only that, but Hardy, didn't let just anyone roll up in there. The Devil's Highwaymen were responsible for almost half of the drugs moving in and out of the state of Georgia, and despite most of the cops in the county being on our payroll, precautions still had to be adhered too.

I looked over at Butch and he shrugged at me without looking away from Gauge, already sensing the question I hadn't voiced yet.

"This should be interesting," Dom said, lighting a cigarette and settling in for the show.

I turned to look back at Gauge as he cut the engine of his bike and pulled off his helmet. He eyeballed Butch and Dom, barely noticing me standing there, and then he climbed off his bike with a grunt. Gauge was around twenty-eight or thirty, with dark hair and a long beard. Most days he wore a little black beanie hat that we all ridiculed him for, because come rain or shine, he always wore that damn hat. He was quiet, never talking when talking wasn't called for, but he was a mean motherfucker underneath his quietness.

Gauge started walking toward us, and then I saw *her*.

I swallowed hard and tried not to stare, *despite* the fact all I could do was fucking stare.

Even at fourteen years old I knew she was fucking special. My kind of special.

Long, straight, dark hair that hung down her back and warm olive skin just begging for me to touch it. She was wearing some little black ankle boots and a pair of cutoff denim shorts and a T-shirt so thin I could practically see her bra underneath. And when she lifted her leg off of Gauge's bike, I swear her legs led the way to heaven.

She paid none of us any mind as she followed Gauge into the clubhouse, her hands clutching onto the straps of the backpack on her back and a hard scowl on her face as she glared at Gauge's back. I followed her with my eyes until she was out of sight.

"Looks like little Jesse is in love," Dom laughed with Butch, and I turned to glower at them both, feeling my cheeks heat up.

"Shut up! She's just a nice piece of ass is all," I said, scratching at my chin and wishing I had a badass beard like Gauge's.

"Wouldn't let Gauge hear you saying that about her," Pops said, cracking open a bottle of beer as he came outside.

Pops wasn't actually our pops, but he was the pops of the clubhouse. He'd been a member since almost the beginning, and though he didn't really get too involved with club business anymore, his vote still counted, and so did his advice. His wife had passed a few years back, and he spent practically all day and every day down at the clubhouse now, drinking and fucking anything he could get his hands on. "Nothing much better to do till I die," he always said. And I couldn't disagree with him.

"She's a little on the young side to be his old lady," Butch said, lighting a cigarette and making the comment that I had been thinking. I reached for his pack of cigarettes and he slapped my hand away. "No fuckin' chance."

I didn't bother to argue with him on it, knowing he never backed down and I had some inside anyway. Pops came closer, downing half his beer in one gulp. Despite his constant heavy drinking, he was still one of the wisest men I knew.

"That's Gauge's daughter," he said.

"Gauge has a daughter?" Dom laughed. "Get the fuck outta here, old man!"

Pops spat on the floor and took Butch's cigarette from his hand. "Sure is. She's about thirteen or so. Her mom was some hooker down in Florida that he used to hook up with some years back. Social services got in touch with Gauge last week after her mom found out she had HIV and wanted him to take care of the kid now that she had one foot in the grave. He didn't even know he had a kid."

"How'd he know she's really his? I mean, if she was hooking the kid could be anyone's," Butch replied.

"Got the DNA test done to prove it. So she's coming to stay with Gauge until he can think of somewhere better for her to be." Pops turned and started walking back inside.

"Why can't she just stay with him?" I said, following Pops and ignoring the wolf whistles from Butch and Dom. We headed back inside and I looked around for her, but couldn't locate her anywhere. The door to Hardy's office was closed and the blinds were drawn, so I guessed that they were in there.

"He don't know how to take care of some kid—'specially not some girly!" Pops laughed. "'Sides, this ain't the life for a kid."

"I'm doing all right and I'm a kid. Ain't nothin' wrong with my life," I protested, already panicking about her leaving before I've even managed to get to know her.

Shit, before I'd even managed to speak to her.

Pops patted me on the shoulder. "You ain't just some kid, Jesse."

"Sure fuckin' feels like it sometimes," I replied, meaning every word of it.

Hardy had no time for me whatsoever. Never had and never would. I wasn't sure what I'd done to deserve such hatred from him, but I'd given up asking long ago. Now I just accepted it and got on with my life. Between Butch, the other club members and the women that came around to cook, clean, and fuck, everyone had a hand in my raising somehow.

Everyone but Hardy.

"Not you, Jesse. There's great things in your future, that's for certain," Pops replied.

He winked at me and walked away before I could say anything else. He walked over to the small bar area that we'd had made for him the year before. One of the club bitches, Rose—a stunning redhead on the right side of thirty and way too fucking young for him—was behind the counter, her long red hair tied tightly at the top of her head, and when she popped open a bottle of beer for him her breasts swayed like Jell-O shots in her top. She handed the beer to Pops as he slid into a seat across from her and patted his knee for her to come and sit on it. It was kinda gross to watch, but I couldn't deny that the man still had it. I mean, Rose was barely thirty and Pops, well, he was as old as shit.

I left them to it, not wanting to watch the live sex show, and headed back to mine and Butch's room, not sure what to do with my day now. I hadn't known Butch was going out of town for the day on business and I'd thought that we'd probably just hang out. But he'd been doing that more and more—club business or hanging with Dom and not me. I got it, and I understood it; I was just a kid and he was practically a man. Didn't mean I had to like it, though.

I shoved my hand down my jeans and scratched at my nutsack as I pushed open my bedroom door, my gaze skipping over to my bed to find a girl sitting on it, one leg curled up underneath her ass, her eyes glued to my small television screen.

Not just any girl, but *her*.

I stopped scratching, my hand frozen in place halfway down my jeans, and I blinked. She started to look up so I quickly took several steps backwards, letting the door shut, and then I stared at the closed door, wondering what the fuck she was doing in my room, sitting on my bed.

"There's a girl…in my room," I mumbled to myself, checking both sides of me to make sure Gauge or Hardy wasn't around. I caught a whiff of my own armpits and grimaced at the smell. "Shit," I muttered.

I took another step away from my bedroom and quickly headed to the bathroom, where I knew the deodorant was, and I lathered myself in that shit so that I didn't stink like the prepubescent teenage boy I actually was. I rolled my shoulders and puffed out my chest and headed back to my room, taking a big breath before I pushed the door open.

But she wasn't there anymore.

I blinked and let out my breath and walked inside, spinning around in a circle and wondering if I'd imagined her sitting there at all. I sat down on the edge of my bed and continued scratching my nuts, my gaze straying to the television, which was still turned on. The news was on about some miracle cure for the common cold that some doctor down in Canada had made. I turned the volume up to listen.

"A simple reprogramming of the DNA to reject the cold virus is all it takes," he said, and I almost laughed. The guy looked like Doc from *Back to the Future*. I flicked the TV off and looked over to my pillow, ready to grab Butch's porno mag from where I'd hidden it that morning. But then I noticed that it wasn't under my pillow anymore; it was open on my bed.

The woman in the picture had huge breasts, with dark round nipples that looked like saucers on them. And someone had drawn lines around them to make them look like glasses. Not just any someone, but her.

I smirked and looked up, wishing she'd come back so I could talk to her, but she didn't.

At least not that day.

In fact, it was two years later before I saw Laney again.

CHAPTER TWO:
Present day
Jesse

"Jesse! Stop it!" Laney cried, her anger and frustration with me obvious by the tears running down her face and the fact that her hands were balled into fists at her sides. "I know you don't mean it—you're still in there somewhere, I know you are."

I paced the room, my whole fucking body feeling like it was on fire because of the anger that was burning through me. I dragged my hands through my hair and gritted my teeth, trying to hold in everything I wanted to say.

I'd regret it.

I always did.

Laney came toward me, her hand outstretched, her eyes beseeching. "I can't deal with you when you're like this, just calm down, baby."

She was close then, close enough to touch me, but of course she didn't. She knew better than to get too close to me when I was like this. I'd never hit her, and never intended to, but fuck knew what I would do.

The anger had been building in me for the past three months—a constant inferno ready to explode. I'd kill everyone when it did,—I knew I would. So I'd held it in the best I could. But it was never enough; it always seeped out a little.

Besides, I wanted her to hate me, didn't I? I wanted that look in her eyes to die. It was for the best—at least for her. The only way to protect her was for her to see what a fucking asshole I was and finally hate me. *Then* she would let me go.

The sound of Casa's bike roaring outside sang to my ears and Laney looked nervously toward the door, her eyes looking even sadder because she knew I was going to bail on her, again. I always did when shit went bad between us. It was my way—our way. It was either that or I'd end up killing someone because I couldn't control my temper.

I rolled my shoulders, feeling them click and pop in their sockets, and I willed myself to calm down. Deep down, somewhere below my simmering rage, I knew that I was being an asshole. My girl loved me—always had—and I was trying to push her away. One day she'd meet someone else, someone that wasn't fucked up like me. She'd get married and have their babies and live happily motherfucking ever after.

That's what I wanted, right?

Yet despite me wanting to do the right thing, I was still a possessive fucker that wanted to kill every other man alive when I closed my eyes and imagined another man's hands pawing at her too-soft skin, her tight ass and flat stomach. And her mouth—those perfect lips that kissed me better every night—wrapped around another man's—

"I gotta get outta here, Laney," I said, turning from her, anger still itching through my veins like heroin.

Laney's soft hand reached out and touched me, gently at first and then firmer, until she pressed herself against my back, feeling bolder by the second. Her hands grazed around my waist, over my leather cut as she clung to me.

"Don't go, Jesse. Stay with me, please," she said between kisses across my shoulders. "I don't know why you're doing this to us, but please stop. There's only so much I can take before you break us."

I even considered it, the temptation of her sweet touch and her hot breath enough to make me feel something other than just anger for a few blissful seconds. I closed my eyes and pressed the heels of my hands to my eyelids, wishing I could push all the bad away so it just left me and Laney and all the good shit we could accomplish together if I just stopped fucking it up for us both.

"I know you're hurting, baby, and I am too. Let me help you," she whispered, and I knew she was crying again.

But she couldn't help me. No one could help me. Not after what I'd done. And if she knew, she'd think the same thing too. So this was how it had to be.

I shrugged out from under her grip and didn't even attempt to rein it back in as I slammed my fist into the wall directly in front of me. Laney let out a sharp cry as my hand went through the dry board, the material crumbling around my fist.

"You just don't fuckin' get it, Laney," I said, pulling my hand free and walking away.

I left the house, slamming the door so hard I thought it bounced back open, but fuck it, I didn't care. My boots stomped over the flowerbeds and grass that Laney had loved so much about this house, and I didn't care about that either.

I didn't fucking care about anything anymore.

Casa was sitting on his bike outside, talking to the piece of ass from next door—Kiera or some shit like that. He saw my stormy expression and whispered something in her ear, and she turned to look at me, her eyes bugging out at my furious scowl. Casa slapped her on the ass and she turned tail and left immediately.

I climbed on my bike, pulled my helmet on and started it, barely able to hear anything but the rushing of my blood.

"Everything okay, brother?" Casa asked.

I looked at the window, seeing Laney standing there, the curtain pulled back far enough for her to look out. Goddamn, she was the prettiest thing I'd ever seen, especially then with the sun starting to fade and casting an orange glow over our house, over her. Her hair hung long and dark down either side of her face, all the way down to that tiny waist of hers, but it was tucked just behind her ears. Tears streaked her beautiful features, and the sick part of me thought she looked even more beautiful with those tears on her cheeks, because those tears were for me. I owned them.

"Nah, brother, things are not okay," I said. "Not at all."

Casa nodded an okay, already understanding and putting a plan together to help me sort out my fucked-up head. He knew me well enough to help me do what needed to be done, and I trusted him well enough to put myself in his hands. Because if there was one thing that Casa knew how to do well, it was how to deal with my shit. He started to ride and I forced myself to tear my gaze away from Laney, and our home, knowing that I was going to regret it.

I followed Casa, and we rode until the sun set and the moon was high, and then we pulled into a small bar just outside our town called The Ranch. It was filled with far too many people for such a small place, meaning there was always way too much testosterone floating around and leading to just what I needed right then: a fight.

I parked my bike next to Casa's, shut off the engine, and hung my helmet, and then we were walking across the parking lot and heading inside. The doorway was already crowded with people trying to get some fresh air while they ironically smoked cigarettes, filling their lungs with the nicotine that got them through the days.

The women's eyes appraised me and Casa as we closed in and the men put protective arms around their waists, letting us know that they had already been claimed, as if that meant anything to either of us. If I wanted one of their woman, I'd have her because no one was fucking man enough to try and stop me. And Casa, shit—panties practically fell at his feet wherever he went. That was just the way it was. The way it'd always been.

We pushed past them all and headed on in. The music was already loud and thumping from outside and practically ear-splitting on the inside. Bodies were squashed against one another, women's skin glistening in sweat as they ground against each other on the dance floor, putting on a full on show for the men watching from the sidelines. The whole place reeked of sweat, stale beer, and pussy, and I fuckin' loved it, immediately feeling myself loosen up.

We reached the bar and I held up two fingers when the barmaid looked in our direction. She nodded and turned away, and a minute later two ice-cold beers were set in front of me. I handed one to Casa and slid twenty dollars across the bar toward the barmaid. She was slim, with curves in all the right places and a mouth that looked like it could suck the chrome off a bumper.

She smiled at me, fluttering her long, fake lashes and hoping to keep the change. I sucked in my bottom lip, seeing her gaze fall to my mouth and her eyes dilate as she watched me.

She was a pretty little thing, though she was wearing too much crap on her face—thick eyeliner under her eyes and bright red lipstick—and with her short skirt and tits practically spilling out of her top, I couldn't help but stare.

"Come on, bitch, get me a fucking drink!" a man, if he could even be called that, yelled from the other end of the bar.

Spell broken, she turned to him, muttering her apologies to both me and him as she grabbed a beer and popped it open. As she handed it to him, he grabbed her wrist and pulled her closer, whispering something into her ear. For all I cared right then, he could have been her old man and he was whispering sweet nothings to her, but I turned and handed Casa my beer and he took it with a sneer, already knowing what I was about to do.

I stormed my way around to the other end of the bar, cracking my neck as I walked, and watching as other people take note of me and get the hell out of my way. I'm a big guy, and most people moved when they saw me coming. If it wasn't the wide set of my shoulders or my six-foot three frame, it was the dark gleam in my eyes that got people's asses out of their seats. Laney once said that she could swim in my blue eyes, that's how deep they were, but right then they were filled with anger and hate, and were probably blacker than the deepest hole in hell.

I reached the guy just as he let go of the barmaid's wrist, almost pushing her away like a cheap piece of meat. Her gaze flicked to me, and I smiled at her and then wasted no time in grabbing the back of his neck before slamming his face into the wooden bar. He grunted out and I smiled in satisfaction as the vibrations from the hit ricocheted up my arm. His body went slack and I dragged him from his stool, letting it fall to the floor as I pulled him backwards and outside into the cool night air.

A path was cleared as I threw him to the ground and he tumbled and rolled, finally rousing as his body came to a stop near the sidewalk. He groaned and put his hands to his face, his eyes not focusing on anything else but the blood on his hands as they pulled away.

But I was only just getting started.

I stormed over to him, enjoying the blood gushing down his face and the fear flashing through his eyes as he saw me and struggled to get back up on his feet. I cracked my knuckles as I got closer and he scooted away, not being able to find the energy to stand up and fight me like a real man.

"Please, I'm sorry," he begged, and I heard Casa laughing from somewhere behind me. "I didn't know she was your woman."

"She's not." I spat on the ground next to him and cracked my neck from side to side.

"Then why do you care?" he yelled, sounding angry.

"I don't," I replied, enjoying the look of fear that crossed his face.

I stood over him, sneering down as he pleaded apologies for whatever it was that he was supposed to have done. Dumb fuck didn't even realize that he hadn't done anything—and even if he had, that wasn't why I was doing this. He wasn't really the reason I was doing this.

I was doing it because if I didn't find some way to get rid of the anger, I'd self-combust.

I kicked out at him, my heavy booted foot kicking him straight in the face, and I watched in satisfaction as more blood gushed free from his nose. Cheers and chants echoed behind me, but I ignored them all in favor of my red-hot fever, the burning self-hatred and anger that ran through me like liquid fire, and I kicked and I kicked and I kicked…

At some point Casa decided that the guy'd had enough, and he was probably right because the dumb fuck wasn't moving anymore and the crowd that was cheering me on had gone silent—a clear sign that I might have gone too far.

Casa laughed and grabbed the collar of my cut before pulling me away. "Come on, loverboy, let's go get you that pussy now, yeah?" He laughed and dragged me back to the bar entrance, slamming the door open and pulling me inside.

Casa pushed to the front of the line, but neither of us could see the hot barmaid from earlier, so instead he ordered us two more beers from the barman, who eyed us both warily but served us regardless.

That time Casa paid, and then we headed further into the bar, my chest finally feeling free of some of the deep anger I'd felt only twenty minutes earlier. My boots were covered in blood, and now that the red mist had cleared I spared a thought for the poor fuck outside who I almost just kicked to death. I patted Casa on the shoulder, glad that he stopped me.

I downed most of my beer in one go before spotting my barmaid collecting bottles at a table near the back, and I handed my almost-empty bottle to Casa.

"You sure about this?" he asked, his couldn't-give-a-shit-façade slipping.

I hated myself.

I hated my life.

I hated everything that I had done to get me to this point.

This wasn't going to make any of that right. The dark days and even darker nights would be a whole lot worse after this, but it was the only way. I'd tried everything else. This was the one thing on the list that there wouldn't be any coming back from.

I patted Casa's shoulder in answer and walked towards the barmaid.

Fuck no I wasn't sure about this. But I was a disease, an' all I did was spread lies and hate and death. I needed everyone I loved away from me before it was too late.

*

I came out from the storeroom, my gaze going over the packed bar until I found Casa. The girl dancing in front of him turned around and leaned in to kiss him on the mouth and as usual he pushed her away.

I raised an eyebrow at him as I picked my bottle of beer up from the table and downed the entire thing in one go.

"Come on, baby," she purred. "Just one kiss."

But she didn't know Casa, because if she did she'd have known he didn't do kissing. He pushed her away again, done with her. "Get the fuck out here, girl," he said, and she stumbled off with a pout.

"Come on, let's go," I said, already done with the place for the night. I was done with everything.

"You get what you need?" he asked, finishing his beer.

"I got fucking something," I replied darkly, the hate settling in my bones further.

If there was a hell, then this was it.

"Probably fucking chlamydia!" he laughed.

"Fuck, don't say that," I groaned, dragging a hand down my face.

Another woman had already slipped in front of Casa and taken the first bitch's place, but Casa slapped her on the ass and pushed her away. "Laters, girl."

I should have apologized for making him miss out on so much pussy that night, but he could get that shit anywhere, and I had no doubt he'd get some by the end of the night regardless. He always did. Hence the name Casa, short for Casa-fucking-nova.

We threaded our way through the overcrowded bar and back outside. The dumb fuck from earlier was still on the ground passed out, but there was a crowd around him by then, and the sound of sirens could be heard in the distance. A couple of people looked over at me as I headed to my bike, but no one said a damn thing to me about it. And no one would say a damn thing unless they had a death wish.

No one fucked with the Devil's Highwaymen and expected to walk away from it in one piece.

I started my bike and pulled on my helmet, feeling shame so bad that my stomach hurt. I looked down at my blood splattered boots and gave a shake of my head.

I was a piece of shit.

I was worse than a piece of shit.

I was shit covered in shit.

I'd promised her I'd never cheat, that she would be the only woman for me till the day I died, yet here I was. That was where I'd had to go to get her to hate me. To make her give up on me. Part of me was scared at the thought, because I knew that once she found out, then that'd be it. It'd be truly over.

I'd die without her. That was a fact.

But she'd live without me. That was a fact also.

And if anyone was worth dying for, it was her.

"Ready, brother?" Casa said, and I nodded.

He'd been with me every step of the way. Lots of brothers tried to stem my flow of anger and hate, but they saw I was a lost cause. But not Casa; he'd stuck by my side through it all. I was gonna have to cut him loose soon too, though.

When your hearts filled with this much hate there ain't no room for much else. Family, friends, they all had to go.

I cracked my neck again, and I pulled out of the parking lot and back onto the blacktop with Casa following me that time.

I was a bastard, I knew I was, but it was too late for me to change.

CHAPTER THREE:
1983
Jesse

I stepped out of the shower and wrapped a towel around my waist before smearing a hand across the mirror and taking in my reflection.

My beard was starting to thicken up, finally. I rubbed a hand across it, thankful.

I had been an early bloomer, already starting to fill out into the body of a man by the time I was twelve years old. But it had been my damn baby face that had always been the giveaway to my age. Still was in many ways. But a beard—a beard would make that all better.

Butch's fist thumped against the door. "Hurry up, Jesse! I need to piss!"

"Fuck off!" I called back, only half-joking.

He'd been out drinking until around five that morning, and had woken the whole damn clubhouse up when he got back in and started to party. Not that I minded too much—it wasn't like I was some good choirboy in bed by nine, and of course he'd brought women and booze back with him, so who was I to complain?

"I'm gonna break it down if you don't open up!" he yelled, thumping the door again.

I ignored him in favor of brushing my teeth and spraying on deodorant, because fuck him, that's why. At some point he started to shoulder barge the door, but I still didn't open up for him. A crack started to form down the center of the door and I smirked at it, knowing he'd catch shit from Hardy when he saw it. I was done then, so I reached over and twisted the lock before pulling the door open and letting Butch fall inside, hitting the dirty floor with a loud crash.

He groaned and rolled onto his back, putting his hands over his eyes, and I looked down at him and laughed. Butch never knew when to stop drinking, and he never could handle his liquor.

"Aren't you supposed to be riding out later today?" I asked, kicking his leg with my foot. He'd only been back two days after a long stint on the road. It pissed me off that he was leaving again so soon, but it was what it was, and I wasn't about to complain like a little bitch. He was my big brother, not my dad.

He groaned again and started to sit up. "Fuck," he mumbled. "Hardy's gonna kill me."

"Yep," I laughed again.

"Why didn't you stop me?" His words were slurred, but his plea genuine.

I helped him up off the floor, and he patted my shoulder and headed to the toilet before pulling himself out and taking a piss, one hand on the wall.

"Old enough to know better, brother," I replied. "Besides, I did try but you were so caught up in snatch that there was no tearing you away."

Butch finished pissing and tucked himself away, a sloppy grin on his face. "Yeah I was." He shoved his long hair out of his eyes and walked toward me, and I high-fived him as he went out into the hallway and headed back to the main clubhouse. I trailed after him, not ashamed to be almost naked in front of any of the bitches there.

Like I said, I was filling out nicely and my almost-sixteen-year-old ass wasn't shy about my body. I headed to the small kitchenette and brewed some coffee for us both before bringing it back out to Butch in the hopes that he'd sober up some more before he took to the road. He was lying across one of the sofas, an arm flung across his face again to blot out the light, and I placed his coffee on the table in front of him after clearing some of the bottles out of the way.

The place was a mess: women and bikers half comatose in every available space, and all of them practically naked. Looked like a damn orgy happened the night before. I wasn't concerned with who was going to tidy up the mess, though; that was the women's job, and they'd be up and sorting it soon enough.

It had been this way for as far back as I could remember. Partying, sex, drugs, alcohol, and then someone else cleaning up the mess for me. Butch and I had raised ourselves when we'd been brought there. Well, between the old ladies looking out for us and making sure we were always fed, and the brothers watching our backs making sure we were safe—but we'd done the rest. Can't say we didn't do a damn good job, either.

Hardy, our dad, practically never spoke to us—not unless it was to bark an order. Though I could tell he had a nicer streak for Butch than me. But most of the time we avoided one another at all costs. Ain't nothing good ever came out of seeing my dad. He made sure we were fed and clothed and that we went to school, but that was where his parental responsibility ended.

Of course it was different for Butch. Now that he was a patched-in member of the Devil's Highwaymen, he had to deal with Hardy much more—taking orders from him, going on runs, club business. But not me; not yet anyway.

I slurped some of my coffee down, and that seemed to rouse Butch. He sat back up and grabbed the coffee before drinking some. I opened my mouth to speak, but a loud banging came from the front door and both Butch and I stared at each other in confusion.

Men began to stir all around us, all of them coming out of their drunken stupors as the banging continued. Butch sobered up automatically, and he pulled out his gun and stood up before telling me to stay where I was. Of course I didn't, and I followed him to the door as some of the older brothers came charging out of rooms, guns in hand. We both looked up at the screen above the entrance, the image showing us who was outside.

"You know her?" Butch asked, and I shook my head. "She looks about your age."

I shrugged. "I ain't seen her before."

"You fuckin' sure, Jesse? Cause she seems about your age, and Hardy will blow his nut if you've got angry teenage bitches coming around here causing shit for him!"

"Dude, I'm telling you I ain't seen her before."

The girl was looking down, her hair covering most of her face, but as she reached up to bang on the door again I got a good look at her face.

Long dark hair trailing down her back, smooth olive skin, dark eyes that sucked me in and a mouth which was begging to be kissed.

"That's Gauge's kid, ain't it?" I said, suddenly feeling self-conscious in only a towel.

"Yeah," Butch replied, unbolting the door, the tension leaving his body. He looked back to the center of the clubhouse. "Back it up, brothers, it's just Gauge's kid."

"The fuck she doing here?" Skinny called to us, looking pissed off—and rightfully so. He tucked his gun into the waistband of his jeans and scratched at his bare chest. His jeans were on, but he wasn't zipped up and he was obviously butt naked underneath, the denim riding low enough on his hips that he was practically hanging out of them.

"Put your junk away," I snapped, hating that she'd see him half-undressed.

Skinny was kind of new around there, barely twenty-five and already fully patched. The brothers loved him because he was a crazy motherfucker who never backed down from a fight and was always the life and soul of every party, and the women all loved him because he was supposedly hung like a fucking donkey.

Without waiting to be asked, Laney pushed her way past us as soon as the door was opened, and I saw right away that she had been crying. Hot tears pouring down her olive cheeks, making them flush pink.

"Where is he?" she said, her gaze on Butch as her chin trembled.

"Who?" Butch asked.

She nodded. "Gauge? Where the fuck is Gauge?"

Butch scratched his head. "Ain't seen him for a day or so now. He's out on club business, but he'll be back tomorrow. You all right? Someone fuck with you?"

Butch looked over to Skinny, who stepped forward, his hard gaze on Laney while he waited for his orders of who to kill and how quickly to do it. Because if anyone had fucked with her, that someone was a dead already.

"No!" she sobbed. "Well, yes, sort."

"Need we to kill someone, darling'?" Skinny said, coming forward.

She looked at the serious look on Skinny's face, realizing that he was serious. And then her gaze traveled down to his near-naked body. "God, you bikers are all the same, aren't you!" She threw her hands in the air and stormed past me and Butch.

Butch looked to me for help, as if I'd know how to calm down a hysterical teenage girl. "I'll go call Hardy. Keep an eye on her," he said, slamming the door shut and bolting it. He patted me on the shoulder as he passed, nodding his head to Skinny to follow him. By the looks of things, Skinny was as happy as a pig in shit watching Laney's tears soak through her white tee. I couldn't blame him either, because goddamn she looked hot as hell right then. Small denim cutoffs, dirty ankle boots, and a T-shirt so tight I could practically see her nipples. I worked hard to control my own teenage hormones and the fantasies that were running through my mind.

"I've got this," I said to him, my teeth gritted.

A slow grin rose on his face and he nodded. "All right, I feel you," he said, and walked away.

I looked back at Laney, unsure what the hell to do to calm her down now that I was alone with her. "Can I umm, get you anything? A coffee? Tissues? Are you hungry?" I asked. I could actually cook—damn good at it too. Not that I'd let any of the brothers know, since they'd be getting me to cook for them all the time. But I'd cook for her if it made her smile.

She stopped crying and looked up to me, and she almost swallowed me whole with those big beautiful eyes of hers.

"Do you have beer?" she asked. "I could really use a beer right now."

Beer.

I could definitely do beer.

Neither of us were old enough to be drinking, but that had never stopped me before, so I figured why the hell not.

"Sure, come on," I said, leading her toward the bar.

I went behind it and pulled out two bottles from the small fridge, popping the lids off and handing her one. She took it from me and drank some, her bottom lip glistening as she pulled the bottle away from her mouth. I took a mouthful of my own beer and looked away from her nervously, watching Butch pacing up and down while he tried to get ahold of Hardy, or Gauge, or fucking anyone who knew what to do with a teenage girl.

I looked back to her, noticing she was staring at me. Her tears had dried up, but their tracks were still blatant down her face. She took another sip of her beer, seeming calmer, thankfully.

"Are you old enough to even drink that?" I asked, already knowing the answer but wanting to get more information out of her. The truth was, I had been infatuated with her since the first time I saw her, yet in reality, I knew barely anything about the girl.

"Are you?" she snapped, her eyes narrowed.

I tightened the towel around my waist and rolled my shoulders before downing half my beer in one go. "That shit don't matter for me," I replied. "But you, you're Gauge's kid, I don't want to catch shit for giving you that." I nodded toward her bottle.

She shook her head and raised her bottle to her lips. Fucking perfect lips they were as well. Pink and fat—no doubt soft too. Fucking perfect for…

She downed half of her beer, just like I had, and I twitched beneath my towel because it was damn hot watching a woman down beer like that. Especially when she dragged the back of her hand across her mouth to wipe away the excess beer. Fuck that was hot.

"I'm Laney. Not just Gauge's kid," she said. "And I'm a big fucking girl who can take care of herself, but if you're afraid of big bad Gauge…"

My eyes widened and I snorted out a laugh, more than happy when she let out a sigh and then retorted with her own laugh.

"I'm not afraid of shit," I replied.

"Everyone's afraid of something," she said with a shake of her head.

I quirked an eyebrow. She was right; everyone was afraid of something, but then most people hadn't lived the life I had.

Laney sighed. "Whatever, look, I'm sorry, I shouldn't take my shit out on you. Gauge just makes me so fucking mad." She screwed up her hands and scowled again, but she looked cute when she was angry, not scary, so I couldn't help but smile again.

"Gauge?" I asked and she nodded. "I think dads are meant to make us mad," I joked, but the joke fell bitterly between us.

I swallowed and started to sweat, not sure what to say then, and Skinny was still staring at us, waiting to see if I was going to make a move on her and practically salivating down himself as he stared at her ass perched on the edge of the stool.

"Name's Jesse," I said. "That was my brother Butch that you just almost killed with the door."

"Sorry about that too," she said, her cheeks turning pink and making me think how pink they'd be after she came. "He was just collateral damage."

I shrugged and laughed. "If he wasn't so hungover, he would have had quicker reflexes, so we'll just blame him for the near-death experience and call it quits," I replied, enjoying the shy smile that crept up her face.

"Near-death experiences seem to follow me around," she said, turning suddenly wistful and looking away.

She was beautiful even when she was sad. Maybe more so. Because when her expression cleared of all the other conflicting emotions, it left her skin smooth for me to see the truth of who she was underneath it all. And what I saw in her was so close to my own feelings that it startled me.

"You sound like me now," I said, and she watched me intently, her gaze almost seeing into my soul.

"You're always here," she suddenly said, her mask slipping back into place just as quickly as it had fallen.

I shrugged again. "It's where I live."

A small frown came across her forehead and I wanted to reach out and smooth it out with the pad of my thumb, but thought better of it.

"You live here? I thought this was just like a meet place or something, and that everyone lived somewhere else," she asked bluntly.

I chugged some more beer, not really wanting to get into it, yet with her I felt like the truth was the only good enough answer to give. And if I was going to be truthful with anyone, I wanted it to be her.

"Butch and I, we're brothers and we came to live here when we were little kids. Hardy's our dad and we uhh, well, neither of us get along with good ole' dad. Never have, and I doubt we ever will." The images swirled just below the surface, but I refused to give too much thought to them.

"Why? Where's your mom?" She knew as soon as she'd asked the question what the answer should be, though I wasn't sure how because I wasn't exactly an emotional guy. "Shit, I'm sorry! You don't have to answer that." Her cheeks flushed pink and she looked away, embarrassed.

"It's okay, it doesn't bother me. My mom died when I was real young and I don't remember much about her anymore. Hardy took me and my brother in, but since he was here practically every night, working until real late, it just made sense to fix us up with permanent bedrooms here. Everyone in the club raised us, so we have a big-ass family, which has its upsides as well as its downsides," I chuckled.

I wanted to ask about her, about what things she enjoyed doing, what things she hated doing. I wanted to know everything from her favorite childhood memory to her favorite band. She was pussy-whipping me without me even getting a scent of her on my fingers. It was fucking ridiculous. No, *I* was fucking ridiculous, yet there was nothing I could do to stop the patheticness from shining bright like a three-hundred-watt bulb in the black of night.

I took another drink of my beer and tried to calm myself down before I said or did something stupid. She looked back to me, her gaze watching the bottle at my mouth. She swallowed when I did, and I swear to God I think we shared a fucking Hallmark moment.

She looked away first, and I cleared my throat and scrambled for something to say to break the awkward silence that had fallen between us again.

"Why were you so upset?" I asked bluntly, because I needed to break the tension between us because all I could think about right then was her nipples and how painfully hard I felt below my towel.

"What?" she asked, turning to look back at me.

"Before—when you got here, you were upset. Why?"

"It doesn't matter now." She looked away, her gaze straying to the sofas where Skinny was sitting, his gaze still trained on Laney, one hand resting on his lower stomach. "Who's he?" she asked, and I felt my anger spike at the hungry look in her eyes.

I clenched my teeth and tried not to sound too pissed off. "That's Skinny."

She nodded in response but didn't say anything. She looked away from him and silence fell between us. I couldn't think of a damned thing to say to the girl—at least not anything that would keep her attention on me and not on Skinny, the club, or anything that was going to upset her. I stared down at my bottle, my gaze straying to hers where she was picking at the label and tearing it off into little pieces. I thought I'd read somewhere that doing that was a sign of sexual frustration, and I looked away, my hard-on hurting even more. The silence continued to grow until it became uncomfortable and I had to speak to break it up before I had a fucking heart attack. Butch was on the phone to someone by then—probably Hardy—and Skinny kept on looking over at us and trying to catch Laney's eye again.

"So, what's it like living with your dad?" I asked, trying to make small talk with her. It wasn't something I was good at, but I wanted her attention on me and no one else.

"My dad?" She snorted and took another sip of beer, and once again my gaze went straight to her mouth. "If you can even call him that. All he does is give me money to buy food and school supplies and tell me to keep out of his way and not cause any trouble for him. I'd hardly call that dad material."

She didn't realize how much I agreed with her on that, but that wasn't the time to get into it with her. All around us, people were starting to wake up, thanks to Laney's sudden entrance. Women were standing up on unsteady feet, still half-naked, and bikers were pulling them back down to be fucked before the day's work began.

Groaning echoed over to us from one of the small black sofas in the center of the room, and Laney turned to look. From our position we could see every fucking thing and Laney's eyes went wide when she saw Pops ramming into some bitch that Butch and Casa had brought back with them the night before. He was holding onto her waist tightly, and she was rolling her hips against every one of his thrusts and grunting.

The woman was old enough to be there, but like always, she was still way too young for Pops. She'd barely woken up properly when Pops had flipped her around and held her legs wide open, his gummy grin leering down on her as she grunted and groaned.

I'd grown up seeing that sort of shit, so I didn't bother me in the slightest, but it was shit that Laney didn't need to see. That was for damn sure.

"Come on," I said, moving from around the bar. I took her hand automatically, feeling an instant connection as our skin touched. Laney looked away from Pops and the woman he was fucking and looked at our linked hands, and then her gaze rose to meet mine. I swallowed, feeling like I was going to have a fucking heart attack with the way she was looking at me.

"Where are we going?" she asked breathlessly.

"No one needs to see old, wrinkly nutsacks first thing in the morning," I replied, and I felt a wave of something rush through me when she laughed. The sound was like fucking birds singing or some romantic shit like that.

Fuck me, I was a pussy.

"He's really old," she whispered on a laugh, her fingers squeezing my hand tightly. "How does he even get it up anymore?"

I laughed back and pulled her down the hallway, not sure where I was heading until we reached my room and I pulled her into it. I shut the door behind us, still laughing. I didn't want to let go of her hand, but there was no reason to keep holding it anymore so I reluctantly let it go.

"Yeah, I don't even know how he still has the energy for all the fucking he does, to be honest," I replied, feeling my cheeks go hot as I looked around the pigsty that was my room. For the first time ever I felt embarrassed by the mess. Dirty clothes were piled up in the corners and moldy plates and cups were edging out from under my bed. And the smell. Good fucking Lord, how had I never noticed the damn smell before? It smelled like ass. Jesus Christ, I wouldn't be surprised if she ran screaming from the room.

"He fucks a lot?" Laney said with surprise. Her face was still flushed pink, but it seemed more from humor than her tears now. And fuck me, I liked it when she said the word *fuck*—mainly because all I could think about was fucking her right then, and her saying the word made me hopeful that she was thinking the same things as me.

"Oh yeah, Pops fucks more bitches than the rest of the brothers here put together, and they fuck a lot," I replied, laughing. My laughter died on my lips when she didn't join in. I'd said something wrong, I figured, but I wasn't sure what. I grabbed the back of my neck, feeling uncomfortable.

"Why do you do that?" she said, sounding angry again, her face screwed up as she glared at me.

Made my dick even harder.

"Do what?"

"Call women bitches. It's degrading, and you're better than that."

I was flustered for a moment because that sounded too much like a fucking compliment for my liking. "I uhh, I don't know, that's just the way it is," I replied, and she shook her head, looking even more angry so I tried to explain further, because for some reason, what she thought made me stand up and give a shit. "The women that come here, they come here for one reason and one reason only. They know what they're getting themselves in for. That's why they're just bitches."

"Oh yeah?"

"Yeah."

"And what do they come here for then?" she snapped, her eyes on fire. Goddamn, I wanted to drag her down to my bed right then.

"To fuck," I said bluntly—probably too bluntly, but I couldn't help it. Her anger was giving me a raging hard-on and I was horny as hell. "Those women out there come here knowing full well that they're only here to be filled and fucked and suck anything that's given to them. They enjoy the party and the lifestyle that we give them. They don't expect anything else. Some hang around for a few months until they realize that sleeping with half the club ain't going to make 'em an old lady, because who wants to make some dirty skank their property when she's been through all their brothers? But some just show up to party, wanting to get with the bad-boy biker. Everyone knows their place and everyone is cool with that. So don't look down your nose at any of it until you understand the way it works." I finished my little speech and clamped my mouth shut. I was defensive of our club because it was all I had ever known, and I was sick of civilians coming in and looking down their noses at our way of life.

She opened her mouth to speak and then closed it again just as quickly, looking shocked that I'd spoken to her that way. She seemed to correct herself and took a step toward me.

"And what's my place, Jesse?" she asked, and I nearly poked a hole through my towel when she said my name because it was the most seductive thing I'd ever heard in my life.

"What?" I asked, punch-drunk on her scent as she closed the gap between us.

"You said everyone knows their place. So what's my place in all of this?" She took another step toward me, and I swallowed and willed my cock to go down before she saw the effect her words were having on me.

"You're Gauge's kid," I said, my words feeling thick in my mouth.

"And you're Hardy's kid," she replied.

I nodded and we both stayed silent, taking in each other's expression. Laney broke the moment first and began walking around my room, looking at the posters on my walls as she did. She was wearing a small backpack that had a shit-ton of buttons and patches all over it. My room wasn't exactly huge, so it didn't take her long to finish the inspection, and by the look of disgust on her face the verdict clearly wasn't good.

She went and sat on my unmade bed, kicking her dirty little ankle boots off and crossing her long brown legs. Who the fuck knew when it had last had the sheets cleaned. Probably fucking never. I decided right then that I'd be getting one of the club bitches to wash my sheets later that day.

Laney took another sip of her beer and looked at the posters of naked women and bikes spread all over my walls, her eyes falling to the one right above my bed—the one she had drawn on almost two years ago to the day—and she smiled.

At some point in the last year, Butch had moved out of our room, deciding that he needed his own space, which was fine. It gave me more room for my things—not that I had much. Just my magazines and tapes, records and clothes. But still, it was good in some ways to have more privacy—especially as I'd grown into more of a man. I'd started getting interested in building bikes in the last six months, and manuals and bike parts filled a large plastic tub in the corner. One day I was going to build myself the most badass beast of a bike.

I realized that I needed to get dressed, since I was still just wearing a towel and my hard-on was blatantly fucking obvious beneath it now. I grabbed my jeans from the end of my bed, the chain that I had hanging from the belt loop to my wallet jangling noisily. I stepped into the jeans, forgoing underwear, and I started to pull them up. My towel was just about to fall when Laney looked back over at me and I quirked an eyebrow at her and smirked.

"Ya mind?" I asked, gesturing with a nod of my head as I let the towel fall at my feet.

"Oh god, sorry," she said, her cheeks flushing even redder as she quickly looked away.

A small smile played at the corners of her mouth as she turned to stare at the poster again. I pulled my jeans all the way up and kicked the damp towel into the corner of the room with the rest of the mess. My hard-on for her seemed much less obvious hidden behind some denim instead of a flimsy towel, but it was still pretty fucking obvious and I willed little Jesse to calm the fuck down before Laney noticed and ran screaming from my room, calling me a pervert.

Laney reached over to the side of the bed and picked up a pen. She knelt up on my pillow, her snatch so close to where I put my face every night that I knew that I'd never wash that fucking pillow ever again. I grabbed my crotch and pulled at my dick, which was pressed up against the zipper, trying to escape from my pants and get into hers.

She leaned up higher, her T-shirt rising enough so that I got a look at the smooth olive skin on her back that was just begging for me to run my hands down it. She drew a smile underneath the breasts that she'd previously drawn sunglasses on, and then she turned back and smirked at me, giving me a little wink and laughing.

I flushed bright red and smiled back. I dragged a hand through my still-damp hair, grabbing the back of my neck where it felt painfully tight. Her eyes traveled over me as if seeing me for the first time. Her gaze strayed to my bare chest, to where I knew the muscles were hard and firm, a *V* forming at the base of my stomach that looked like a fucking arrow pointing toward my dick. She swallowed, watching as I lowered my hand from the back of my neck and took a step toward her, and her tongue darted out to wet her lips.

I opened my mouth to say something to her when my door opened and Hardy filled the space. He took one look at Laney kneeling on my bed, beer in hand, and her perfect ass practically hanging out of her cutoffs, and then he took in me with my own beer and just a pair of low-hanging Levi's hanging from my hips.

"Are you fuckin' kiddin' me, Jesse?" he growled out, and if I could have shriveled up and vanished right then, I would have. "This is Gauge's kid, and you're thinking of fucking around with her? Have some fuckin' respect, boy!" He reached over and grabbed me by the shoulder before pulling me around to face him. He glared right into my face, anger pouring from his hellish eyes and boring straight into mine.

"It's not what it looks like, Hardy," I gritted out. "I was just trying to get her away from the shit happening out there." I jerked a thumb out the door, but I already knew it was pointless arguing with him. Shit had been getting worse with us the older I got—as if the more I grew into a man, the more he hated me. Clearly he saw something in me that he didn't like, but I'd be damned if I knew what it was.

"The shit out there?" he snarled, his dark eyes boring into mine like he was trying to drill a hole through my fucking skull.

"The fuckin' and shit," I responded, desperately trying to contain my anger.

"You puttin' your brothers down now too, boy? There's somethin' wrong with what they're doin'? I know you ain't popped your own cherry yet, but you tryin' to tell me you're a faggot, boy? That you don't like pussy?" He sneered at me, and though my chest burned with an anger so fierce that all I wanted to do was lash out, I refrained, knowing it would be pointless.

My dad had been a fucker to me my whole life, and I had never known why. We'd come to live with him as boys, me more of a boy than Butch, and I had never felt anything but hate coming from the man, no matter how much I'd tried to please him.

The man hated everyone and everything, and never had a good word to say about anything—me especially. And up until then, I'd never really cared. I stayed out of his way and he stayed out of mine. The way I figured it, soon enough I'd be a prospect and I'd force some damn respect from him, one way or another. Ain't nothin' I did gonna change the way he felt about me until I did—that much was obvious.

But right then a hatred I'd never felt before blossomed to life in my gut, roaring its way up my spine.

And he fuckin' knew I'd popped my damn cherry too! Bitch named Apryl did that for me when I was barely fourteen years old.

"No, sir," I replied through gritted teeth. "Nothin' wrong with fuckin' women, and nothin' wrong with what my brothers were doing, just didn't think Gauge would want his kid seeing Pops banging some twenty-year-old bitch with her tits and cunt hanging out."

"Also, sir, if I can interrupt," Laney said, coming forward with one hand on her hip. "Only uneducated fucking idiots use the word faggot, Sir—you're not an uneducated fucking idiot, are you? I mean, this is a time for spreading love, not hate. At least if the sixties taught us anything. At least that's what my mom used to say."

I saw the change in Hardy's face—the look of utter shock that she had just spoken to him like that, because *no one* spoke to him like that, ever. I don't think his own mother ever got away with speaking to him like that. And if it had been any other woman, she'd have felt his hand across her cheek and more, but Hardy couldn't do shit to Laney because she was Gauge's daughter. Though I had no doubt in my mind that Gauge would catch shit from Hardy for this mess.

We were at a standstill: Laney with one hand on her hip and her eyebrow quirked like she hadn't just called the meanest fucking president this side of Georgia a fucking idiot, me still held in Hardy's grip and more in love with that woman than I was with my own dick, and Hardy looking like he couldn't decide whether to kill me, kill this chick, kill us both, or walk away.

Decisions decisions…

"If you weren't Gauge's kid, I'd make you regret talking to me like that, girl," he growled out, glaring at her, but she only smirked in response, clearly not afraid of anything.

"For once I'll be glad that I am then," she retorted.

"I should slap some respect into you!" he said like a dark promise. And I don't know what happened. A switch flipped inside of me and I took a step toward him.

"You ever fuckin' touch her and I'll kill you myself, Hardy," I spat out, meaning every word of it.

Hardy's eyes went even wider, and if I thought he'd hated me before, it was nothing compared to what he felt for me then. His face went red and his grip tightened on my shoulder until I knew it'd leave bruises for days, his eyes practically popping out of his head. But I refused to show any weakness. Instead, I gritted my teeth and held his stare as he squeezed harder and harder until I thought he was going to break my shoulder. And even then I refused to back down.

"Hardy?" Butch came to the doorway, his nostrils flaring and his eyes growing dark when he saw Hardy's grip on me. "Gauge is on his way," he said tightly.

Laney was so close to me that I could feel her own anger radiating from her body. Hardy glanced between us, his features softening fractionally as he took in my expression before he finally let me go with a push. I stumbled but righted myself and held his stare, my shoulders back and feeling like I had a renewed sense of power.

"If you've laid one hand on her—" Hardy began, his eyes still narrowed on me.

"He didn't," Laney interrupted. "I believe in free love but I'm not about to get myself knocked up like my mom did."

My face was hot, my heart pounding in my chest so hard it hurt. I kept my hard gaze on him, not willing to back down that time, and I could see that it was getting to him, but neither of us were willing to break.

Laney pushed past all three of us and out into the hallway. "Men are pathetic," she mumbled as she walked away.

I kept my gaze on Hardy and he kept his on me. Eventually he tapped the side of my face with his open palm, his mouth turning up into a sneer, before he turned away and followed Laney.

Butch looked at me seriously. "You okay, Jesse?"

My mouth turned up into a wide smile. "I've never been better," I replied truthfully.

He smirked before turning and walking away too, and I closed my door behind them all and went and sat down on my bed. I looked up to the poster and the new doodle Laney had added to it and I smiled, despite myself and despite everything that had just happened.

And then I reached over and grabbed my pillow, pressing it against my nose and hoping that I could smell her on it.

Something had changed that day.

I knew it and Hardy knew it.

What the repercussions of that change would be were anyone's guess.

CHAPTER FOUR:
Present day
Jesse

Hands beat at me and Laney's hysterical voice broke through my sleep and tore me from my drunken dream. Something hit me hard in the back of the head, and I rolled over to face her.

"You bastard! How could you? How fucking could you?"

I was lying on the practically new sofa in our living room, the cushions that Laney had so lovingly picked out barely six weeks ago either squashed to hell beneath my body or cast to the floor.

"What the fuck, bitch? Are you crazy?" I grumbled and blinked up at her, wondering what the hell her problem was.

She threw another shoe at me. "Don't you dare fucking say that to me!" she screeched again. "And don't call me 'bitch!'"

"Fuck, woman, stop already!"

I looked up to see Laney standing in front of me, hands on her hips and eyes full of fire. But damn, she looked hot as fuck in her little gray AC/DC T-shirt and black panties. Her hair was wild around her beautiful face, and I must have still been drunk because I reached for her with a droopy smile, hoping to get a little action before I had to go down to the clubhouse. She slapped my hand away but I reached for her again.

"Come on, baby."

She screeched and threw another shoe at me, the heel just missing my face by an inch.

"What is wrong with you?" she screamed, batting my hand away, and then she dropped the rest of her ammunition—an armful of shoes—and stormed away from me, her hair flying up behind her like a dark cloud.

I sat up and scratched at my beard, a little pissed off that she'd cock-blocked me so brutally. I pulled a shoe from next to me and flung it to the floor before reaching for an open bottle of beer on the coffee table and taking a swig. I looked down, seeing my clothes in a heap on the floor by the sofa that I was sitting on. I rolled my shoulders, my body tense and stiff after sleeping on the sofa, and I reached around to rub my neck when I felt the scratch marks on my back.

"Fuck," I murmured, dragging a hand down my face as I remembered the previous night.

Losing my shit with Laney for no goddamned reason.

Nearly kicking someone to death.

Fucking some random piece of ass in the bar.

Yeah, it was all coming back to me now, and I didn't like any of it.

"Fuck," I muttered again, standing up. Though why I was so surprised by any of this was anyone's guess. This was what I had wanted, right?

I turned in a circle, taking in the mess I'd made when I got home—half-eaten pizza and empty beer bottles, but no Casa. I'm guessing he found warm space in someone's bed last night. Down the hallway I could hear Laney crashing around, drawers and doors slamming open and closed, and I reached down and grabbed my jeans off the floor and stepped into them and then headed to our room to try and calm her the fuck down before she ruined our new furniture.

I pushed open our bedroom door and found her suitcase open on the bed, several items already thrown inside it, and my heart slammed against my chest so hard that I thought I was going to pass out from the pain of it.

She was leaving me. Finally.

The pain in my chest tightened until I couldn't see straight. This was what I had wanted—what I had been pushing for. I wanted her to leave me, get away from me before I ruined her like I ruined everything else. Yet, the thought of her leaving brought a fresh wave of pain. Almost physical in its strength.

Fuck, I couldn't do this. I couldn't lose her. I grabbed my head in my hands, my dirty hair falling in front of my face. I had wanted to do the right thing—I'd tried so hard to, but I couldn't after all.

There was no way I was letting her leave me.

That was not fucking happening.

Laney came out of the bathroom at that moment and looked over at me, guilt flashing through her eyes before she quickly looked away from me and threw the items—her shampoo and makeup—into the case. She turned and headed back into the bathroom.

"You ain't goin' anywhere, Laney," I called to her, but all she did was snort in disgust. "I'm fuckin' serious, babe. You're not leavin' me."

I heard her movements stop in the bathroom, and could almost imagine her standing there, waiting for my next words. Her hands balled into little fists by her side like the proud, strong-ass woman she was. Her eyes squeezed closed, trying to stem the flow of tears that she was fighting against.

"If it helps, it meant nothing to me," I said after several moments of total silence from her.

She came back out of the bathroom, staring at me with so much contempt it shocked me. "It meant nothing to you?" she said, her voice shaky when she talked.

"Of course not," I said, reaching for her.

She stared down at my hand, her forehead creased in frustration. When she looked up at me, her frustration was gone and all that was left was anger and hate for me.

"You say that like it means it's okay, Jesse,"

"Lane—"

"Like I should just pretend it didn't happen then, I mean, if it didn't mean anything, no harm no foul, right?" She cocked her head to one side and looked at me.

"Right," I agreed, nodding my head, regretting it as soon as I saw the spark of hatred flare even brighter in her eyes. "Laney, come on, you know how it is. You know me. It's just the way club life is."

I was saying the words, but I had no idea why I was fucking saying them. It *was* club life, but it had never been that way for us. Never. It wasn't *our* club life. Never had been and never would be. That's what I'd always promised her, and up to six months ago I had kept that promise.

She shook her head like she couldn't believe what I was saying, and I couldn't blame her. I was being an asshole—a grade-A asshole—and I was losing her because of it, no doubt.

"I'm done with your bullshit. I've tried, lord knows how I've tried to make this work, but I can't do it any longer." She threw the things in her hands into the suitcase. "There's no fixing your kind of fucked up—not anymore."

"You don't mean that."

"I do," she replied, eyes full of fire. "I don't know who you are anymore, Jesse. But you're not the man I fell in love with."

I was standing, frozen to the spot, not sure what to do with myself. I couldn't let her go, fuck that, I *wouldn't* let her go, no matter what happened. My heart was beating again, faster and faster as the panic began to pump through me. If she went I'd be all alone, and there'd be nothing left and no reason to carry on. I had to fix this, despite knowing I shouldn't.

"I can make this right," I said, sounding every inch like the fucking pussy I was. "I can, but you can't go. I won't fuckin' let you leave me, Laney. That ain't happenin' so drop that thought right the fuck now!" I shouted.

She shook her head in exasperation and turned around to face the dresser, and pulled the top drawer open before grabbing some more clothes. When she turned back around she glared at me defiantly. "You don't get it, do you?"

"I get that you're not leavin' this fuckin' house," I snarled, feeling the familiar roar of anger inside me.

"You don't own me, Jesse. You never did. I stayed because I wanted to, not because I had to. That hadn't changed until last night. But now I'm done putting up with your bullshit, and I'm done listening to your apologies. It's over." She put the clothes in the case, her face twisted in pain and anger at me. Her shoulders began to shake as she finally let the tears come, and when she looked back up at me a small piece of me died. My heart stopped, time froze, and the lifeline rang in my ears—a high-pitched ringing that signaled a flat line.

"Laney—" I started, but she held up a hand to silence me, and I shook my head no. Fuck no, she wouldn't silence me. No one fucking silenced me.

I moved then, reaching her in two big strides, my large frame towering over hers, domineering the space in the room and demanding her absolute fucking attention. And then I dropped to my knees right in front of her.

"Laney, I'm beggin' you, woman, don't do this to me. I'm fuckin' sorry, okay? I'm sorry!" I grabbed at her legs and her hands went to my hair, her fingers running through it and making me feel like maybe this would be okay after all.

"I'm sorry," she whispered. "You need help."

"I do, I need help. So help me!"

I looked up at her, hating that I'd hurt my woman like this. This wasn't how it was supposed to be. Not for us. But then nothing was as it should have been. Everything was wrong and fucked up now.

"I can't help you, I've tried but you won't let me or anyone else in. I love you, but it's over, Jesse." She started to pull away from me and I shook my head, desperate as I grabbed at her legs.

She tried to pull away from me but I grabbed at her over and over, ignoring her slaps that rained down on me until I got a firm grip and I pulled her down and onto my lap.

"Get off me, Jesse! Just get off me!" she shrieked and cried, her hands still batting at me, hitting me anywhere she could land a punch or a slap. I didn't try to stop her; I took each hit, knowing that I deserved each and every one of them, and then some more. Fuck, I deserved a gun to the temple for the shit I'd done to her. The things I'd put her through these past months.

"It didn't mean shit, you know that. I don't know why I did it!" I whispered into her hair as she quit fighting me and started crying again. And the crying hurt more than the hitting ever could.

A man was supposed to take care of his woman, but I had done nothing but hurt her. I was fucked up and spiraling out of control, and I couldn't blame her for wanting to leave me—fuck, it was what I'd been trying to get her to do for months now: leave so that she would be away from me and my poisonous world.

But if it was really what I wanted, then why couldn't I just let her go? And why the fuck did it hurt so damn much? Never known pain like I had these past months. Didn't know things could hurt so much that you couldn't catch your breath. Didn't know that pain wasn't just about the physical, but the mental too.

Didn't know a lot of things until these past few months.

She cried and cried until I couldn't take anymore and I would have rather cut off my own fucking ears than listen to my own woman crying anymore because of me. Again. God-fucking-damn it, I wished I could take it all back. Wished I could make it all go away. But I couldn't. The pain that lived in me was as fresh that day as it had been six months before. If anything, it was more so.

"I'm sorry, baby," I whispered against her hair, my hands running down her back.

"So stop it, Jesse, just stop doing it," she finally pleaded, her words coming out between hicuppy sobs. Her body was tense and unmoving, not loving and soft like usual, and I kissed the top of her hair and breathed in her scent, willing her to forgive me.

"I will, I promise I will. Never again, I swear, Laney," I begged and pleaded. "Just give me another chance, baby."

I continued to stroke my hands up and down her back, my fingers tangling through her long hair until finally I felt her soften in my grip. I held her against my chest, feeling my T-shirt damp with her tears, and then I held onto her arms but pulled her away from my chest so I could look her in the eyes. It was like a thousand needles stabbing me in the heart, seeing the hurt on her beautiful face.

Her pain was the only thing that made me feel a damn thing anymore.

"I love you, Jesse—"

"I love you too, so much, baby, I—"

"Then stop breaking my heart before you kill me," she pleaded.

Tears trailed out of the corners of her eyes and blazed tracks down her cheeks and I reached over and wiped them away with my thumbs, stroking down the side of her face. I dropped my gaze from hers, feeling the familiar shame flood through me.

Shame and guilt and anger. They were the feelings that I had lived and breathed for the past six months. They were my air, my sustenance; they were what kept me awake late at night. And I felt them like a mantra in my skull.

Shame.

Guilt.

Anger.

All the love had gone. Doused out by the waves of those three other emotions. There was nothing good left inside of me. Only darkness.

Laney's hand reached up to touch my cheek, and I looked back at her and she leaned in and kissed me softly, soothing me from the outside in.

"I know you're hurting, baby, I get that. But you can't keep doing this and expect us to stay the same. It doesn't work like that," she cooed as her kisses moved from my mouth to my cheek. "It can't work like that."

One hand gripped her hair, tilting her face up as I jerked her mouth to mine, possessing her as my tongue stroked along hers and she sighed, her body relaxing. Her hands moved over my body, stretching over each hard muscle and tattoo I had. I laid her backwards on the bedroom floor, the new carpet we'd had laid only months ago still soft underneath her as I pushed up her ratty AC/DC T-shirt to reveal her perfect breasts.

Her hands reached down between us but I batted them away, pulling them up above her head and pinning her in place with my body. I tilted my head and kissed along the side of her neck and jaw, feeling her chest rise and fall as she panted underneath me. I shoved one knee between her legs and pushed her thighs apart, settling myself into my favorite fucking place in the world. She stared up at me, a pleading, needy look in her beautiful eyes, and I pressed a hand between us. Finding her panties already soaked, I slid them down her legs and then pressed my hand to her, feeling her arch her back against me, wanting to get closer to me, wanting to feel me inside her. I slid a finger in and she gasped. I leaned over and took the breath from her mouth, kissing her forcefully as I pushed another finger inside, wanting to taste her so bad but needing to be inside her more.

I pressed a third finger inside and she groaned against my mouth, her body clenching around me as my thumb circled her clit and she moaned loudly. My jeans were already undone and I let go of her hands to push them down, freeing myself of the restraint of clothing as I settled between her thighs, my cock nudging her opening where my fingers were working her.

Laney's back arched as my fingers sped up, and her back arched as she chased her climax. I pulled my hand out of the way and replaced my fingers with my cock, pushing inside of her and forcing her to tumble to the other side as her orgasm gripped her and her body squeezed me. She cried out, her body clinging to me as I pounded into her, chasing my own high.

I sighed as I looked down on her goddamned beautiful body, knowing how fucking lucky I was to have her in the first place—never mind after all the times I'd hurt her with my asshole ways. I leaned over and took her nipple in my mouth, sucked it softly and then harder before biting it just hard enough to feel her arch her back in response. I slid into her over and over as I cupped her other breast, pulling on the nipple until she gasped in pleasure, forgiving me over and over with her little sighs and moans.

She looked at me, her face blotchy and red from all the crying she'd been doing, and I squeezed my eyes closed, hating myself for what I was doing to her. Hating myself so much for everything that had happened.

"Hey, come back to me," she whispered, her hands stroking up my chest and across my shoulders.

I opened up my eyes as she wrapped her legs around mine and pulled me tighter against her. She draped her arms around my neck before pulling my mouth back to hers as I rocked back and forth into her, slowly, taking my time, showing her how much I fuckin' loved her with every thrust of my hips.

I felt her start to tighten around me, her mouth opening in a silent *O* as she dropped her head back and closed her eyes. I sped up, holding her hips almost painfully as she cried out loudly, her body exploding around me for a second time. I plunged into her harder, keeping pace and hitting her deep as her body continued to shudder around me. And then I brought myself home, riding the wave that was Laney until I could barely see straight, never mind fucking breathe.

I lay down next to her, cradling her small body in my arms, pulling her closer and closer until it felt like we were one person, and then I fell back to sleep. Happy that she'd given me this last chance.

Happy that I hadn't totally fucked things up between us, yet.

But not truly happy, because I didn't think I could ever truly be happy.

I knew I'd hurt her again.

Knew I'd ruin the last fucking good thing in my life.

And knowing that there was fuck all I could do about it, because not even Laney could end the torment I suffered.

The torture that I deserved.

CHAPTER FIVE:
1985
Jesse

I sat at the bar talking to Pops. He was telling us some old war story from back in the day. He clearly didn't realize that I'd seen the movie *Deer Hunter* several times, and Pops was definitely no Robert De Niro. Not even way back in the day.

But I played along with him, part of me enjoying the story and part of me worrying that maybe the old guy was slowly beginning to lose his damn mind.

Skinny—one of the drivers for the club—was in that day, waiting to speak to Hardy about the next shipment, and he obviously hadn't seen the movie either, because he was just as enthralled as Rose. The pair of them were staring, completely engrossed by everything Pops said.

"And then Nicky, aww he was crying like a little bitch, but so was I. In those days, a man weren't afraid to cry. Ain't nothing wrong with crying, ya know, Jesse? So the Jap, he slaps my face over and over and he's screaming at Nicky to put the gun to his head and fire the gun, but of course Nicky's scared. Russian roulette ain't no joke! And me, I'm practically pissing in my pants not wanting him to do it either, but we ain't got no choice. And so I stand up and hit the Jap in the face and then we all scuffle, but in the end it's all for nothin'." Pops shook his head and swallowed his whisky. "All for nothin'…" His words trailed off and he went silent, his gaze far away as he thought back to the memory, even though it wasn't real. It was to him.

"And what happened then, Pops?" Rose asked, eager for the end of the story. She was sitting next to him, leaning on one hand, her eyes wide as she imagined all the things he was telling her, believing every word and eating it up like candy.

Pops came out of his daze and looked at her. "What?" He looked over at me and then back to Rose before sliding a hand up her thigh and under her skirt. "Oh, oh, we killed those Japs good. Shot one right between the eyes and then Nicky and I got the hell outta there," he laughed.

Rose fluttered her eyelashes as Pops slid his fingers into her panties, and I took that as my cue to leave. I patted him on the back as I stood up, and he grunted something to me. Skinny followed close after, heading to Hardy's office and looking jealous as hell that Pops and Rose were about to get it on.

I was halfway to my room when the clubhouse door opened and Hardy, Gauge, and Rider all walked in. Rider was a new member to our charter. Though he'd been a Highwayman for as long as I could remember, he'd always been a nomad; but just recently he'd decided to come in and settle with a club.

Trailing behind all three men was Hardy's latest woman, Silvie, and then Laney. Her shoulders were back and her she was walking tall and proud, her mouth pinched in a way that told me she took no shit from anyone. Not even Gauge.

I stopped walking and tried to act casual about seeing her again, though there was nothing casual about the way I was looking at her, that much was for sure. But Rider saw my stare and patted me on the back as he passed me by.

"Down, boy," he said, and I'm grateful that Gauge didn't hear him or I'd have been a dead man.

"Silvie, fix us something to eat, we've got visitors coming in later," Hardy called as he walked to his office without giving me a passing glance. The three men followed him in, shutting the door behind them and closing the blinds to give them some privacy, and Silvie and Laney headed into the kitchen.

I stood there wondering what the hell to do. I hadn't seen Laney in a long-ass time—not since Hardy'd made a damn fool of me in front of her and she'd practically saved my ass from a beating. I swallowed, looking at the door to the kitchen and wondering if Silvie would let me speak to her or if she'd been ordered not to even let me in.

Silvie was pretty cool—a little older than Hardy normally liked 'em, but she had spirit and she cooked a damn good pie. I kinda hoped that Hardy would make her his old lady at some point, but you never knew with him. One minute he'd be blowing hot and the next not so much. Either way, I liked her. I liked the way she tried to cover for me when I fucked up, and the way she always made sure my clothes were clean and I ate breakfast before going to school. Shit, I even liked the fact that she made sure I *went* to school. No one other than Butch ever gave a damn before, so it was kinda nice to have a mother figure around, if I was being honest.

A couple of minutes passed and I was still standing in the center of the room with my proverbial dick in my hand, wondering what to do with myself, when Silvie came back out. She glanced at me before quickly looking away.

"Need to go get some more beer and potato salad," she said before heading to the exit with her keys in her hand.

I nodded at her retreating back and watched as she left, and then I took a deep breath and walked into the kitchen, letting the door swing shut behind me. I looked around for Laney, finding her chopping salad next to the pantry. She looked up as I entered, a small smile playing on her lips. I was practically thrown back to her kneeling on my bed and drawing a smiley face on my poster—a poster that still hung above my bed, not for the topless woman on it but for the connection to Laney that it now held.

"Hey," she said, quietly. One hand was holding a head of lettuce and the other was using a large kitchen knife to chop it in half. Her hair, as usual, was hanging down her back in long, dark waves. And I couldn't help but wonder what her hair would feel like trailing down my chest as her lips moved across my stomach and down to my cock.

"Hey," I replied, going forward, my mouth suddenly dryer than it'd ever been before. "Not seen you in a while, how've you been, darlin'?"

She looked up at me and raised an eyebrow, a sexy smirk hanging from her mouth that made me want to reach over and kiss her. "Good, I guess. Gauge is letting me stay with him, finally." She kept on cutting the lettuce, and I swear to God I'd never seen someone cut lettuce and look so sexy. I wasn't sure if she was doing it on purpose or if she was just naturally gifted one thing was for sure though; I'd never look at lettuce the same after today.

I leaned back against the kitchen counter, arms crossed over my chest casually. "So, you're stayin' with him now, huh?"

She made an agreeing noise without looking up, and her hair fell over one shoulder.

"Guess I'll be seeing more of you then."

I swear it was casual when I said it, and it wasn't obvious that inside I was cheering like I just won a gold fucking medal, but when she looked up at me, her gorgeous brown eyes soaking me in, I knew she must have been a witch because it was obvious that she could read my damn mind and knew exactly what I was thinking.

"If you're lucky," she replied, winking at me.

She'd finished chopping the lettuce and she piled it all into a large silver bowl and went to the sink to rinse it out. The water sprayed back against her white T-shirt and I almost came in my pants when she turned around and I could see the outline of her breasts.

She opened the pantry and took out some more food before placing it on the countertop, and then like a scene from some soppy romance movie, she dropped the package of tomatoes and they went rolling in all directions as they hit the floor.

"Crap," she muttered, getting down on her hands and knees to pick them up.

I automatically did the same, and I started helping her collect them. Some rolled around the counter, and before I knew it that was where we both were—on our hands and knees behind the counter—and she laughed as we both reached for the same tomato and end up squashing it between our hands. Tomato juice was everywhere; oozing down our hands and between our fingers, and we were both laughing when we heard the kitchen door slam open.

"Laney?" Gauge's rough voice called for her, and she looked at me with worry in her eyes. She placed a finger against my lips and it took everything I had not to suck that finger into my mouth. She stood up, the kitchen counter hiding me from view.

"I'm here," she said, lifting the squashed tomato up. "Dropped one," she laughed.

"Fuck me, jailbait," Skinny called out with a wolf whistle. Red rage almost blinded me as I thought of him looking at her like that, and Laney must have sensed it too because she pushed her leg up against my side, practically tucking me against her, and her smooth skin and the scent of whatever lotion she rubbed down those beautiful legs wafting over me was the only thing the stopped me from standing up and ripping Skinny's throat out.

"That's my fuckin' kid, brother!" Gauge growled.

"I know that. If she weren't, I'd have her over the counter already!" Skinny laughed back. "But mmmm, you're going to have to watch your back with this one, Gauge. She's got trouble written all over that body of hers."

"Get the fuck outta here before I shoot you in the motherfucking head," Gauge snapped back, and moments later I hear the door swing open and closed again, the tail end of Skinny's laughter growing quieter.

"Where's Silvie?" Gauge asked, his footsteps coming closer.

"I don't know, she left," Laney huffed out.

I looked up at Laney, watching as she reached for the knife again and started chopping the remaining tomatoes. Her leg was right by my face, and I swallowed and reached out my hand until it was touching her calf, the skin so smooth that I almost groaned loudly and gave myself away. I saw the small smile on Laney's face as I slid my hand over her bare skin, though she tried to act like I wasn't there.

Fuck knows why I was even hiding, it's not like we were doing anything wrong, at least not before. Now I was thinking the dirtiest thoughts that any man could have and ready to blow my load in my boxers.

"I won't be home until late tonight, so I'll get a prospect to drive you home."

"I can stay here until you're ready to leave."

"Fuck that, no kids are allowed!"

"I'm not a fucking kid!" Laney snapped.

"Yeah, you are. And watch your mouth!"

"You're an asshole!"

Gauge chuckled. "Yeah, an asshole that don't want no kid still up when I bring some bitch home later. So be a good girl and be in bed."

"You're disgusting."

Gauge was eating something because I couldn't make out his next words—or maybe I couldn't hear them because the blood was rushing too loudly in my ears as I stroked my hand higher, reaching to the back of her knee and watching her try her damndest not to grin again.

Another tomato rolled off the counter, almost hitting me on the head before it landed on the floor, and she put down her knife.

"Shit," she murmured.

"Language," Gauge replied.

"Fuck off," she snapped back before casually leaning down to get the tomato. Her eyes met mine and she leaned in with a smile, and then she surprised me by placing a quick kiss on my lips, stealing my breath away before she stood back up.

I thought I was going to pass out from my desire for that woman, and I had to let go of her leg before I really did cum in my pants. The door swung open again and I heard Silvie come back into the kitchen.

"Where've you been?" Gauge asked.

"Potato salad," Silvie said, putting her groceries and keys down on the counter and going around to stand by Laney. She glanced down, her eyes widening when she saw me on my hands and knees by Laney's legs. "I got more beer—it's in my car. Can you help me grab it, Gauge?" she asked, heading back around the other side of the counter.

"Sure thing," he replied, and then the door swung open and closed as they headed out of the kitchen.

Laney looked down at me and I finally stood up, my body invading her space.

"Why'd you want me to hide?" I asked. "I'm not afraid of Gauge."

She laughed almost bitterly. "Are men always like this?"

"Like what?"

"Full of testosterone and macho bullshit."

I grinned in reply. "I'm serious. I can handle myself."

"You might not be afraid of Gauge, but you probably should be. You might be friends now, but he does not like men speaking to me. Apparently he sees me as his little girl that needs protecting, thanks to the rep my mother left me with…" Her words trailed off at the end of her sentence, her expression going sad.

I reached over, my hand touching the bottom of her chin and lifting her face so she was looking at me again. "Hey," I said and I watched as she forced a smile and pushed her previous dark thoughts away.

We were face to face, nose to nose, and I put my hands on her arms and leaned in. Because this was it. I couldn't not kiss her then, no matter what the consequences would be, or who might walk in on us.

Her eyelids fluttered closed as I pressed my mouth to hers and kissed her with everything I had. She groaned and leaned into me, and I thought it was the best damn day in my whole sorry fucking life until I heard my father's voice out in the clubhouse and the spell was broken.

She pulled out of the kiss first and we stood there looking at each other, both breathless, both taken aback by this thing that was growing between us. Her tongue darted out to wet her lips and my gaze followed it, staring at the glisten that it left behind. I leaned in, sucking her bottom lip into my mouth, and she moaned against.

My hands reached around, cupping her ass and pulling her crudely against me. And there was nothing soft or gentle about it. It was rough and urgent, almost desperate as I ground against her, squeezing her ass-cheeks and she panted against my mouth.

The sound of Hardy talking to Gauge stopped us both in our tracks and I pulled out of the kiss, feeling lost in the adrenaline of the moment. The door swung open and Silvie came in, making sure to kick the door closed behind her.

"You better go before he sees you in here, Jesse. He's in a shitty mood today," she said seriously. Her gaze washed over me and Laney, and I saw her mouth pulling into a smile. "Go on, get."

I stepped back from Laney, unashamedly straightening my jeans as I walked away from her because of my raging hard-on. I didn't even feel embarrassed as her hand covered her mouth and she tried to hold in her laugh.

"Young love," Silvie laughed with a roll of her eyes.

I smiled wider because I knew she was right.

I was in love with Laney and I wasn't letting her go, not for anything or anyone.

Even if it killed me, I would have her in my bed and on my bike.

Because that girl was gonna be my old lady one day.

CHAPTER SIX:

Present day
Jesse

I woke to the cold silence of an empty home, and even before I was fully awake, I knew that she was gone. But what was worse was that I knew I deserved it.

I lay on the floor, the smell of her still clinging to my skin like a taunt, and I stared up at the cracked ceiling and felt empty—dead and empty like there was no meaning for anything anymore. And there wasn't, not without her. She was all I'd ever wanted, all I ever really needed, and now she was gone.

It was for the best, I tried to tell myself. It was for the best.

But it didn't feel like it. Not even a little bit. It felt like acid, wrapped in hell and then shoved down my throat. My chest hurt with every breath I took, my lungs wanting to give up on life. And maybe I should have. Maybe that was it—the solution to the fucking pain and misery. But I knew I couldn't.

Highwaymen weren't made that way, though I wished we were. It'd be a hell of a lot easier than trying to survive.

I lay there for what must have been hours, listening to the occasional car door slam somewhere out on the street and the sound of voices fading and then disappearing completely. I lay there stewing in my own self-pity and wondering what I did to deserve such torment as the light of day faded into night. I wasn't a good man, not even close, but I must have been real fucking bad in a previous life, because all this life had shown me was misery with the occasional splash of hope thrown it to tease me.

The sound of my cell ringing from somewhere in the living room roused me from my dark thoughts and I somehow found the energy to get up off the bedroom floor and go retrieve it. I grabbed my jeans and stepped into them as I walked down the hallway. It was the club phone so I knew I couldn't just ignore it, no matter how much I might have wanted to, but I take my time, my thoughts still drowsy from my Laney hangover.

The sun had long since set, so everything was dark, barring the glowing of my cell on the coffee table. I picked it up and checked the screen, seeing that it was Hardy, and I took a deep breath before I took the call because it was never a good thing when Hardy called me.

"What?" I said, holding the cell to my ear and sitting down.

"I've been trying to get ahold of you for hours! Where the fuck have you been?" he yelled down the phone at me.

"Must have been on silent, what do you need?" I replied, not having the energy to deal with him right then. I pushed my hair out of my eyes and sat down on the sofa, my body feeling almost drunk with weariness.

"What do I need? What I need, you little motherfucker, is for you to pick up the fucking phone when I call! That's what I need! You hear me? I'm your president, and when I call you stop everything to take my call. If you're in the middle of taking a shit, you answer your phone. If you're fucking your woman—you take my damn call mid-thrust and tell that bitch of yours to hold off on the orgasm she's got building until I say she can fucking have it, you got it?"

I pinched the bridge of my nose and tried to control the rage I felt burning inside my chest. "You wanna tell me why you called, Hardy? Or you wanna keep riding my ass?" I growled out, the words almost sticking in my throat like razorblades. The line went silent for a moment and I could only imagine that he was working out which way he was going to kill me. "Can we just get on with it, Hardy?"

Finally, he went on speaking like I hadn't even spoken. "Listen here, and you listen fucking good. There's a deal going down in Atlanta tonight, and I need some eyes on the situation," he said, and I could tell he hated asking me to do this for him. "As you know, Gauge and I are out of town dealing with the shitstorm that Skinny has caused, so I can't do what needs to be done. And Rider took Axle down to Charleston to deal with the Blood Bastards situation." He sighed heavily. "Shit is getting more fucked up by the second."

Skinny was one of our nomad members. He drove trucks for us, moving shipments across the country—only the poor fucker got caught a few months back and he ended up in the DOC. If that weren't bad enough, brother got mixed up with another club and their dealings while he served his time and ended up losing an eye in the process. Hardy and the others had gone to clear the air and try and sort some kind of truce out before Skinny found himself losing even more body parts.

My forehead scrunched up in confusion and I brushed my hair out of my eyes again, wondering what was going on. Hardy never asked me for anything—any orders I got came from Gauge or Rider—and it was obvious by his tone that asking this of me was definitely fucking painful for him.

"Intel good?" I asked, because for another club to try and cut us out of business was bad fucking news. For them, at least.

The sound of a motorbike in the background had Hardy cursing down the phone. "Yeah, the intel is solid. Look, I gotta go, I can't get there in time myself and I'm pretty sure they knew that when they arranged the meeting. I need to know that the Highwaymen are getting their cut outta the deal and someone isn't trying to screw us over. And if they are—"

"It'll be the last thing they do," I cut in, almost eager for the fight.

"Exactly. But I need this on the down low for now. Last thing the club needs is someone getting wind that another club is getting brave and trying to cut us out. Loyalties get tested, and brothers come out of this worse off. You hear me?"

"I hear you," I replied. "Who's the other club?"

"Not sure, but you'll know when you get there, I'm told. I'll be back tomorrow, and I'll see you then. Remember, keep this shit quiet."

"I'm on it," I said, trying to wake my damn mind back up. Because if he was asking me to do this, then shit was serious and I needed to be ready to do what needed to be done, or risk getting killed. I stood up and rolled my shoulders, the scratches on my back from the bitch in the bar last night reminding me that Laney was gone. And for good that time. It didn't matter though; I could feel sorry for myself when this was done. Right then I needed to get my head in the game. "I'll call you when it's done," I said, readying to hang up.

I heard Hardy sigh down the phone, and I was about to hang up when he said my name. "Jesse?"

"What?" I barked down the phone, my tone cold and hard.

He was silent for a moment before replying. "Thanks, son." And then he hung up.

I pulled the cell away from my ear and stared at the screen that had gone black, even more confused than before. Hardy had just called me *son*, something he'd never done before. Just when I thought my life was fucked up enough, it went and got even weirder.

I swallowed, unsure what to do with that new development. On one hand I should have been glad; it was about fucking time he showed me something other than disdain.

But on the other hand, whatever relationship I ever could have had with my father was long since dead.

Or maybe I was reading too much into it. Could have just been a slip of the tongue. Maybe he forgot who he was talking to and thought I was Butch. Hardy fucking loved Butch. Brother couldn't set a foot wrong in his eyes. It was my turn to sigh then, already wishing I could go get drunk in a hole somewhere because I was fucking over this day—this week—this month.

I pressed some buttons on my cell and called Casa. He picked up on the second ring and I heard him lighting a cigarette and the sound of Casa's footsteps as he starts walking.

"What's up, brother?" he said. "You get shit off Laney about last night?" he chuckled.

I shook my head, not wanting to go into details about how fucked my relationship was right then. Casa and Laney had never been each other's fans—mainly because she thought he was a womanizing pig, and well, because Casa was in fact a womanizing pig. He couldn't understand why a man would ever want to stay with the same woman for the rest of his life when there was so much pussy out there, but he was a good man. Reliable, loyal as hell, and he had an evil streak you could see from space. A pretty face didn't mean he was pretty on the inside, that was for damn sure.

"Never mind that, we got business to take care of," I snapped.

"Yeah? What's up?"

"Someone's pulling a meeting while Hardy is away. He wants me there to make sure the Highwaymen get their fair cut."

"Well that's...surprising," he replied, and the sound of his footsteps stopped. He was either in as much shock as I was or he was sitting on his bike and ready to roll out.

"Ain't it just, brother, ain't it just." I paced the room, my muscles feeling wound up tight. Something was definitely off about the whole thing, but I couldn't figure out what.

"So who the fuck is it?" he asked.

"He doesn't know. Intel only gave him so much, but he's out of town dealing with the Skinny situation so he asked me to go check it out—keep it quiet too." I grabbed one of the half-empty bottles of beer off the table and took a long drink of it. It tasted disgusting, the beer warm and flat, but I needed alcohol in my system regardless.

"I'll reach out to Dom and Pipes, get them down there with us, okay?" Casa asked. "They'll keep this shit quiet, and no one should be going into that meet alone."

"I agree. Meet me at the Clubhouse—we'll be rolling out in thirty." I ended the call and slipped the cell into my pocket.

The house was quiet and far too empty without Laney filling the space. The sound of her feet padding over the carpet. Her humming coming from the kitchen. The sound of her calling my name as she walked into the bedroom, smiling at me because she knew exactly what I wanted.

I turned in a circle, looking at our things: the furniture that we'd picked out together, the cushion covers she'd chosen to match the rug—or was it the curtains? Fuck, I couldn't remember. It hadn't seemed important at the time, yet now it seemed like the most important thing in the world. I pinched the bridge of my nose again, thinking of her face and letting the scent of her fill my lungs.

She'd squealed when she saw the cushion covers—that was what I remembered—and then she'd thrown her arms around my shoulders and kissed me long and hard before telling me how perfect everything was. And then we'd fucked for what felt like days, right here on this fucking floor. And in-between the fucking, we'd talked about us.

How we would be happy forever.

Always together.

She was my old lady and we were going to start a family together.

Everything was fucking perfect, just like she'd said.

But neither of us had a fucking clue that months later our whole lives would be fucked up forever, and I would be here all alone after pushing her away.

The now empty bottle of beer was in my hand, my palm wrapped around it tightly, and I let out a guttural roar and launched it across the room. It smashed into the wall above the fireplace, and splinters of glass littered the carpet.

I didn't know how I was going to cope without her. She was the only thing keeping me grounded, holding me in place when all I wanted to do was float away into misery. My life had been a series of horrors and misfortunes, and Laney had been the only good thing in it. Now she was gone and that left me with nothing. What would anchor me in place now? What would keep me from spiraling down the tunnel to hell and ending up like my own fucking mother?

I needed to get the fuck out of there before I tore the place up, or burned it to the fucking ground. I reached for my T-shirt on the floor, pulling it over my head, and then I put on my cut and rolled my shoulders. I stalked to the front door, catching sight of my reflection in the hallway mirror. I was a fearful fucking sight. Built like a tank, thick muscular arms covered in tattoos, with shoulder-length dirty blond hair, and a scraggly beard that was two days past needing shaving. But it was my eyes that held the true darkness. Where normally they were a clear dark blue, they were instead red-rimmed and looked almost black, as if my very fucking soul had been sucked out of me and replaced with the devil himself.

I pulled open the front door and stepped outside before slamming it closed behind me. The echoing silence taunted me. I walked to my bike and straddled it before pulling on my helmet and setting off for the clubhouse.

Regardless of what was happening in my personal life, I needed to pull my shit together for that meeting. If not, I probably wouldn't make it out of the meeting alive, because if there was a meeting being held without the Highwaymen, that meant someone was trying to cut out the middleman. And when he saw us pull up, expecting our cut of the action, it could likely start a war.

A war that Hardy was sending me right into.

I arrived at the clubhouse ten minutes later. Casa and Pipe weren't there yet, but Dom was. I'd mostly avoided him the last couple of months, making sure there was never any time for us to talk, but sooner or later we'd have to—that much I knew.

He nodded at me as I walked inside, and I nodded back.

"Casa fill you in?" I asked, sliding onto the stool next to him.

"Yeah, he called and it doesn't sound good," he replied.

The club was pretty empty, since most of the brothers were down either dealing with the Skinny situation or in Charleston trying to sort out a deal with the Bloody Bastards MC. They'd had offers coming in from other clubs to supply them with product for a fraction of what we charged, and Hardy had decided that the threat of losing their business was big enough to warrant him going down there and dealing with that shit directly. It wasn't just the loss of money that bothered him, but the fact the new product wouldn't be half as pure as they shit we supplied.

And a dirty product meant dead bodies.

And dead bodies always meant heat from the cops.

Being the Mother Chapter of The Devil's Highwaymen, it always made our lives easier to keep the cops out of our business—even the ones on the payroll.

A couple of the newer prospects were lingering, clearly looking for something to do other than just hold their dicks in their hands while they waited for Hardy to get back.

I stood up, making a decision that Hardy might not like, but making it all the same. I nodded for the two young prospects to get over to me, and they did, both of them eager to help.

"What's your orders while Hardy's away?" I asked, feeling Dom stand up behind me.

"Watch the clubhouse, watch the warehouse, and watch the bikes," the eldest of the two replied, sounding deeply pissed off at having to wait around while everyone else had important shit to do. "You need some help with something?" he asked eagerly.

"Cutter, right?" I asked and he nodded. I looked to the other guy, but for the life of me I couldn't remember his name. The kid barely looked seventeen and had only been with us for a month or two, but I'd seen him around, and just like Cutter he was a hard worker and eager to please. "There's a meeting going down tonight, caught everyone by surprise."

"You think it was purposeful?" Cutter asked.

"Sure as shit it was. Could get messy."

"I'm in," Cutter replied, barely letting me finish my sentence.

We both looked at the other kid, but it was Cutter that asked him.

"Max?"

Max nodded and cracked his knuckles. "Yeah, I'm down for that."

I wasn't sure he was ready for it, but decided it was the best way for him to learn. Besides, it was better to go down with a crew than just me and Casa, so the more people I got on board, the better. Hopefully the other club would see us as a big enough threat and not try to kill us.

"All right, we're rolling out as soon as Casa and Pipes get here. Get your shit together, and make sure you're carrying. This ain't a party we were invited to." I held out my hand and they both took turns in shaking it before stalking away to gather their things.

I turned back to Dom and he nodded and looked away, a look of pride shining in his grey eyes. Before I could say anything else, Casa and Pipes walked in, looking serious.

"Ready?" Casa asked.

He reached out and I shook his hand, pulling him into a rough hug before letting him go. I did the same with Pipes, and then Cutter and Max joined us.

Pipes eyed the prospects before looking at me questioningly. "Think it's wise?" he asked, and we all knew he wasn't being disrespectful to me or the prospects. Going in with two or three of us was one thing, but turning up with six or seven brothers— well, we were sending a message, that was for sure.

I nodded. "Yep, think it's about time we show the other clubs that the Highwaymen aren't to be fucked with. Hardy said to make sure we were getting our fair cut, but I think we need to be going in and asking for more now that they've shown their hand."

My brothers all watched me, their eyes dark and their expressions grim. They nodded and grunted in agreement.

"I'm thinking we show them what respect really fuckin' means, and what happens when someone disrespects our club like this."

I smiled grimly, because it wasn't what Hardy had asked me to do, but I knew it was the best decision for the club regardless. Hardy was biding his time, readying for retirement. Long after he was gone, the club would still be going, and I needed to secure our position with the other chapters—make sure they really knew not to fuck with us, or try and cut us out of any deals in the future.

"Let's roll out," I said, and my brothers followed me out of the clubhouse and to our bikes.

We'd be in downtown Atlanta in under thirty minutes, and then we'd see what was what. I hoped we'd all make it back alive, but none of us were under the illusion that death wasn't a possibility. But more importantly, after everything that had happened in the past twenty-four hours, I'd come to the conclusion that I wouldn't be letting anyone walk all over the only thing I had left.

And if that meant starting a war, or going head to head with Hardy after all of this, I was ready for that too.

CHAPTER SEVEN:
1988
Laney

I had sworn to my mom on her deathbed that I would never get involved with a biker. Yet there I was, living with one, working for a club, and fantasizing about another.

Sure, one was my dad—if you could call him that—and the job part was just while I saved the cash to help me through college, even though Gauge said I didn't need to worry about that.

But the fantasizing part, that one was all on me.

"Sorry, Mom," I muttered, swinging my hips as I followed Gauge through the clubhouse.

"You say something, Laney?" Gauge asked, looking back over his shoulder, his dark eyes moving over my face. I could see what my mom had loved about him so much—thick dark hair, dark brooding eyes, and a body made of steel—what wasn't to like? Of course, I could just as easily see why she hated him too: he was a selfish, womanizing asshole, who only thought with two parts of his body—the hand that was shooting, and his dick that was fucking.

My mom's heart never stood a chance against him.

I scowled at him. "Yeah, I said 'fuck off and die,'" I snapped and stalked away from Gauge.

"Fucking bitch!" he called as I stormed away.

"Eat shit, asshole!" I yelled back. I held up my middle finger to him without bothering to turn around, and I could barely contain my grin when I heard some of his club brothers laughing at him.

Good.

I hated him. I still had no idea why my mom had thought I would be better off living with him than with any of her friends. I was a capable woman, and I'd once been a capable child. I could handle my own, and what I couldn't handle, her friends had always helped me with. Sure, they were all prostitutes, but they were people too—good people—and they loved me like a daughter.

Gauge mumbled something in return, but he'd backed down—which was good, because I was lucky in that I got both my mom's and my dad's stubbornness, and Gauge never won a fight against me. Ever. Stubborn genes and the perks of living with a group of strong, independent women: I wasn't afraid to stick up for myself.

I passed by Pops at the bar and gave him a little wave. He was looking sick, I realized. Not just old, but actually sick. His paper-thin skin was sallow and pale, and his eyes didn't hold that spark like they once had.

"Everything okay?" I asked him, pausing before I went through to the kitchen.

Pops raised a beer bottle in my direction. "Never been better." He grinned, but it was obvious he was full of shit and not feeling good at all.

"Maybe hold back on the beer today, and let me grab you a coffee instead, huh?" I asked, genuinely concerned.

He scowled at me. "Next you'll be offering me some green tea and some brown fucking rice to help keep my blood pressure down! I'm fine, girl, now leave me to my beer!"

I rolled my eyes. "All right! No need to be a dick about it, Pops!" I snapped back and pushed open the swinging door to the kitchen. No point in arguing with a man intent on killing himself. Because that's what was happening, though no one else seemed to notice. Either that or they weren't too concerned by it. But I'd seen that type of thing once before. I was little—real little—but the image still haunted me even now.

The kitchen was a hive of noise when I walked inside. Some of the old ladies were already there working on fixing a large meal for everyone. Gauge had said that there was a big meet that night—a couple of different clubs meeting up to party and discuss business. He said he'd be getting a prospect to drop me off at home later, before the party started, but for the time being he wanted to know exactly where I was and what I was up to. The safest place for me was apparently there.

Silvie—Hardy's girlfriend—looked up and smiled. "Get your skinny butt over here and help me out, Laney."

I smiled back, because I liked her—always had—and I really hoped that Hardy intended on keeping her around. He hadn't made her his official old lady yet, but all the men knew to keep their hands off of her or they'd lose them to one of Hardy's butcher knives. That man did not like people messing with his stuff, and whether Silvie was wearing Hardy's patch or not, she was definitely something of his.

I made my way over to her, shrugging out of my black hoodie and dropping it onto an empty work surface before taking the knife she handed me. I continued chopping up the steaks she was prepping, while she seasoned them and put them on a big plate ready to be barbequed later that night.

She leaned in and kissed the side of my face, and I blushed. "How you doing, sweetheart? We haven't seen you for a while," she asked, walking to one of the cupboards and opening it.

Silvie was a beautiful woman, in a classical sense. She didn't wear much makeup because she didn't need it. She had thick long dark hair, and dark brown eyes which were always practically covered by her thick bangs.

"I'm good," I replied, really not wanting to go into details. My life was pretty much an open book, thanks to the club. It was like being part of a small town, and everyone knew everyone else's business. And of course, everyone always had an opinion. The only things private were the things I kept locked up inside my head, and I was certain that Gauge wanted to know those thoughts too. As I'd gotten older, he'd got worse, always stating that I needed to cover up because he'd end up going to prison for murder due to the way other men were looking at me.

River and Charlie, two of the other old ladies, came out of the big walk-in pantry giggling. Their eyes lit up when they saw me and I smiled over at them.

"That dad of yours still riding your ass about school?" Silvie asked.

"Yeah," I groaned, though if I was going to be completely honest with Silvie—which I wasn't going to be, of course—I was glad Gauge was riding my ass about school all the time. At least when he did that it felt like I had a real dad and I wasn't really all alone in the world.

We'd been visiting colleges over the past couple of weeks, and I couldn't help but get a little excited about the prospect, though of course I kept that shit under wraps. I didn't want Gauge thinking he was doing a good thing for me. He might have started getting the wrong idea and thinking he was doing a good job of raising me—which he wasn't.

"School is important," River—Axle's old lady—called over.

I scowled at her, but she saw right through me.

"Don't look at me like that. You're getting older, and the boys have been looking at you like you're something to fuck for far too long. The fear of Gauge's wrath won't put them off much longer. You need a plan if this isn't what you want for your life, because before you know it, this club will suck you in and never let you go. Or worse, it'll spit you right back out." She brushed her blond hair away from her eyes and smiled sincerely.

"As if any of the men here would be stupid enough to dump her fine ass after getting a taste!" Rose replied as she came into the kitchen. She winked at me as she dumped some groceries on the counter. "Besides, ain't nothing wrong with this life."

"It can't always be about getting drunk and hooking up, Rose," River scolded, glaring at Rose.

Charlie—Rider's old lady—snorted out a laugh and we all turned to look at her. She looked up sheepishly, but couldn't contain her laugh.

"What? River, I'm pretty sure your motto in high school used to be 'this life is all about getting drunk and hooking up,'" Charlie snorted on another laugh.

"What the fuck, Charlie? You're supposed to be on my side," River laughed back and threw a dish towel at her.

Charlie laughed again, her cheeks blushing red. She wasn't much of a talker, though I suspected she'd loosen up once she got to know everyone a little more. She'd only been with Rider a couple of months, and I knew more than anyone how over-the-top this life could feel when you weren't used to it. Though to look at her, she just screamed *biker bitch*. Heavily done makeup, a piercing through her septum, plus the tattoos she had going down both arms—yeah, she was made for this life; she just didn't know it until recently.

I hadn't known that Charlie and River had known each other back in high school, though. That was definitely news to me—and to Silvie, by the looks of her expression. I'd kind of pieced together that Rose and River had known each other previously, but I guess it shouldn't have come as too much of a surprise, since the town was so small.

River rolled her eyes. "Fine, getting drunk and hooking up is all well and good, but only when you're someone's old lady. Up until that point you're no better than one of the club whores around here, and you know how fondly we think of those bitches." She winked at me, her gaze sliding snidely over to Rose, who shook her head and left the room.

"Well, I don't have much say in it anyway. Gauge says I have to go, so it's been decided," I replied soberly, feeling guilty for how River had just spoken to Rose. Rose was a good woman—beautiful, reliable, and loyal. I had no idea why she hadn't ever been made into someone's old lady, or why she stuck around. Club girls came and went all the time. Once they realized they weren't going to be wearing someone's patch, they took off. Or they went working in the club's strip club, The Pit. But not Rose.

There was a long story there, but I figured I'd probably never hear it.

"So, when do you start?" Silvie asked.

"This fall," I fake groaned.

Silvie reached over and squeezed my shoulders. "You're going to do great," she said. "I guess we won't get to see too much of you, though."

I groaned again, sounding every bit of my eighteen years. "I bet you will. I'll be home every weekend, apparently." I put down the knife I was using, thinking I might throw it at Gauge if he came in the room right then.

"Wait, what?" River asked. "So he's sending you away to college, but you have to come home every weekend?"

"Uh huh," I grumbled. "It's like he doesn't want me to have a life."

"Or he wants to make sure you have a life and don't waste it," Silvie said kindly.

"Stop being so motherly, bitch," River snapped, pointing a red-nailed finger at Silvie. "Laney needs to get laid at some point, and the best college parties are Friday nights. Gauge can't be serious in making her come home every weekend and miss out on all those hot college boys!"

River genuinely looked annoyed for me, which only fueled the hilarity of the situation. She was right—I'd never get laid if Gauge kept me under lock and key constantly, though I wasn't too concerned about missing out. After all, there were men that I'd rather spend my time with at the clubhouse than at college. Unfortunately, he was pretty much out of bounds, since Gauge had given me a *no biker* clause when I first moved in with him. I'd agreed at the time, not realizing the severity of my decision, or that several years later, biker would be the only thing that would do it for me.

Charlie and Silvie were still laughing about the unfortunateness of my situation when Gauge came into the kitchen. They cracked up even more when River glared at him.

"What the fuck did I do now?" he grumbled. He glanced over at me. "What did you say?"

"Don't look at me. I was just telling them how you expected me to be a virgin until the day I died," I smarted.

"Not till the day you die, just until you don't live with me anymore!" he grumbled back, and I just bet he was blushing beneath that dark beard of his too. Good.

"This is unacceptable, Gauge!" River said, heading toward him, one hand on her hip and her red-tipped finger now directed at him and not Silvie. "A girl as pretty as Laney deserves to be—"

Gauge lifted a hand up to River. "Don't want to hear this shit right now, River!"

"Well I don't care. You need to hear it, so listen up!"

I grinned when Gauge looked over at me helplessly, because what could I say? I liked to make him suffer. And listening to one of River's lengthy tirades was definitely going to make him suffer.

Axle walked into the kitchen at that moment, blissfully unaware of the drama unfolding until he took in the scene before him. He quickly stepping into River's path.

"Woah, baby, what's up?" He wrapped his arms around her waist and roughly pulled her body flush against his when she tried to get away.

"Gauge is a pig," she mumbled as Axle leaned down and pressed his mouth to hers, and Gauge took that as his cue to shoot me an evil glare.

"I know, baby, I know," Axle replied. "Total pig." He kissed along her jawbone and she practically mewled as his hands grabbed hold of her ass and squeezed. "Want me to shoot him for you?"

"Uh huh," she mumbled against his mouth, her hands moving to his hair, where she threaded her fingers through his thick hair.

"Thanks a fucking lot, brother," Gauge mumbled and headed back out of the kitchen as quickly as possible.

Everyone made themselves busy as River and Axle made out like a couple of college kids, and when the heavy panting got too much and Silvie looked like she might ask either them or us to leave the kitchen to get some privacy, Axle hoisted her up over his shoulder and carried her laughing and screaming from the room.

I turned to look at Charlie and Silvie. They looked at each other, grins on both of their faces and a glint in their eyes that showed me I was missing out on something—something I always would be missing out on unless I got myself an old man like one of these. A pretty college boy wasn't going to kiss me like that, or carry me away to fuck me like that. No, a pretty college boy was going to take me home to meet his mom and dad, and then what? Then I got to introduce Gauge as my dad? Maybe tell them the tale about how he met my mom, the beautiful hooker from Cali, and how he left her high and dry once he'd had what he needed, but now he had to take some responsibility for me because Mom was dead and he was all I had left in the world?

Fuck, no.

That wasn't going to be my life, and no pretty college boy would be good enough for me.

I knew exactly what I wanted, and I knew who I wanted.

Unfortunately, it was the same biker that had been avoiding me for the past two years.

CHAPTER EIGHT:
1988
Laney

The party was in full swing, and I knew that at any moment Gauge was going to ask me to leave, so I was doing what any rational teenage girl would do: I was hiding.

It was ridiculous, really. I should not have been hiding at a party. Even if it was a biker party that I wasn't technically invited to. I should have been out there, drinking and having fun with the rest of the women. Instead I was hiding in the kitchen with a bottle of beer I'd managed to get from behind the small bar area.

I unscrewed the lid and drank a quarter of it down before needing to belch. The door to the kitchen swung open and I heard Silvie humming as she walked to the pantry to get another tray of buns for the barbeque.

She saw me sitting on the floor and gave a little scream before I had chance to hush her, and a couple of seconds later I heard Hardy come into the kitchen.

"What the fuck was that?" he snapped.

I held a finger to my lips and Silvie nodded and walked out the way she'd just come in. "I thought I saw a spider," she lied easily. "False alarm. Go back to the party, Hardy."

It was silent for a couple of moments before I heard him speak. "Everything okay with you, Silv? You've been quiet all week." He breathed out a heavy sigh, and I wondered what bothered him more—the fact that she was keeping secrets from him or the fact that she seemed unhappy. Hardy was true to his name in every sense of the word—he was hard. And mean. And definitely cruel. Yet I had seen a softness with him when he was around Silvie, and I wasn't sure what to make of that.

He treated Butch like an employee, and he was downright hateful to Jesse, but with Silvie he was almost like a different person—a man without the weight of the world on his shoulders. And Silvie obviously cared about him a great deal. Why else would she stick around and put up with his shit?

I didn't mean to listen in on Silvie and Hardy, but I was a people watcher. That was what my mom used to say. I couldn't help that I noticed things that others didn't. Like I noticed that Axle clearly had a thing for Rose despite being married to River. But I also knew that Rose clearly had a thing for Pops, despite the age difference between them. And what an age gap that was.

I also saw the way Butch looked at Dom sometimes. And it wasn't in a best friend way.

I zoned back in, listening to the sound of Hardy groaning. Either I had missed Silvie's reply to him or she was reassuring him that she was okay by giving him a blowjob. Either way, it seemed enough to satisfy him and stop him from going in there to look for the fictional spider.

"Fuckkk, Silv," he grunted.

I took another mouthful of beer, wondering what the fuck I was doing with my life. I was almost eighteen, and hiding in a walk-in pantry at my dad's biker club, when really I should have been out partying with my girlfriends. Not that I had any, but that would change when I got to college, for sure. Once I hit college I was going to put this whole part of my life behind me and make a new beginning up for myself. My mom wouldn't be a dead hooker, my dad wouldn't be a sleaze ball biker, and I would be a strong, independent woman making her way in the world.

But for now, the beer bottle was empty, I was still sober, and I was still hiding and listening to Silvie and Hardy do whatever they were doing. Which meant that I was still a loser.

The music was getting louder from the other room, and I wished like hell that I was in there dancing and partying, having some fun like the other women. I hated my life, even more so now that I was stuck with Gauge. My mom had warned me about him, telling me the sort of man he was and the life he lived. She'd even warned me away from this life. So I'll never understand why she wrote to him and told him about me.

I could have stayed with my Aunt Kate—not technically a real aunt, but she may have well as been. She was the closest thing I had to family, much more so than Gauge. Yet for reasons unbeknownst to me, Mom had contacted Gauge and finally told him about me. The asshole didn't want to know until he found out that Mom was dying. That's what a great guy he was.

He found out he had a daughter and didn't give a shit. Not until he thought I'd be thrown in the system. Why that mattered to him, I didn't know, but it was what had changed his mind, and two weeks later Mom was packing up my stuff and Gauge came and collected me, taking me away from my home, my family, and my mom.

It wasn't long after that that Mom had passed.

He took me to the funeral, but I blamed him for the fact that she had died alone in the hospital, without me by her side.

I hated him with every molecule in my body.

The sound of grunting and skin slapping against skin coming from the kitchen was getting louder and louder, and I was guessing that the kitchen countertops would need some serious sterilizing after Hardy and Silvie finished fucking on them. Or maybe not. Bikers were disgusting, so they'd probably get off on knowing their food was made on surfaces that had been fucked on.

Hardy grunted loudly and Silvie let out a little squeal, and the sound of skin slapping against skin came to a stop as Hardy panted.

"You good?" Hardy asked, but I didn't hear Silvie's reply.

However, a few moments later I heard the music get louder as the kitchen door swung open, and then I looked up as the sound of footsteps got louder.

"You okay, kiddo?" Silvie asked as she poked her head around the door.

"Yeah," I replied, standing up.

She came toward me and pulled me into her arms, and I let her, because being hugged by Silvie was almost like being hugged by my mom. She wore the same perfume as she had, and she was the same height and build. If I closed my eyes and drowned out the world, I could almost pretend that things were how they should have been and I was back home watching *The Wonder Years* with Mom. But soon enough the world came crashing in and brought me back out of my fantasy.

"You know you can always come to me, don't you?" Silvie asked, looking down into my face. "If something's bothering you, or you need something."

"I'm fine, I just needed some space."

"Okay, well, in that case I'll leave you to it." She turned and grabbed one of the trays of buns and then backed away. "Unless you want to grab a tray of steaks from the refrigerator and come help out? You're not supposed to be here, so I can't promise you can stay for long, but it has to be better than sitting in here alone."

"Sure, I can help," I replied quickly with a smile. I grabbed the tray of steaks but Silvie swapped with me and then I followed Silvie out of the kitchen, hoping I could avoid Gauge and stay a little longer. Either way, I was out of beer and couldn't stay in the kitchen all night.

We left the kitchen and headed through the clubhouse and out to the large yard, where the barbeque was. People were everywhere, the party in full swing by then. Women were wearing practically nothing, men were drinking beer and talking, or fucking. Fires had been lit for atmosphere as much as warmth, and it gave the whole party a dirty, seedy look.

"Stick close to me," Silvie said when she noticed I was dragging behind a little, so I hurried to catch up.

I had heard about biker parties, so I knew what to expect—at least in theory—but hearing about them and being at them were two very different things, and I found myself staring at everything as we walked. For an almost-eighteen-year-old whose mother was a prostitute, I suddenly felt a little intimidated by so much naked flesh on display.

I blushed, and when I looked up Silvie was grinning. "You'll get used to it," she said. "Trust me, this is nothing compared to what happens when the women go home."

"Does it not bother you?" I asked, watching a woman in the corner drop to her knees and start unzipping Skinny's jeans. I looked away as he smiled at me, because yeah, I remembered the way he had looked at me the first time we'd met. He was bare-chested, and full of muscles, and I watched them move as he grabbed the woman's head and shove it against his crotch, his eyes never leaving mine the entire time. I looked away, my cheeks flushing hot.

"No, Hardy is the president of the club and he's my old man, pretty much. He has a lot of pressure on him, and I understand that, and he'd never do anything with someone else while I was here, and what I don't know can't hurt me."

I shook my head. "I would want my man to be faithful to me," I replied matter-of-factly. "I wouldn't care who he was."

Silvie stopped and turned to me, her expression suddenly serious. "I know it's hard for you, it always is for newcomers, but I trust Hardy not to do anything stupid, and it's me that he comes home to every night. I'm happy with that."

I looked down, embarrassed—not just because I had spoken out disrespectfully to her, but because I was embarrassed for Silvie as well. Because I meant what I'd said: my man would be with me and me only. I knew my worth, and it was more than what she gave herself credit for.

"Sorry, I didn't mean to offend you," I said, though I wasn't really sorry at all.

"That's all right," she replied and we kept on walking.

We placed the food on a large table that had been set up, and I watched Pops flip a couple of steaks like an old pro.

"This the last?" he asked Silvie, his gaze sliding to me briefly before he frowned. "Should she still be here?"

Silvie looked at me with a concerned look, and I felt instant guilt in case I'd gotten her into trouble.

"Yeah, she's with me, helping out," Silvie replied, covering for me, even though she knew damn well that Gauge wouldn't want me there. She winked at me and turned back to Pops, and I decided that I liked her even more.

I had started opening up the burger buns, ready to put the burgers on, when a large hand reached out and grabbed my ass, before squeezing it harshly. I yelped and looked up as shock covered Silvie's face.

"All right, sweet thing! That ass is tight!" someone whistled from behind me, and I turned around to punch whoever it was in the face as they grabbed another handful. "Why don't you bend over for me, pretty thing?"

But when I turned around, it wasn't some greasy no-named biker that I didn't know, it was Gauge—my dad—and we both looked horrified and disgusted as the other. I backed up a step as he wiped his hand down his jeans as if he could wipe away the feel of my ass from his palm.

"Laney! What the fuck are you still doing here?" he bellowed, suddenly sober as a judge.

"Having fun, asshole. Or I was until you turned up!" I yelled back at him. "God, you're such a pervert!"

"I didn't fucking know it was you!" he yelled, throwing his hands up in the air and almost spilling the beer in his other hand.

Gauge was standing with two other bikers that I couldn't remember the names of, but both of them were laughing hysterically as if this was the funniest thing they'd ever seen.

I cocked an eyebrow at him and glared at the other two. "As if that makes a difference, Gauge!"

"Of course it makes a fucking difference, Laney. I can grab any ass I want, except yours. So yeah, big fucking difference!" He looked like he was about to blow a gasket.

"It shouldn't matter, because you shouldn't be such a fucking pervert and be grabbing women's asses all the time. Ever heard of consent?"

"Ever heard of shut the fuck up because you're a kid who doesn't know what you're talking about?" he retorted angrily, throwing his beer to the ground.

We'd started to get attention from other people now, and I could feel their stares on us, which only made the situation ten times worse. Not only had he caught me at the party I wasn't supposed to be at, but he'd grabbed my ass—disgusting us both—and now we were seconds away from ripping each other apart.

"Eat shit!" I screamed, and grabbed the nearest thing to me and threw it at him, and suddenly thirty empty burger buns—and the tray they were on—were raining down on Gauge's head.

Gauge roared in anger and stepped forward, but Hardy came over and dived in-between us both.

He placed a hand on Gauge's chest. "Gauge! Enough, she's just a fucking kid!" Hardy bellowed, pushing Gauge away from me.

"I am not a fucking kid!" I screamed at Hardy.

He turned and glared at me, one hand staying on Gauge's chest. "Yeah? Then stop fucking acting like one."

Gauge glared at me over Hardy's shoulder. "Should have fucking left you to go into care," he snarled out darkly.

"I wish you would have!" I screamed at the top of my voice.

"Bitch, just like your goddamn mother," he snarled nastily, and I clamped a hand over my mouth to stop myself from crying out as his words cut me.

Suddenly no one was laughing. This wasn't just a father and daughter arguing; this was worse than that, and I couldn't help the tight knot that wrapped itself around my heart and squeezed. He didn't even look like he regretted his words, so I lifted my chin and narrowed my eyes, refusing to acknowledge the pain his words had caused me.

"I wish she would never have met you, because you're a piece of shit man and an even shittier dad," I snarled back, not feeling any satisfaction from saying that despite the hurt I watched flare to life in his own eyes.

"Yeah?" he goaded.

"Yeah!" I snarled.

"Good, because I'm hoping you'll get the fuck out of my life soon then!"

I opened my mouth to say something but realized that for once my temper had given up, and all it had left behind was a hole in my chest. Tears blurred my vision but I refused to let them fall.

"Silvie, get her the fuck out of here," Hardy yelled, and I felt someone grab my arm and start to pull me away.

"I've got her," Silvie said.

"Crazy bitches everywhere," Hardy muttered as Silvie pulled me away.

Gauge called me something else as I was leaving, but I drowned him out, refusing to hear anything else he had to say. He'd said and done enough damage for one night. We both had.

Silvie's grip was firm, but not tight, and when we were far enough away she let go of me completely, trusting me to follow her and not run back to Gauge for round two. We walked toward the exit. A couple of prospects were standing by the bikes, and they looked between themselves as we got closer.

"One of you needs to take Laney home, please," Silvie said firmly. She looked down at me apologetically. "You need anything, you call me. Okay?"

I nodded okay and looked back down at my feet, knowing that no matter how much I cared about Silvie, I wouldn't call her. I could handle it on my own, just like I always had.

"I'm fine," I mumbled.

"Hey, it's going to be okay," she said softly, her hand reaching down to tug my chin upwards.

"I said I'm fine! Stop treating me like a kid. I'm practically eighteen, Silvie," I said, pulling my face free. "I just want to go home."

And I did want to go home. But not to Gauges house. I wanted to go back to Cali, back to my mom. I wanted to be home with her, not there in that shit-hole town, or that shit-hole club, with my shit-hole dad. But I could never go back home again, and that killed me the most.

"Well all right then," she said, and I knew that I'd offended her, again. "Which of you can take her?"

"I'll take her," a deep voice said from close by.

I looked up, recognizing the voice instantly. My face was still puckered in anger and frustration, and I looked straight into the eyes of the blue-eyed boy that had stalked my dreams for so long. No, *boy* was the wrong word. He wasn't a boy anymore, he was a man now. And damn, what a man he was. His hair was shoulder length and dirty blond, and he had a short rough beard that just begged me to run my fingers over it. His arms were thick and roped with muscles and tattoos, and his shoulders were wide and strong.

"You sure, Jesse?" Silvie asked. "You been drinking?"

Please say yes, please say…

"Sure, it's fine," he replied, barely looking at me. "I haven't had anything to drink yet. I only just got back into town."

"You good with that, Laney?" she asked, looking at me doubtfully, but I nodded quickly—possibly too quickly, because I saw the corner of her mouth crinkle up in a knowing smirk and her uncertainty vanished. "Okay, get her home safely, and Laney, let me know if you need me. I'm always here for you, sweetheart."

I nodded again, watching as she walked away and feeling awful for how I had just spoken to her. She was just trying to be nice—just trying to help me—and it was a lot more than most people had ever done for me. But as usual, I'd pushed her away like I did with everyone else. I sighed and took a deep breath knowing I would have to speak to her tomorrow and apologize.

I finally looked up at Jesse. I was short and he was tall, and I had an athletic, slender frame where he was broad and bulky; we looked almost comical standing together. He looked down at me, his deep blue eyes roaming over my body and back up to my face, his jaw twitching as he clenched and unclenched it. Something hot blossomed to life inside of me and I looked away, feeling embarrassed all of a sudden, as if he could see the things he did to my body without even touching me.

Ughhh, I'm pathetic.

"You want me to take her in the truck, Jesse?" one of the prospects asked, his gaze wandering over my body like Skinny's had.

Jesse scowled, his expression hardening until the prospect took a small step back. He looked back down at me. "Come on, my bike's this way," he said, wrapping his hand around my bicep and tugging me. He let me go after several steps, but I could still feel his grip on me, the way his fingers had squeezed a little too tightly—almost possessively, as if he wanted to get me away from the other men—and the way his rough skin had felt on mine.

I let him guide me over to his bike, my gaze fixated on the sway of his hips as he walked and the firmness of his ass, and I practically walked right into his back when he came to a stop and turned to look at me.

"You okay?" he asked, a small laugh in his words.

"Umm, yeah, I'm fine," I said, shaking my head. "Just tired is all. It's been a long day."

He climbed on his bike, one long leg stretching over to the other side, and then he watched me, waiting for me to climb on behind him. He handed me a helmet and I wrapped my arms around his middle, almost tentatively until he grabbed my hands and pulled them tighter—tight enough to feel the bands of muscle around his waist.

"Hold on tight," he said, his voice rumbling through his chest.

And I did.

I held on as if my life depended on it. I pressed my face against his back, taking in his scent of old leather and musk and sweat, and I watched the world pass me in a blur. I got lost in the sensations of the bike and of Jesse, the humming of the bike through my legs and the feel of his muscles tight under my hands, rippling with every corner we went round. I got lost in the ride, but mostly I got lost in Jesse. It was just what I needed to clear my head and soothe my heart.

When he pulled up to Gauge's house twenty minutes later, I was breathless and I held onto him tightly, not ready for it to end just yet. My cheeks felt flushed, my adrenaline pumping even though for the first time in years I felt calm and relaxed. It was Jesse, I realized. He calmed me—my soul. He made me feel safe, and like I belonged. And for the first time since moving there, I realized that I wasn't homesick and I didn't feel lonely.

"We're here." His deep voice cut through the thoughts in my head, and his hand reached down to give my knee a small squeeze, his hand staying on my skin. A shiver trailed up my body and I swallowed, loving the feel of him next to me.

We sat in comfortable silence, the darkness surrounding us and keeping us trapped in the bubble that we found ourselves in. I held on tighter when I felt his muscles move, and I think he chuckled, though it didn't feel like he was mocking me.

I closed my eyes, banishing the view of Gauge's house, because Gauge was the last person I wanted to think about—especially with the way my body was feeling right then.

"Laney?"

"Yeah?" I replied, still not moving, still content to just sit there, the heat from his bike burning through my thighs and his scent wrapped around me.

"You maybe wanna go for a ride somewhere?" he asked, sounding almost shy.

"Yeah," I replied instantly.

"Good. Because I'm not ready to let you go just yet," he said, and I think my heart skipped a beat.

His muscles tightened again and then we were peeling away from the sidewalk and heading back out on the road, and I smiled contentedly, never wanting that feeling to end.

CHAPTER NINE:
1988
Laney

Time had lost all reasoning by the time Jesse pulled up to a small lake. The trees rustled in the light breeze, the night air still hot and sticky despite it being after two in the morning.

Jesse pulled the bike to a stop and then reached down and gave my knee a small squeeze again. I slowly unwrapped my arms from his waist and sat up straight.

"You okay?" he asked. "I think I might end up with handprints on my stomach from where you've been holding on," he chuckled.

I blushed in the dark and climbed off, realizing how stiff my muscles had gotten after sitting on his bike for so long.

"Sorry about that," I mumbled, embarrassed. I started to turn away and head to the lake when he grabbed my arm and tugged me back to face him.

His deep blue eyes burned into mine with an intensity that swallowed me whole. "Don't ever be sorry for holding onto me, Laney. I wasn't complaining."

His tongue darted out to lick his lips and I watched the small movement, my gaze transfixed, and my own mouth desperate to feel his lips pressed against mine. I swallowed and looked away.

Was I imagining the way he was looking at me? Or was he feeling the same thing that I was? I couldn't decide if it was real, or if I was just becoming infatuated with the man that I couldn't have. I had sworn to my mom that I wouldn't date a biker, and a biker from my dad's club was a definite no-no. But there was something about Jesse—something different. Something I couldn't help but think my mom would approve of in some small way.

He seemed just as broken and lost as me. And I wondered if we would fit together like a jigsaw if we tried. Because sometimes, two lost pieces are just made for each other, regardless that they weren't from the same place.

Jesse stood up and took my hand in his, and then he guided me down to the lake's edge and pulled me down to sit with him. There was no reason for him to hold my hand, but he held it all the same, and the butterflies in my stomach grew more restless the longer he held it. We sat and stared out at the silent water, watching the small ripples move across the surface, the moon the only light.

I was calm sitting there with him, calmer than I'd felt in a long time. Anger and sadness normally gripped me, squeezing my heart and making me lash out at anyone within hitting distance—normally Gauge. But there with Jesse there was none of that—just a comfortable and blissful silence that sat between us. I mean, sure, my heart was thumping in my chest and I was having trouble breathing at a normal rate—he was a gorgeous biker, after all—but despite the lust that traveled through my body, I was peaceful.

The night air was still and humid, and I pulled off my small jacket, feeling hot. I folded it and laid it on the ground behind me, and then I lay back to stare up at the sky. A second later Jesse lay back too.

Above us was an expanse of black sky, dotted with thousands of stars, and we watched it silently, our bodies so close that I could feel the heat radiating from him. His thick thigh was pressed against mine, his arm so close that when I stretched my fingers out to find his, we locked hands almost instantly. There was a spark between us, a magnetism that I couldn't deny, and I hoped to God that he felt it too because it would be a damn shame if not.

His hand squeezed mine as if he was reading my thoughts, and I smiled up at the sky—the first genuine smile I'd had in a long time.

How could this man, that I knew so very little of, make me feel like this?

I turned my head to look at him, and found that he was already looking at me, and I felt heat crawl up my cheeks. Even in the dark his eyes shone out like blue beacons, drawing me in and pulling me home.

Jesse leaned up on one arm and stared down at me, pausing for several seconds as if deciding on something. It was a long moment as the silence encompassed us and I get lost in his blue eyes, and then he sighed heavily, one hand reaching out to tuck some of my hair behind my ear. My breath caught in my throat as his hand skimmed my face, and then I watched as his tongue darted out to wet his lips once more. My own mouth opened so I could take a breath because I was pretty sure I wasn't breathing properly anymore, my chest heaving up and down as he stared at me and I grew more and more intoxicated in him.

"Fuck it," Jesse mumbled, and then his hand tangled in my hair and he leaned over further before pressing his mouth to mine.

I stiffened at first, the kiss harder and more brutal than I expected, but then I relented, giving in to the heat that flared inside of me as it came to life.

His fingers gripped tightly to my long hair as I opened my mouth to him, letting his tongue invade me, and I groaned, the sound coming from somewhere deep and primal inside me as my body clenched in desire and need for him. It seemed to spur him on as he gripped me harder, the heat from him pouring over my body. But it wasn't enough—for either of us.

I needed more of Jesse: I needed all of him. I needed everything, and I reached up with both hands and wrapped them around his neck and pulled him closer until his entire body was covering mine like a thick blanket of male dominance, his masculine scent washing over me and making me shiver. His thigh pushed between mine, spreading my legs wide and letting him press his body closer to me. The hardness between his legs dug into my most sensitive area and made me gasp as he ground his hips against me.

I bucked against him, wanting more. No, needing it. But as soon as I did he rolled off of me, settling on his knees, and dragged both his hands through his hair. I looked over, hurt flashing on my face before I could cover it.

"Did I do something wrong?" I asked.

Of course you did; you misread the signals. You're not good enough for him. He can have any woman he wants, so why would he want you? The little voice inside me mocked.

Jesse reached out, his hand cupping the side of my face. "Fuck no, you did everything right. It's me, I ain't good enough for you. I don't want to spoil you." His thumb trailed down the side of my face, and even that small movement—combined with his heated words—sent shivers through my body. "I want you to live a little before you come into my world. Have fun, make mistakes, and then when the time is right, I'll be here. Waiting."

I didn't know what to say to that. It was both the stupidest and sweetest thing anyone had ever said to me.

"Jesse, I'm a big girl, I can handle this—whatever it is. One night with you is fine. I know how you bikers work," I said. I was lying through my teeth, though. I couldn't handle one night with him. One night with him would be like achieving ecstasy and then never having it again. I would be forever ruined for other men, constantly craving the high that only Jesse could give me.

One night with Jesse James would never ever be enough, but I lied because if I could only have one night, then that's what I'd take. "I want this," I said, sounding needy and desperate.

A wolfish smile flashed over his face and he leaned in and kissed me hard again. I opened my mouth and let his tongue in, my hands reaching around to touch him, to hold him, to feel him. I shoved my hands up his tee, desperate to feel his skin beneath my fingers, as his own hands held my face and he kissed me like his life depended on it.

I reached around to the front of his pants, feeling the swell beneath the zipper, and my body clenched at the thought of him pushing inside of me and taking my body, using me anyway he chose to. I fumbled for a second, trying to pull the zipper down, when Jesse pulled out of the kiss for the second time. He reached down and pulled my hand away.

"Another time," he said, his voice thick and gravelly, his breath washing over me.

I swallowed and nodded, when really all I wanted to do was have him then. I had no clue why he didn't want this right then, but I couldn't force him to have sex with me if he didn't want to.

"We should get back," he said, standing up and pulling me with him.

I nodded but didn't say anything, not trusting myself to speak. Instead I reached down and grabbed my jacket and let him guide me back toward his bike.

Jesse climbed on and waited for me to do the same. I wrapped my arms around him, and once again he grabbed my hands and pulled me tighter against him. I pressed my face against his back as he started the bike and I breathed in his smell.

Jesse drove me home, and when we got there he walked me to my front door, his large frame filling the small porch of Gauge's home. He looked like he wanted to say something but couldn't find the words, so instead he pulled out his cigarettes and lit one, and then he backed away from me with a smile. I noted the small dimple in his right cheek and I bit down on my bottom lip to stop the huge grin that wanted to escape.

"I'll be seeing you, Laney," he said with a nod, and then he turned around and walked to his bike.

"Yeah you will," I whispered to him.

I unlocked the front door and went inside, leaning back against it as I shut it behind me, and I stared into the dark hallway with a smile on my face.

"Sorry, Mom," I mumbled, looking upwards. I took a step away from the door and jumped as something thumped on the other side of it three times. I turned back around and threw it open to find Jesse standing there.

He took one look at me and then his arms reached out and grabbed me by the waist, pulling me to him as he slammed his mouth on mine once more. And then we were kissing, tongues moving against each other, hands groping at one another's bodies, teeth clashing as we greedily took from each other. He pushed me backwards until we was in the hallway, my back pressed up against the wall. Whenever my hands strayed to his dick he grabbed my wrists and held them above my head and instead he ground his hips against me, torturing me with his body and chuckling when I begged for more.

His mouth moved to my neck, kissing along my throat, and then he was pulling away again. "Gotta get back to the clubhouse," he said, his eyes sparking with mischief.

"You're fucking kidding me, right?" I bit out breathlessly.

"You and that mouth of yours," he goaded, rubbing his thumb across my bottom lip. "Gonna get me into trouble one day, no doubt," he laughed again.

I blinked, sexual frustration running riot through me. "You can't kiss a girl like that and then just leave," I said with a breathy laugh.

"But if I didn't, then how would I know she wanted me for my mind and not my body?" he smarted, giving me a wink.

And I couldn't help it—I had to laugh. Even as he backed away, one hand rearranging his jeans because of his obvious hard-on for me. I laughed louder and he shook his head and laughed back before sucking his bottom lip into his mouth and letting it go. He cracked his knuckles and turned and walked away, and I watched as he got on his bike and rode away that time.

I had no idea why Jesse didn't take me that night, when I was so clearly begging for it and he so obviously wanted to fuck me until I couldn't walk straight for days. But it only made my infatuation with him stronger.

Mom had made me promise I wouldn't get involved with bikers, but there was no chance in hell I was staying away from that one.

CHAPTER TEN:
Present
Jesse

The ride down to Atlanta was uneventful, giving me more than enough time to plan how it was all going to go down once we arrived. Every once in a while my thoughts would stray to Laney and where the fuck she was.

One thing was for certain: there would be no talking my way out of it this time. I'd made sure of that.

Couldn't say I blamed her. Hell, that was what I'd done it for. I'd tried to scare her away the past couple of months, but nothing had worked. She'd stayed time and time again. But I knew what would do it.

Too many thoughts whirled through my head the closer we got to the meet—thoughts of death, thoughts of killing and surviving both equally, and everything in between.

And of course of Laney.

I glanced over at Casa, feeling his gaze on me, and he frowned, clearly wondering what the fuck was wrong with me. I shook my head and looked back to the road, pulling ahead of him so as not to have to look at his questioning stare anymore.

Half of me wanted to blame him for this fuckup. He'd been the one to drag me out to that bar and encourage me to fuck that barmaid. But I knew it wasn't Casa's fault, really; it was mine, and I was man enough to admit that. Casa wasn't a one-woman man, never had been, and I didn't see that ever changing, so I couldn't blame him for my mistakes because he didn't see what was fuckin' wrong with them. But I also couldn't look at him just then, knowing how glad he'd be that Laney and I were over.

I might kill him if I had to see that.

The roads were busy when we drove into Atlanta, but they grew quieter and darker as we drove toward the meet point—a large warehouse district to the north of downtown—and my muscles started getting tenser the closer we got.

"Jesse? You seeing this?" Casa asked as we slowed our bikes down.

Tall buildings rose up on either side of us, dark and ominous, but I was more focused on the road up ahead that was closed off. A couple of prospects that I recognized had pulled some old construction signs into the middle of the road to block the path ahead, and they were standing armed and waiting.

Waiting for us? I couldn't help wonder.

I slowed my bike to a crawl. Casa, Dom, and the others did the same until we were all lined up side by side. Reverend's prospects seemed calm under the circumstances, leading me to believe once more that us showing up like that was expected.

"You catching this, brother?" Dom asked, his voice hard as tension wrapped itself around him.

"Yeah," I replied darkly, eyeing up the buildings on either side of us. I wasn't sure what I was looking for, but right then I didn't like our odds.

"Smells like bullshit to me," Pipes said, calling it as it was.

I didn't know what to say to any of them. The whole thing stunk to high heaven. Weren't nothing right about the whole damn thing, from them cutting us out of the meet to Hardy asking me for help. And now there we were being eyeballed like candy by two of the Reverend's fucking prospects.

The Reverend was a mean motherfucker, nicknamed because he'd been a reverend in another lifetime but had flipped his shit one night, for reasons unknown, and never looked back. Broke his vows and turned to a life of crime. The rest, as they say, is history. Yet there he was, cutting the club that helped put him on the map out of a deal. Bad fucking news for him. One thing for certain was that those boys needed to learn who the real men were around there. I took another look at the buildings on either side of us, but didn't see any movement.

"Let's move," I said, finally making the call. "Be ready for anything." I looked over at Dom, Pipes, and Max, and they all nodded in agreement.

I pulled forward toward the roadblock, the sound of our bikes echoing loudly. I kept my gaze on as many places as possible. We were one of the largest distributors of coke in and around Atlanta, so Rev must have been fucking crazy to try cutting into our profits, but stranger things had happened.

Unless, a thought came to me, *the shit that went down with Butch was all leading up to this.*

There'd been talk of a new player coming in, ready to take over for some time. The Reverend was ready to retire; he'd been in the game long enough to know when to get out while you still could. Still, he wasn't about to walk away from his empire without making sure he had all his cards on the table for his upcoming withdrawal from the rat race first. Couldn't blame a man for that, that was for damn certain.

So if this was about a takeover, who the fuck was it and why didn't they want us involved? Why cut out your biggest supplier?

Because you're not needed anymore. I scowled at the thought.

We came to a stop a couple of feet from the prospects, and despite the dark lighting and the front they both tried to put on, there was no denying the fear that worked its way through their bodies now that we were right in front of them. Prepare all you want, but when you have five angry-looking Devil's Highwaymen in front of you, you'd better be prepared to die.

"Heard there's a meet tonight, brother," I said, taking in the older-looking prospect.

He couldn't have been more than twenty, a fucking kid really, and the other one looked even younger. He also looked like he was about to piss himself, and I noted that he shifted uncomfortably, his gaze traveling to the building to our left every once in a while.

"Invite only, Jesse," the prospect replied darkly.

"The Rev really cutting out the Highwaymen? That how it's really going to go down?" I asked, side-eyeing Casa and making sure he noted exactly what I had. By the hard look on his face, he wasn't blind to the fact that we probably had shooters on us right that second, which was exactly what I had worried about.

"Nothing to do with the Rev. New club in town don't want the Highwaymen involved in this," the prospect replied, swallowing noisily.

"Since when does the Reverend take orders from a new club?"

"Since the new club holds all the cards."

"What's your name?" I asked him.

"Anthony," he replied, raising his chin to me.

"Well listen up, Anthony. We need into that meet, and we need in right the fuck now—direct orders from The Highwaymen's president Hardy. I don't care who this club is or who the fuck is running it. Right now, I don't even give a fuck what they've told you to do. This is about respect, and if we don't get in there's going to be a whole world of problems, for you, for your club, and for whoever else is at that meet. You feel me?"

Anthony looked over at the younger kid, who was sweating and looking like he might pass out any second. Goddamn it, poor kid hadn't signed up to go to war; he'd wanted to join a club and belong. That's what the fucking brotherhood was all about—riding and having a family that would do anything for you. But he'd fallen in with the wrong side, and now he was going to pay for it. I hated this shit.

"I feel you, but I can't do it, Jesse," Anthony said, looking regretful. "We got orders to follow from our president, and those orders say it's invite only." He looked uncomfortable, despite his hard stance. I had to respect that; at least he showed loyalty and a backbone. Those were things you couldn't teach a prospect. They either had it or they didn't.

"Let's just blow this shit to high hell," Pipes snarled from next to me. "Brothers gotta be expecting it if they're going to be disrespecting the Highwaymen like this."

Anthony and the nervous prospect looked to one another, their fear pouring from them in bucket loads. Poor fucks.

I turned to Pipes. "Now just hang on a minute, Pipes. No need to start blowing shit up. I'm just talking to Anthony, and I'm pretty certain that we can come to an amicable solution that doesn't involve anyone dying tonight." I looked at Anthony, watching him white-knuckle the gun in his hands. Fucking hoped he had the safety on. "At least for now, right, Anthony?"

He grunted a yes, but his gaze was fixed on Pipes now, the real threat in his eyes. Good thing too. The two men were glaring at each other, and I had to hand it to the prospect—he'd make a good brother when he was fully patched in, because it was obvious that he wasn't backing down for nothing. Well, he would if he lived that long that is.

I looked up to the left again, catching sight of a shadow moving from within the building, the small sliver of moonlight reflecting back of the eyepiece of a sniper. A sniper that was aimed on us.

The whole thing was worse than I'd first realized. If we had guns on us on either side we were pretty much fucked, but there was still a chance. But this was snipers. That was some serious shit right there. And it spoke volumes to me about the sort of men we were dealing with. Because that wasn't the Rev's way.

I looked back to the prospects, noting that Anthony had seen my stare. He almost looked relieved, like he'd been hoping I'd notice someone was up there.

"All right, brothers," I said finally, making my decision. "We're leavin'."

"Jesse?" Pipes said my name, his voice tinged with total confusion. A Highwayman never backed down from a fight, yet there we were driving away with our tails between our legs. Or at least that's what it looked like.

"It's all right, brother. Gotta trust me on this one," I replied calmly, hoping he'd follow my orders, because if he didn't we were all going down. No sense dying for nothing. I was in this for the long game, and we'd achieve nothing if we opened up on those prospects then. If anything, it could be more damaging to our club.

"The Highwaymen don't fear, but the world should fear the Highwaymen," Pipes quoted our motto to me as he turned to glare at me, and I wanted to punch the stupid fuck in the head. Who did he think he was, quoting my own shit back to me? I knew the words, and I knew what they meant. Damn things were etched into my skin, right across my back. But at the moment this was bigger than just standing up to a couple of pissant prospects.

Every inch of me was vibrating with the urge to break some bones, but it was more important to hold my shit together right then so I gritted my teeth and glared back at Pipes, waiting for the stupid fuck to back down. Man didn't know who he was talking to if he thought that shit was okay.

"Okay," Dom said, taking the lead. "You heard Jesse, now let's get the fuck out of here then."

"Tell me one thing," I said to Anthony as my brothers turned their bikes around.

Anthony nodded his head, relief flooding his features.

"What's the name of the club back there?"

Anthony smiled, like he had been waiting for the question. He put his hand in his pocket and pulled out a piece of paper and handed it to me. "Been told to give you that," he said.

I shoved it in my pocket, none too pleased with how things had turned out, but someone was in those buildings to our left and right and I didn't feel like dying without finding out what the hell was going on. For the sake of my club, I'd sort this shit out.

"I'll be seeing you, Anthony," Pipes said, looking back over his shoulder, his deep voice gravelly and full of unspent rage.

I took one last look over my shoulder before we sped back off the way we'd come in. About a mile down the road I pulled over to one side and my brothers followed suit. I climbed off my bike and walked over to Pipes before reaching out and dragging him from his bike. He clawed at my hands and kicked out, but I threw him to the ground and pulled out my gun before aiming it at his head.

"Stay down!" I growled out as he attempted to get back up.

Dom and Casa flanked me, their guns out too. Max sat on his bike looking like he was about to piss himself and completely unsure what the hell he was supposed to do.

I kicked Pipes in the ribs and he groaned and curled up in a ball. I slammed my foot into his side three more times and then stopped. He slowly uncurled from his ball and looked up at me, hate and rage burning through his gaze.

With my gun still aimed at his head, I spoke clearly and calmly. "I'm the motherfuckin' enforcer of the Devil's Highwaymen. What I say goes, you hear me, brother?"

Pipes nodded and I sneered down at him.

"You ever fuckin question my authority again and I'll put a bullet in your brain. You feel me?"

"Yeah," he groaned, the anger finally retreating from his face.

I reached down, my hand outstretched to him, and he gripped it and allowed me to pull him back up to his feet. I pulled him in and patted him on his back before pulling away. One hand reached around his waist to cradle his bruised ribs. I'd kicked him hard, but not enough to break anything—just enough to teach him a lesson.

"This shit is bigger than what we thought," I said, looking across at my brothers. "Anyone else spot the sniper in the building?"

"A sniper? You serious?" Casa asked, pulling out his cigarettes and lighting one.

Dom let out a heavy breath and shook his head. "You think that fucker the Reverend is in bed with the heat?"

I shrugged. "Not sure, but I know I wasn't getting us all killed without knowing exactly who was shooting us in the back. That shit won't do the club any good." I pulled out the piece of paper that Anthony had given me and unfolded it. I read it twice and then handed it to Dom.

"Who the fuck are the Razorbacks?" he said, handing the paper to Casa.

"The Razorbacks will be expecting a thirty percent cut of all Highwaymen profits delivered to—" Casa looked up at me. "What the hell is this bullshit?"

"The start of a war, brother," I replied. I turned away and pulled my cell out and called Hardy. Because he needed to know right then what the hell was going down. His cell rang seven times before it went to voicemail and I hung up.

When I turned back around my brothers were standing by their bikes and watching me expectantly. But I had no idea what to tell them. Hardy would be pissed that we'd walked away, but he'd be even more pissed at the idea that someone was giving out orders to us.

"What now?" Pipes asked, his arm still around his ribs.

I used my cell to call Beefcake, the president of the West Side Bangers. He picked up on the second ring.

"Jesse fuckin' James, as I live and breathe. What can I do for you, brother?" he drawled down the phone.

Beefcake was a sound enough man, and he ran his club like a well-oiled machine. If something was going down in his area, he'd know what. I'd only ever met him once, but he'd treated me with respect, and clearly he had a good memory.

"Me and a couple of brothers are in town. Needing some hospitality for the night, if that's good with you?" I asked.

"Got a party going down tonight. Brothers just got out of DOC after a dime, but you and your boys are more than welcome to come and join in the celebrations, as long as you aren't bringing trouble to my door. Not tonight." I listened to Beefcake walking, the crunch of gravel underfoot and the music fading as he walked outside.

"No trouble, but I do need to discuss business with you. Some shit is going down in your area that I think you should know about." I turned back to my brothers and nodded to them and they all climbed on their bikes.

"All right, we'll discuss it when you get here, then we'll party," Beefcake replied, his voice serious.

"We'll be there soon," I replied and hung up. I climbed on my bike and started it up. "The West Side Bangers are sharing their hospitality for the night while we deal with whatever shit this is. Brother of theirs just got out after a ten-year stretch, so it's a celebration. Bit of an awkward time, but I'll discuss it with Beefcake when we get there."

My brothers nodded and we pulled away, heading toward the clubhouse of the West Side Bangers. I wasn't happy about leaving there without getting into the meet, but at least we knew the name of this other club. Now we just needed to know what their fucking play was going to be, because cutting us out of business and demanding a percentage of our taking wasn't going to go down well. For them, or for us.

CHAPTER ELEVEN:
1990
Jesse

Butch strutted through the room, proudly wearing his cut that now bore the colors of our club. Asshole was being a smug son of a bitch about it, too—not that he didn't deserve it, of course.

Two bitches walked over to him, one standing on either side to drape themselves across him, and he reached down to grab their little asses in their tiny hot pants and squeeze painfully tight. They both squealed but leaned further into him, giggling even louder.

"All right, brothers," Hardy called, coming to stand in the middle of the room. He pulled out his knife and tapped it against his bottle of beer. "Ring-a-ding-ding, fuckers!" he bellowed louder, until the room went silent, barring the pounding music, and everyone turned to look at him. "Let's give a Highwaymen welcome to our latest fully patched-in brother, my boy—Butch." He turned to look at Butch, an actual smile on his face—the first I'd seen in a long time. Shit, maybe ever.

The Highwaymen all cheered loudly, raising their beers to the air and calling Butch's name, and I couldn't help but find a smile and I raised my beer also. Butch was my brother and I loved him more than anyone else in the whole damn world—not that I'd tell the stupid fuck that, of course. He'd been working his ass off as a prospect for a long time to get this honor, and now it was his. He was a full member of the Devil's Highwaymen. Not only that, but Hardy had made him Road Captain for the club since Eight-Ball had been sent down and wouldn't be seeing the sun for a long fucking time. Poor bastard.

"I couldn't be any prouder of you, boy," Hardy continued, moving toward him.

The two bitches took a step to one side to allow Hardy to pull Butch into a hug that shocked all of us. When he pulled out he dragged a hand over Butch's head and ruffled his hair like he was a little fucking kid. Shit was weird to watch, but Butch was basking in the attention, and rightly so. Hardy was a hard man and he never showed affection, of any sort. Bet the sorry son of a bitch was stony-faced even when he was fucking. Hadn't when we were boys and it was unlikely he would now that we were men—except today.

"Let's fucking party!" Hardy called, laughing and walked away from Butch, heading toward Silvie, his old lady.

The other brothers cheered, and then some dumbass put a thumb over the neck of his beer and shook it until it started to foam and spray and then he aimed it at Butch, covering both him and the two bitches that had sidled back up to him in frothy, warm beer.

The girls screamed and Butch rubbed the beer over their bodies before leaning into kiss one of them on the mouth. Dom, Butch's best friend, was in a foul fucking mood and he stormed through the clubhouse and out the front door. I laughed and looked away, heading back to the bar to grab another beer. I downed what I had and set the bottle on the counter, and Rose handed me another one with a smile.

"He's a good man," Rose said, and I raised an eyebrow at her. "Butch," she clarified, pouring herself a shot of tequila and throwing it to the back of her throat. "He'll make a great old man for some lucky bitch one day." She smiled and walked away.

I turned back around, leaning on the bar with my elbows, and watched as Butch dragged the two giggling bitches into the back room. Casa walked over to me, pulling up his zipper as he did. Hadn't seen him all night, but I had no doubts on where he had been.

"Gimme a beer," he called to Rose, and she obliged, giving her usual smile. Woman was a goddamned saint to put up with our shit. Beautiful, too. Casa leaned over and clinked his bottle against mine. "Cheers, brother."

"Yeah," I said, giving him a nod.

"Butch sure knows how to party," he said, taking a long swallow of beer. "I swear some bitch almost sucked me dry back there—mouth like a vacuum! Thought she was going to swallow my balls whole at one point! Where the fuck does he even find them?" He laughed and nudged my elbow and I laughed with him.

"Everyone loves Butch." I grinned. "Fucker could talk a nun into putting out. I remember him taking me out to a party up near Smoke Rise, and as soon as he walked in it was like the prime pussy was released from somewhere and the dried-up old bitches scattered like cockroaches," I laughed. "Fucker had me join my first train that night."

Casa laughed loudly. "Like I said, man knows how to party, that's for damn sure."

I grinned and nodded before taking a swig of my beer. We both looked up as the door to the clubhouse opened and Gauge walked in, followed closely by his daughter, Laney. Casa nudged me, almost making me fall over, and then he burst into laughter as I almost spilled my beer down myself. Goddamn fucking idiot.

"Pussy-whipped and you ain't even got any yet." He laughed harder.

"Fuck off."

"Too many offers to fuck bitches to find time to fuck myself, brother," he snorted.

"Offers from your mama!" I bit out.

Casa stopped laughing and scowled at me. "That shit's just disrespectful."

"That's what your mama said, you pussy!" I flashed him a grin and strutted over to where Laney was. Pretty sure he called me something, but I drowned his voice out in favor of taking in Laney's beautiful figure. She was wearing something different from her usual denim cutoffs and tee that night—a lacy, white, figure-hugging dress that skimmed her golden thighs. Course, she still wore her little black ankle boots. Her hair was up on top of her head in one of those weird knot things that women wore, and I had the urge to reach over and let it down. Not that the look didn't suit her—it did, anything would fucking suit her—but there was something about the way her dark hair sashayed over her back that always turned me on.

"Keep an eye on her tonight, Jesse, she's feelin' particularly bitchy," Gauge said, patting me on the shoulder.

"Go fuck a cow!" Laney snapped back.

"Cunt!"

"Limp dick!"

Gauge looked between us both and shook his head before walking away, grumbling something under his breath. Things were not getting any easier between them. If anything, they were getting worse. Little did Gauge know that soon enough Laney wouldn't be his problem, but mine. I smiled at the thought.

"I hate him," she said, still watching after him.

"Ain't no secret about that." I grinned.

Her cheeks flushed pink at the sight of me, and I could tell she was restraining herself from smiling. She brushed her hands down her dress nervously and I watched appreciatively. Goddamn, she looked beautiful. Could only imagine what she would feel like wrapped around me—at least for the time being.

"You wanna beer?" I asked and she nodded and smiled again. Beautiful. Fucking beautiful.

We headed to the bar and Rose popped open a beer and slid it over as we got close. "Looking real pretty tonight, Laney."

Laney blushed and looked down at herself, and that time there was no mistaking that she was trying to hold back a smile. "Thanks, Rose, just something I threw on, nothing special."

"Really? Well, darlin' you scrub up good. Ain't that right, Jesse?"

Both women turned to look at me and I had to hold back on my eagerness to reply. "Don't think I've ever seen Laney look anything but good," I said, looking between the two women.

Rose's eyes sparked with mischievousness. "Well, that goes without saying," she replied.

Laney picked up her beer and cleared her throat loudly before taking a swig, and I could barely tear my gaze away from her damp lips wrapped around the end of the bottle. I shifted uncomfortably, needing to rearrange my junk but thinking better of it. Pussy-whipped before I'd even gotten any. Casa was fucking right.

I turned to Laney. "You wanna go for a walk?"

"Sure," she replied, tucking a loose piece of hair behind her ear. Christ on a bike, even her ears were beautiful. How was that even possible? "See you later, Rose," Laney said as I placed my hand on the bottom of her back and started to guide her away.

"You two kids have fun," Rose called back and I shot her a look.

We headed outside, away from the noise and the crowds, and into the humid September evening air. The sun was setting, casting an orange glow over everything, and little insects were buzzing around. I walked us over to the trees to the left of the clubhouse, intending to sit down at one of the small picnic tables we'd set up earlier that year, but when we got there Laney reached down and took my hand before leading us further away and out of sight.

Her hand in mine felt like fuckin' heaven, her grip both soft yet strong. And goddamn, being this close to her I could smell whatever shampoo she used and I'd be damned if she didn't smell like strawberries. Strawberries and cream, goddamn. My jeans grew tighter, and while still holding my beer, I reached down and rearranged myself.

The music faded the further away we walked, until it felt like we were the only two people left in the world. I smiled, knowing that I wouldn't have minded that for one minute.

"What's the smile for?" she asked.

I turned to her, sucking in my bottom lip and letting it out again. "I was just thinking about what it would be like if we were the only two people left on earth. Think I'd like that."

"Well, aren't you the poet?" She smiled and nudged my shoulder.

I pulled her to a stop and looked down at her. Goddamn, she was turning into something spectacular. She had always been sexy as hell, but she was a beautiful fucking woman now, and one that I wanted. Didn't matter how many women I fucked, my mind always strayed back to Laney. My hands weren't on those other women's hips and my dick wasn't ramming into their bodies. It was always her and her beautiful body that I felt wrapped around me. Her that made me come so hard my knees fucking shook.

It was always her.

I'd nailed so many women in an attempt to try to forget about her, but it wasn't working. Not even a little bit. I knew it was wrong; she deserved better than me. Ain't nothing that I could give her that would be good, but there was only so much one man could take before he cracked. And I had reached my limit.

I leaned over and kissed her hard, my teeth nipping at her lips before my tongue slid into her mouth and claimed it for my own. I was hard in my jeans, so hard I was sure I was going to poke a fucking hole through them any minute.

We were by one of the back walls of the clubhouse and I pushed Laney up against it, and tilted her face upwards so I could kiss across her neck and down to her breasts. She moaned and rolled her hips as I pressed my body against hers, grinding against her hard enough to hurt, but all she did was sigh.

I pulled out of the kiss and pressed my forehead to hers. "I'm no good," I said. "I need you to know that right from the start, because there's no going back after tonight. There's only so much one man can take before he just takes what he wants."

Her pupils dilated and her breathing hitched. "And what is it that you want, Jesse?"

"You," I growled out, swiveling my hips and grinding myself against her. "I want you."

CHAPTER TWELVE:
1990
Laney

"I want you," he said, his voice thick and full of untamed hunger.

I nodded, ignoring the flutter in my stomach as I held on tighter to him, letting him know that it was what I wanted too. Jesse leaned in and kissed me almost desperately, as if both of our lives depended on it. He stole me with that kiss, stole every part of who I was with every roll of his tongue and every nip of his teeth on my bottom lip. I would never be the same woman after a kiss like that. How could I be? The kiss was an all-devouring promise.

And it was just a taste of what was to come.

His pelvis ground harder against mine and I arched my back to meet each roll of his hips with my own, my mind reeling with what was happening. He reached up and untied my hair, letting g it fall about my shoulders and then he shoved both of his hands were wrapped in my hair and he pulled almost painfully on it. But it was a good pain, the sort that reminded you that you were alive and this was what your body needed.

That *he* was what my body needed.

My hands slid from his shoulders, moving down his back to where his T-shirt had come loose, and I pushed my hands underneath it, needing to touch his heated skin beneath. A spark of electricity hit me as my fingers touched him and he stilled momentarily, feeling it too. I slid my hands up his back and then his own hands were out of my hair and moving over my body and gliding down to the slope of my breasts. He pulled at the thin straps on my dress, pushing them down my arms until he could see my bra, and then he was pulling my breasts free of their confines and rolling my nipples between his fingers and making me whimper and sigh in pleasure.

I arched my back and groaned and he pulled his mouth away from mine, his possessive kiss leaving my lips to trail his tongue down toward my right breast. He sucked my hard nipple into his mouth, one hand kneading the other breast, while the other held me firmly by the waist, his hips still grinding and rolling against me until I felt the pleasure I was searching for, just out of reach, begin to move toward the horizon.

His was rock hard between my legs, his length pressing against the part where I needed him the most and grinding against my body to give me the friction that I so desperately wanted. With every thrust he gave me I thrust back against him until our bodies were in sync, and my back arched as pleasure rolled through me, pushing me over to the other side as I called out my release with a drawn-out cry, stars exploding behind my eyes.

He didn't stop. Instead he continued to press against me harder and harder, rolling his hips against me, hips that knew exactly what they wanted and how to get it, and taking what they demanded as he chased his own release, which came in the form of him grunting and holding my hips so tightly I knew I'd be bruised from his touch. I felt him pulsing against me as he ground his hips against mine in one long, torturous move that must have been shown to him by the devil himself because that last movement sent me over the edge once more and I clung to him, crying out as bright flashes of pleasure flashed behind my eyes once again.

"Fuck, Laney," he called out against my mouth, absorbing my cry.

He took my pleasure, swallowing it down as he kissed me, holding me close. And then he stilled me against him, slowly lowering me back down to the ground. We both opened our eyes at the same time, sharing the same expression on our faces. His gaze dipped lower, to my chest, and a moment of sexual hunger sparked in his eyes when he saw my naked breasts. His left hand came to trail down between my two peaks, making me shiver once more and my nipples go even harder.

I realized then, as Jesse looked down at me with both wonder and lust in his eyes, I realized that this would never be enough. I wanted more, and from the looks in his eyes, so did he.

"Are you okay?" he asked me, his voice like rough gravel.

I nodded, "Yeah."

My heart was still pounding in my chest, and I was unable to tear my gaze away from his. I was more than okay, but couldn't find my voice to put it into words just yet. I'd had orgasms before, but they were nothing compared to this, and it only made me greedy for the knowledge of what it would be like to actually have sex with him. When no clothes were separating our bodies and his body was sliding into mine, over and over again. I gulped, my body clenching at the thought.

Jesse reached over and pushed my long hair behind my ears, his fingers getting tangled once more in the thick strands. He dropped it, the hair floating down over my shoulders and collarbone and making me shiver and my nipples peak so hard that they were painful. His tongue darted out, wetting his lips, and then he leaned over to kiss me again, taking my mouth softly.

The kiss was gentle this time, but still filled with the hunger that seemed to accompany all of his kisses. I opened my mouth and let him in, taking his tongue and letting it move against mine as I nibbled at his lower lip, enjoying the feeling in my stomach like I was slowly unraveling. His muscled chest pressed against mine as he covered my body with his, and I let myself get lost in his kiss…

In his arms. ..

In his scent…

In him.

When I couldn't take any more, when I thought I might combust if he didn't take me right there and then—tear my panties off and slide himself deep inside me in one swift move—he pulled out of the kiss and pressed his forehead to mine, both of us panting in need and desire.

We stayed that way for several minutes and then he pulled away, kissing me once more, softer that time, less urgently, as if he'd found some self-control from somewhere, his thumbs trailing down the sides of my face.

The kiss ended, like all great kisses end, slowly and smoothly. Jesse looked at me, the hard angles of his face seemed softer somehow, even though I knew that was impossible. I smiled up at him, my cheeks feeling hot, and he smiled back. There were no words to describe what had just happened, no feelings to explain how my body called for him, and how his called to me. Or how, like magnets, we kept colliding no matter how hard we tried to pull apart.

There was no need for anything right then but the comfort of each other's arms wrapped around one another, and the realization that things had changed. After that night, nothing would ever be the same again.

CHAPTER THIRTEEN:
1990
Jesse

H-O-L-Y FUCK!

What the actual fuck was that? I looked down at Laney, her cheeks flushed and her eyes bright, watching as she opened her mouth to say something but then closed it again as if lost for words.

"Are you okay?" I asked, my words coming out heavy and thick, and meaning a hell of a lot more than *are you okay*.

"Yeah," she replied, her own voice breathy. She swallowed, her tongue darting out to lick along her lower lip, and I felt myself hardening in my jeans again as if I hadn't just fucked her through my jeans once already.

What the fuck was happening to me? She was driving me insane; that was it. This woman with her goddamned perfect body and dirty mouth was driving me insane. Her gaze was full of an almost insatiable hunger, her body and mind clearly wanting what I wanted.

Her dark hair was lying across her pale shoulders and I reached over and to tuck it behind her ear, but instead of letting go I watched her body shiver under my touch and I groaned at the sight of her full lips opening to release a small sigh. I hardened even more, painfully so, and I let her hair fall from my hand and gently fall back to her skin. I could make out her hard nipples beneath the thin material of her bra and dress since she'd covered herself back up, the little peaks begging to be licked and sucked on. I leaned over her, wrapping my fingers in her hair, and I pulled her in for a deep kiss.

I kissed her softly at first, but it didn't last long before I was kissing her hard, my tongue moving against hers, enjoying every nibble on my lips and her groans of need in my mouth. My pants were too tight, and I wanted inside her, no questions asked. I wanted to take what was mine, right there and then. Because there was no doubt in my mind that this woman was mine now. I was claiming her, and fuck Gauge and fuck Hardy and fuck anyone who tried to get in my way. I'd put a bullet in the skull of any man who tried to keep me away from her now.

I'd been the good guy. I'd left her alone, but time and time again we were drawn back to one another. So fuck that now. Fuck all of it.

This woman was mine.

I was claiming her right the fuck now.

"You're mine now, you hear me?" I said, pulling out of the kiss and pressing my forehead against hers.

She nodded beneath me, her fingers digging into my waist. "Okay," she whispered breathlessly.

I reached down between us and placed my hand between her legs, feeling her soaked panties and growling territorially. "And this is definitely mine and no one goes near it—or you—but me. You got it?"

She nodded again and I sighed with relief. There was never any question after that night of her not being mine, but the realization that she wouldn't fight me on it, that she wanted me as much as I wanted her, soothed me. No, not wanted, needed. I fucking needed her like I needed air. I needed her kisses as much as I needed to eat and to drink and to breathe.

Laney was life, and from that moment on, she would be my life.

I pressed a hungry kiss to her lips again, wanting to take her right there, because I desperately needed to feel her sweetness wrapped around me, but I also wanted more for her than this. She deserved more. I pulled out of the kiss, knowing that if I didn't there would be no stopping me, or her. I pulled her down to the ground and we both lay back on the grass. I tucked her body tightly against mine, fighting my urges every step of the way.

We lay back and looked up at the stars, my heart hammering against my ribs and my cock aching something fierce in my jeans. Her breaths slowly evened out, and when I looked down at her, her eyes were closed, her face calm and serene.

Goddamn, but she was beautiful. The most beautiful fucking woman I had ever laid eyes on. From day one of seeing her, I had known there was something about her that was made just for me, but now I had the proof. Her slender body fitted in effortlessly next to my bulky frame, and her full lips connected with mine perfectly.

And that fierce mind and dirty mouth of hers were just the icing on the cake.

Laney was perfection and she was all fucking mine now.

CHAPTER FOURTEEN:
Present
Jesse

The West Side Bangers clubhouse was lit up like the fucking Fourth of July when we pulled up outside.

The music was obnoxiously loud, and bikes were riding up and down the street outside with bikers and women standing around drinking beer from bottles and generally not giving a shit what kind of noise they made. Their clubhouse was in downtown Atlanta, in a real shitty neighborhood, to say the least, but at least their neighbors knew to keep their noses out of other people's business, and by the looks of things they weren't the sort to call the cops at every small opportunity. Good to know.

The party was in full swing as we parked our bikes in a long row next to the other thirty that were already there and duck-walked them into position. We eyed the prospects in charge of guarding them as we walked by, giving them a small nod. Women were huddled in groups, giggling and jutting out their chests as we passed through the main doorway, their long-nailed fingers grazing my bare arms as they rubbed against us like cats in heat.

"Hey," a little blond thing said as we walked inside and I looked her up and down, noting her tiny waist and even tinier shorts barely covering her pert little ass.

"Hey," I replied, walking away. Sure as shit had enough women drama for one day.

Beefcake stood up and walked toward us and pulled me in for a hug, patting me on the back before pulling back to look at me, a wide smile on his fat face. Beefcake was a big man in both height and weight, easily passing six feet and two hundred and fifty pounds of pure flab. His hair was long and dark and always pulled back into a long braid down his back. But the fat fucker never had a problem getting a woman on his arm.

"Welcome, Jesse." He nodded to my brothers. "Make yourselves at home, brothers, *mi casa es su casa.*"

I nodded to my brothers, setting them free to party for a couple of hours while I dealt with the shit that had just gone down. Dom eyed me warily before nodding and heading to one of the kegs to grab himself a beer. Man just seemed worn out those days—never smiled, never laughed, just constantly brooded about life and the universe or some shit. And though he was still a part of the club, he'd taken a step back from most dealings. I was lucky that he'd even come tonight.

Casa stayed behind with me, and I was grateful for his presence.

"Let's talk," Beefcake said, and put his hand on my arm and started guiding us across the room.

He led us through the center of the party, passing bikers and bitches who all turned to stare at us.

Beefcake waved them all off with a wave of his fat hand. "Don't mind them. Think they're still in shock from everything and wanting to pay their respects at some point. Told them to give you time to settle in before they spoke to you about it all." He pushed open the door to his office and we stepped inside

"Appreciate that," I replied.

"No problem." He pulled out a chair behind his desk and sat down, gesturing for me and Casa to sit opposite. "So what's this shit going down in my charter you were talking about?" He steepled his fingers together and waited for me to speak, and I glanced across at Casa before replying.

"You ever heard of the Razorbacks MC?" I asked, feeling him out for information first.

His look turned serious. "Heard whispers about them—nothing set in stone, though. They seem more like ghosts than anything else. No one has seen them or spoken to them, but we've seen their tags. Why? What's going on, Jesse?"

"There was a business meeting tonight, seems that the Highwaymen weren't invited." I watched Beefcake's face to see if he looked surprised or not by that. He did, which was good for him and his club. "In fact, there were orders to keep us out completely. And we got given this," I said, fishing the note out of my pocket and handing it to Beefcake.

He took it and opened it up, reading it quickly before placing it down on the desk in front of him. If his look had been serious before, it was nothing compared to now. Beefcake stood up and walked to the door before opening it and calling outside for Bridge, his VP.

A few moments later Bridge came in and the door was shut again. Beefcake went and sat back down and Bridge stood next to him, looking expectantly at his pres.

"Looks like the Highwaymen are going to war," Beefcake said, looking across at us and nodding before looking back to Bridge. "Club called the Razorbacks are trying to cut them out of their own business. Shit won't stand when Hardy finds out, that's for damn sure. Need to make sure it's clear what side the Bangers are on." Beefcake looked over to me and nodded respectfully. "We clear?" he asked.

"Crystal," I replied. "You should know, though, the Reverend was there tonight."

Bridge stepped forward. "Seriously?"

"Serious as a fucking judge on a murder rap, brother," Casa replied. "Heard he was looking to retire to the Bahamas or some shit like that. Never thought he'd betray his brothers, though."

"That change anything for you?" I asked Beefcake.

He looked up at Bridge and they exchanged a look which I took to mean that it did, but Beefcake surprised me by looking back at me. "Not a damn thing. Two things I can't stand are disloyalty and assholes who think they're above everyone else. Looks like the Rev just crossed both those lines. The Bangers have the Highwaymen's back, brother, no problem on that front."

"Appreciate that," I replied.

Beefcake stood up and came around the desk, and both Casa and I stood up too. I reached out my hand and Beefcake took it before pulling me into a manly hug and slapping my back. When he pulled back, his expression had softened from serious to sympathetic.

"This shit with Butch, real sorry, Jesse. The whole club is still in shock. None of us saw it coming."

I nodded, not really wanting to talk about it, but I had known I would have to when I came here. All the other charters had been desperate to talk about it too, but I'd so far avoided it. Clearly that wasn't going to happen for much longer.

Not that I could blame them.

"Thanks, the club appreciates it," I replied, my throat feeling tight.

He reached into his cut and pulled out a cigar before handing it to me. "It's the life we choose to lead though, right?"

I took the cigar and nodded at Beefcake. "Damn straight."

"Anything I can do, you let me know," Beefcake added.

"Think we could do with a drink," Casa said, knowing me well enough to cut in.

"Of course, of course, let's go get a drink. You still with that woman of yours?"

We headed to the door, and he pulled it open and we all filtered out, heading back into the main clubhouse.

"Yeah," I replied, lying through my teeth.

"Woman is fucking beautiful, but we've got plenty of bitches here if you wanted a break from the usual, brother. Take what you need," Beefcake said before heading off to his seat.

Bridge patted me on the shoulder and stalked off, leaving me and Casa alone. I pulled out my cell and tried to call Hardy again, but it only rang out and went to voicemail. I hung up and slipped my cell in my pocket and looked around, finding Dom, Pipes, and Max sitting together drinking beer out of red plastic cups. A sexy little brunette was draped across Dom, her face buried in his lap where she was bobbing her head up and down while she gave him a blowjob—not that you could tell from the blasé look on his face. He saw me and Casa and pushed the brunette away, ignoring her angry glare. Instead he tucked himself back in his jeans and zipped them back up. He walked toward us, with Pipes and Max following close behind.

"Everything cool?" he asked, his tone devoid of emotion.

"Yeah, the Bangers are with us, no matter what goes down," I replied.

"Any news on Hardy?" he asked.

I shook my head. "Nothing. Just ringing out constantly." I frowned, wondering what the fuck else could go wrong with that crazy-ass night.

"I tried Rider and Gauge but there was no answer from either of them," Dom said, dragging a hand down his beard. "I don't like this, Jesse. Something ain't right."

"I feel you, and I agree, but fuck knows what's going on. Meeting they were going to was nothing but a meet and greet. Nothing heavy."

"Let's wait it out, see what Hardy says in the morning. We'll figure it all out," Casa said and Dom nodded in agreement.

The blonde from earlier had spotted me and was on her way over, her eyes making their way up and down me. "Fuck me, I could really do without this shit tonight."

Casa turned to look and then he grinned. "You want me to take care of that problem for you, boss?"

"Fuck yeah, go knock yourself out," I laughed and patted him on the shoulder.

"No problem. All in the line of duty and all that shit." He laughed and took off, cutting into the blonde's path and directing her in the opposite direction.

"Yeah, you're a real fucking saint, Casa." I shook my head and laughed. "Let's get a beer. Not much I can do until I get ahold of Hardy and find out what he wants to happen."

We walked outside to where another keg was and I got myself a beer, downed it in one, and then got a second, feeling better as the shitty beer sank into the pits of my stomach. Pretty sure I hadn't eaten anything since the night before. Not that I remembered it, because I'd been so fucking drunk—drunk enough to cheat on Laney—but I'd seen the pizza boxes scattered across my living room table.

Goddamn, I was an asshole, but that was what I'd aimed to be. Had to make her see that I was no good for her. Had to make her understand that she needed to get away from me. Couldn't blame her for leaving my sorry ass; it was more than I deserved and then some.

Someone had started a couple of fires in the metal drums around the place, and an orange glow lit up the dark sky. I stared into the flames, wondering what the hell I was going to do. It was turning out to be one of the craziest nights in a long time. First I fucked up my relationship with Laney, and I had no doubt that it was well and truly fucked this time and I wasn't delusional in thinking I couldn't come back from it. Then Hardy asked for my help, which was fucking unheard of, and then the Highwaymen got a declaration of war from a start-up charter and we found out we'd been betrayed by the Reverend, of all people.

Shit was crazy.

Nah, this shit was more than just crazy; this shit was fucked right the fuck up.

I downed my second beer and threw the plastic cup to one side, needing more than just warm beer to get me through the rest of that fucked-up night. I needed to keep my head in the game and stop thinking about Laney—for a little while, at least. Too much was going on and too much was at risk to be distracted. Yet I couldn't stop myself, because if I didn't think about Laney I would think about Butch, and when I thought about Butch, bad shit happened around me. As usual, Laney and Butch dominated my very being. They were the two most important people in my life—or they had been. Now, through one thing or another, I had lost both of them.

"You okay?" Dom asked, coming to stand by me. He handed me another beer, and I took it because there was nothing else there to get me through this shit and I needed something.

"Not really," I replied, still staring into the flames. "You?"

"Nope," he replied. Dom had been Butch's best friend and they'd known each other way back before we'd even moved in with Hardy, back when we lived with my mom and she was a crackhead junkie and we were half-starving to death because she'd spent our family allowance on drugs. Dom's mom had fed us, helped clothe us; even though she had six kids herself, she helped me and Butch like we were her own.

Even after Mom died and we went to live with Hardy, Dom and Butch had stayed friends. Fucking nothing could keep those two apart. Not distance, not the club, nothing. Or so we thought. Now Dom was as lost as I was, going off the rails while he tried to sort out the rage that was filling him from the inside out.

Rage I knew only too well, because I lived and breathed right alongside him. Most of his shit went under the radar because he was always fucking quiet and moody anyway. Shit, maybe I wouldn't have noticed too much either if I didn't know him so well.

Because for me, it was his eyes that gave him away. Where once they had held a certain ferocity now they were cold and dead, just like Butch. They were grey, like slate or marble or some shit Butch had once said, but now…now they just seemed empty. Dead of anything.

At least for Dom the only thing he couldn't fuck up was his relationship, because he didn't have one. The man barely glanced at bitches, his time having been taken up by the club and caring for his brothers and sisters for as far back as I could remember. He was a goddamned saint as far as I was concerned, because most of his siblings were crazy fucked up too.

But Dom was a good man, and he was the biggest connection I had to Butch now, and vice versa. We stood in mutual silence, both of us watching the flames, drinking our warm, shitty beer and thinking of Butch, my brother, and his best friend, and wishing shit would have turned out differently.

We both missed him like crazy, and we would both probably never get over his death.

But at least Dom didn't have to live with the guilt like I did.

CHAPTER FIFTEEN:
Present
Jesse

I woke to the sound of water dripping into a metal bucket somewhere in the room. I was lying on my back on a bed that had seen better days, given the amount of springs that were digging into my spine. Rubbing at my eyes, I yawned and rolled onto my side before realizing that my bladder was on fire and I needed to piss.

"Fuck," I mumbled, stumbling up to my feet and crossing the room. I threw open the door and looked around, not having a clue where the bathroom was in this place. A couple of bitches were still up and drinking, though they should probably have quit a couple of hours ago, by the state they were in.

"Bathroom," I barked out to the closest one—a tiny redhead with tits bigger than my head.

She pointed behind me and I turned and headed back the way I had just come, intending on going back to visit her as soon as I was done. There were several closed doors along the corridor, though it was easy to spot the ones that were occupied, given the snoring or the grunts coming from behind them. I found another door right at the end of the hallway and pushed it open, praying it was the magical room with a piss pot, and lo and behold, it was.

"Thank fuck." I closed the door and stumbled over to piss, holding onto the wall for support.

Didn't remember much about the previous night after the twelfth or so beer and Beefcake bringing out the whisky. Dom had disappeared around that time—fuck knew where, though—and Casa had returned from fucking some bitch and joined me in taking shots in memory of Butch.

It was blank after the memory of sucking whisky out of some blonde's navel.

I finished pissing and shoved my junk away, desperate for coffee and some fresh air, when I felt my cell vibrating in my pocket. I fumbled around trying to grab it, and stared bleary-eyed as Hardy's name lit up.

I slid down to sit on the floor and tried to clear my head as I answered the cell.

"Hardy, I've been trying to get ahold of you," I said, and dragged a hand through my hair.

There was silence on the other end of the line before Hardy replied. "Jesse?"

"The one and only," I said, stealing Butch's line.

"Don't get smart. I've been calling all morning, why didn't you pick up?" He sounded strange; more confused than pissed off.

"I was sleeping. I was calling you all last night. Gave up around two a.m. Where the fuck were you?" I did not need him giving me a lecture at the moment; too much other shit was going down that was more important than whatever his feelings for me were.

"I'm the president, Jesse, I'm not at your beck and call!" he yelled down the cell, making my ears ring and my head swim.

I pulled the cell away from my ear while he continued to shout and I tried to contain my own anger. Arguing with him wouldn't get me anywhere, I knew that, yet right then my head didn't give a damn who he was. All I could picture was slamming his head into a brick wall.

I put the cell back to my ear. "Will you shut the fuck up?"

"What did you just say to me?"

"I said shut the fuck up, Hardy, we got bigger problems than whatever it is between you and me. The Reverend betrayed us and we've got a new player in town, call themselves the Razorbacks."

The line went silent and I wondered if he'd gone, but the sound of his breathing made it obvious he was still there.

"Hardy?"

"What?"

"We need to put the Rev to ground and then we need to pull all the charters in to take out these Razorbacks. Fuckers had snipers on me and the boys last night."

"You and the boys?" he asked. "Who did you take with you?" Now he sounded angry. Really fucking angry.

"Dom, Casa, couple of prospects—Pipes and Max. Thought it would be better going in with bodies," I replied, confused by his anger. Seemed pretty obvious to me that we go in with a small crew, show force against being cut out.

"I told you to go alone," he said darkly.

"No, you told me to be discreet, and I was." My brain was wide awake now and I stood up, my senses alert. "I made a judgment call," I replied. Something was wrong, off somehow, something that, in all my brilliance, I hadn't picked up on the day before.

"Where are you?"

"Why?" I asked, unsure as to why I felt so uneasy about the whole conversation.

"Because I fucking asked, that's motherfucking why! I'll be back at the clubhouse around noon and I want you in the Chapel, Jesse. Tell your brothers that, okay?" he said. He cleared his throat. "So, where the fuck are you?"

"Doesn't matter. I'll meet you at the clubhouse at noon," I said, hanging up quickly before he could ask me again where I was.

I slipped the cell into my pocket and walked over to the sink before running the taps and filling it. When it was full of ice-cold water, I leaned over and took a deep breath before dunking my head under. My heart sped up as the cold water shocked me, but I stayed under for as long as I could, waking my brain up and straightening up all my thoughts. Shit was fucked up, but out of everything that had happened, Hardy's reaction bothered me the most.

When I couldn't hold my breath any longer, I pulled the plug on the sink and stood upright, letting the cold water trail its icy tendrils down my chest and back. I rubbed at my face, my cheeks feeling numb from the cold, but my mind was awake and alert. And I had a feeling that today I would need that.

I stepped out of the small bathroom and into the hallway and headed back to the main clubhouse. Dom had finally shown back up and he was standing at the bar talking to the redhead with the huge tits and drinking a coffee. He draped a jacket over her shoulders and she picked up a mug of coffee and took a tentative sip of it before laughing at something he'd said.

I raised an eyebrow as I got closer, and he raised his chin to me.

"Mornin'. Any more of that coffee going?"

"I'll go get you one," the redhead said, sliding off her stool on unsteady feet.

"I got it." Dom put down his mug, and with one swift movement he'd hoisted her back up on the stool. She blushed profusely and looked down into her coffee, her red hair framing her face. Looked like Dom had staked some sort of claim on her, which could be added to the list of crazy shit going on right now.

Dom wandered off to what I presumed was the kitchen and I stared down at the redhead. She looked young—not jailbait, but close enough—and she was beautiful, too. Plump mouth, little upturned nose, and high cheekbones. She looked up at me through her lashes, obviously feeling uncomfortable but also feeling too much like shit to do anything about it. Her makeup was smudged under her eyes, like she'd been rubbing them and forgot she was wearing makeup, and even though Dom had covered her up with a jacket, her huge breasts were still on display for anyone to look at through her low-cut top.

Dom came back and handed me the mug of steaming coffee. There was no milk, but I didn't care too much.

"Where's Pipes and Max?" Dom asked, sitting down opposite the girl.

She looked over at me and I jerked my head to one side, making it clear she needed to go so we could talk. Dom grabbed my arm and started guiding me away instead, which was even more fucked up than anything else.

We headed across the room and I shrugged out of his grip and glared across at him. "What the fuck is that about?"

"Nothin', bitch just looks like she needs the seat more than you," he grumbled out.

"You sweet on her?" I laughed.

Dom raised an eyebrow and shook his head, a coy smile on his face. "I miss your brother even more when you come out with stupid shit like that, Jesse," he said, and I frowned, wondering what the hell he was talking about.

As we pushed open the clubhouse door, Casa groaned from one of the sofas and stood up, one hand grabbing at his head.

"Gotta stop drinking whisky," he grumbled, and stood up before following us.

He grabbed my coffee as we sat down at a small table outside, and after a long gulp he put his head in his hands and groaned again. I looked at Dom and we both laughed.

"You seen Pipes or Max yet?" I said, banging the table right next to his head.

"Fuckkkk," Casa yelled without looking up. "Not since last night. Saw them outside talking to the Bangers prospects. Pussies probably complaining to each other about not being patched in yet," he said with a chuckle which morphed into another groan.

I looked over at Dom and he took a swig of his coffee and shrugged. "Probably. I know Pipes is ready for it. Not sure Max is yet, though."

"I'll speak to Hardy," I replied. "Speaking of Hardy, I got a call from him this morning."

"Yeah?" Dom asked, pulling out his cigarettes and lighting one. "How'd that work out?"

"Same as usual," I replied, thinking back to the conversation. I dragged a hand down my beard thoughtfully. I trusted both Dom and Casa, but I also didn't want them getting into any shit with Hardy because of me. I didn't know what was off with the conversation with Hardy yet, but I knew something wasn't right. And until I knew what, it wasn't fair to put that on my brothers.

"You tell him about the note from the Razorbacks?" Casa asked, raising his head to look at me. His eyes were red-rimmed and his skin was pale and sweaty—not to mention that he stunk to high heaven. His skin was almost leaking out last night's alcohol consumption, yet I had no doubt that he could stand up right then and pick the prettiest girl around and get her on his bike. Man was pussy magnet, that was for sure.

"Nah, didn't get into it. He wanted to know where I was and said he would be back around noon. Sounded real pissed that I had you all with me last night." I looked over to my bike longingly, ready to ride out of there, but also not knowing where to go. I trusted my instincts, and my instincts were telling me not to go to the clubhouse just yet.

"Why? A brother needs backup for meets, especially ones we're kept out of," Dom said, his brow furrowing. He threw his cigarette away and crossed his arms in front of him, his muscles twitching. Man was a fucking beast and he knew it. Never had to get into many fights because most people took one look and went in the opposite direction. Funny, really, considering he was a lover and not a fighter—at least if he could help it. His appearance was his camouflage. At least that's what Butch had once told me.

"That's what I said. He didn't agree, though," I replied.

All three of us sat in contemplative silence for several moments before the clubhouse door opened and Pipes and Max came out. They both seemed in a lot better state than Casa was in, that was for sure. Pipes sat down, a shit-eating grin on his face.

"We rollin' out?" Pipes asked.

"Yeah, let me go find Beefcake and give my regards." I stood up and headed back inside and Dom caught up to me. I looked across to him. "You my chaperone now?"

"Just wanna check on Harlow," he replied.

"Harlow? She the chick with the huge—"

"Yeah. She's a good girl. She's better than what she thinks," he replied.

I stopped and turned to look at him. "You sweet on her? You know she's just a sweetbutt, right?"

Dom's jaw clenched, his eyes going dark. "No one is ever *just* a something, Jesse. You should know that more than anyone." His fierce gaze burned into mine, all familiarity gone out the window. I take back what I said about him being a lover and not a fighter.

However, he might have been older and stronger than me, but that made no difference as I squared up to him, because I was a cocky motherfucker who was done taking shit from anyone a long time ago.

"First off, I don't know what the fuck you're talking about. And secondly, that chick is a hangaround. A club whore. A sweetbutt that's taken more dick in all those little pretty puckered holes of hers than we'll ever know. Bitch has probably taken it up the ass so much her shit slides right out. But if you want to have a ride, you have at it. I won't judge you, brother. But remember to cover up before you blow your load, because bitches like that are always looking for a free ride." I finished my angry speech and stared at him, but he didn't reply. His eyes had no fire left in them and I wondered why I was pushing him on this. Why it fucking mattered to me who he fucked or staked a claim on.

I was a walking talking bomb, and I was ready to fucking explode, that's why. And it didn't look like I gave a shit who I hurt in the process.

"That's what I fucking thought," I gloated with a sneer. With that I pushed open the door and went inside the clubhouse, leaving Dom outside.

Harlow, or whatever the fuck her name was, was still sitting at the bar, her head drooping, but she perked right the fuck up when I walked back inside.

I headed down the hallway and thumped on Beefcake's office door twice and waited.

"Gimme a minute," he called.

I pulled out my cell phone and looked at the time. It was a little before nine, too early to be waking a brother up, but we needed to get back on the road—though by the sounds coming from in his office, he was already wide awake anyway. A few little yelps sounded out from inside Beefcake's office, and he gave out a long, throaty growl that made me smirk. A minute went by before the door opened and a barely dressed woman walked out with an obvious limp in her step as she smoothed out her too-short skirt. She gave another one of her little yelps as he slapped her ass and she wandered off.

"Come on in," he said, giving me a sly grin, his eyes following her ass down the hallway. "Bitch will be walking with a limp for days after that," he said rearranging his junk.

I grinned back and walked inside. "Just letting you know that we're headin' out. Wanted to thank you for putting us up last night, and for your loyalty to the Highwaymen, of course. I'm sure Hardy will be in touch when the time comes." I held out my hand and Beefcake took it, pulling me in to a quick hug before he pulled back out.

He looked at me uncertainly for a second, dragging a hand across his chin.

"Well, what is it?" I asked, because clearly the man had something to say.

"I put the feelers out last night, about the Razorbacks," he replied.

"Any bites?"

"A couple—mostly nothin' though. They're ghosts, it seems—clean up real well after themselves too. But I did get one lead. Heard that the name—the Razorbacks—it's code for something. Not sure what, but then I'm shit at anagrams so there's no surprise there." He reached over to the table and grabbed the bottle of whisky he had there before taking a swig of it. Man hadn't even been to sleep yet, but I had no reason to doubt him.

"All right," I finally said once he'd quit filling me in. My brain was turning around the different outcomes of it all, and none of them looked good at the moment. One thing was for certain: things were about to go south. Way south. "This stays between you and I," I said.

Beefcake nodded. "Not a problem. You gonna need our help?"

"Probably," I replied.

"I'm gonna want compensating for that. Hospitality is one thing, but war is a whole different game."

I nodded, already knowing that had been coming. "All right. Keep your cell on, and I'll be in touch. The Highwaymen have the club's back when you need us, as long as you have ours, but that goes without saying."

Beefcake rubbed a hand across his sweaty head and looked over at me.

I sneered. "What else?"

"The Bangers will want a cut in at some point," he replied, almost regrettably.

"Thought the Bangers dealt in weapons, not drugs," I said.

"Let's just say we're expanding."

I nodded, but both of us knew that it wasn't up to me to answer. It was up to Hardy and the club. "I'll speak to Hardy," I finally said. "Put in a good word, and then it'll go to vote. Not much I can do other than that."

Beefcake didn't look totally happy, but he also knew I couldn't speak for my president or the club. I also knew that it wouldn't go down well if Hardy said no to cutting in the Bangers, but maybe Dom could help sell it to him. For sure it would work in our favor to have another distributor that side if we'd lost the Reverend.

The Highwaymen had dealt in the gun trade with the Bangers for several years, and up until that point they'd stayed away from drugs. Really, though, it was the next logical step for the club if they wanted to continue to grow—especially since it looked like a hole had been made. Though Beefcake would have problems with some of the older members who had always stated they didn't want near the drug trade, that wasn't my problem.

"All right, well, I'm heading out. I'll look into the Intel and I'll speak to Hardy as soon as I get back. Might be a couple of days before it goes to vote, though. Brothers are scattered all over at the moment, but I'll get right on it." I shook his hand and headed out of the office. "Thanks again for the hospitality."

I left clubhouse and headed back outside. Everyone was waiting for me, and I climbed on my bike and slipped on my helmet. I looked over at Casa, who still looked sick as a dog, and then I looked over at Dom. He was on his bike and behind him sat Harlow, her arms wrapped around his waist and her tits pushed up against his back.

"You know what you're doing, brother?" I said, anger and resentment bubbling inside of me for some reason.

"I do," he replied, holding my gaze and letting me know that it wasn't up for discussion.

I started my bike and pulled out of the grounds of the clubhouse with my brothers following me. I wasn't sure why Dom bringing Harlow with him bothered me so much. Perhaps because it was like he was moving on with his life, taking the next leap into the unknown. I'd never thought Dom would take a woman, yet there he was with a sweetbutt on the back of his bike and his head up his ass over her. Couldn't work it out. Sure, she was beautiful, but so were thousands of other women.

Why her and why the fuck now?

Or maybe I was just a jealous asshole. I had fucked up my life and Laney had left my sorry ass and I was pissed that Dom was finally getting the thing that I'd actually had. Couldn't blame the man for wanting to be happy. I just wished I could be happy for him too.

CHAPTER SIXTEEN:
1991 / New Year's Eve
Jesse

Laney slowed to a stop and turned back to face me, her tongue darting out to lick her pink lips. "Thought we could use some privacy," she said, her voice a soft breath.

I smiled, knowing exactly why she wanted privacy. My girl was trying to seduce me. I must have been the luckiest fucking man in the world, right then, and I'd be damned if I wasn't going to drag it out and then make her scream my name afterwards.

We'd left the party—my party—and gone to get some fresh air outside, our bodies automatically taking us away from the noise and the lights of the clubhouse and to our own secluded area behind the clubhouse where the ground was soft and the trees stood tall and proud against the sky.

"Yeah?" I said, taking a swig of my beer. "What for?"

Her cheeks flushed red, and I wondered if the rest of her would be as pink as her cheeks. Damn hoped so.

"Well, there's a lot of celebrations tonight," she said, and I smirked. "Thought we needed some time together."

Damn right there were a lot of celebrations that night. That night I had been patched in. Hardy had made it as difficult as fucking possible for me, and strung it out as long as he could, but it had been decided and there wasn't shit he could do about it. Not only that, but it was New Year's fucking Eve, and Laney was back from some trip that Gauge had sent her on with her college friends.

Between the club and her school, I hadn't seen her for more than a few minutes at a time for almost six months. I'd been determined to get her under me the next time I saw her, but weeks had passed and life had stepped between us. The club had been busy with some bad shit going down, and she'd been busy at school and shit. Thought for a while that she'd had second thoughts, but then she'd turned up at the club with Gauge one day and I'd dragged her into my room and she'd given me the best blowjob I'd ever had.

I'd wanted to tell Gauge about us. Shit, I'd wanted to tell the whole world who owned her, but she'd begged me not to—not until she was ready. Hated every minute of it, but she swore it was to do with Gauge and their relationship and not me.

But after tonight, there was no way this shit was staying secret anymore. I wanted in her, and I wanted the world to know who she belonged to. No matter what the fucking consequences.

She let go of my hand and took a swig of her own beer. "Gauge watches my every move," she said after a hesitant moment. Thought she was going to chicken out for a minute there. I grinned.

"Man knows what his brothers are like," I replied.

"Yeah?"

"Yeah."

"And what are they like?" she asked, testing the waters. She took another drink, and I could barely speak for a second when a drop of beer slid down off her bottom lip and she licked it away. My blood rushed away from my brain and straight to my dick.

I cleared my throat. "Horny motherfuckers, all of them."

"All of them?" she asked, one eyebrow lifted questioningly, a small smile on her mouth.

"Every. Last. One," I replied.

She stared at me, her pupils dilating as she swallowed. "And what about you?"

"What about me?" I took a swig of my beer.

"Are you a horny motherfucker, Jesse?"

I spat my beer out on the ground in front of us, her words catching me off guard, and she burst out laughing. I wiped at my chin, clearing my beard of the warm beer, and I barked out my own laugh.

"Damn fuckin' right I am," I replied, watching the hunger in her eyes grow, and enjoying it too. "But only for one woman."

Laney lifted her chin and stared at me, her gaze burning into mine. "And who would that be?" she breathed out.

I threw my bottle to one side and reached across to her, my hand gripping her waist tightly and dragging her body to mine.

"Think it's pretty fuckin' obvious who, don't you?" I said, grinding myself against her.

Her lips parted to let out a small sigh. She threw her own bottle to one side and I leaned down and pressed my lips to hers, taking her mouth hard and fast. She groaned against my mouth as I wrapped my arms around her, my hands moving up and down her back, desperate to feel her hair trailing through my fingers.

I reached up and pulled out a couple of clips from her hair, my mouth never leaving hers, and her hair came tumbling down around her shoulders. She panted against me, her firm body going weak in my arms as I pulled her tightly against me, pushing her legs apart so I could wedge myself between them and grind against her.

Her own hands roamed down my body until they found my ass, and she squeezed almost hesitantly, making me laugh. She pulled out of the kiss and looked up at me, her gaze dreamy and far away but with that fire in it that turned me on so much. My mouth quirked as I watched her, turning up into a full smile as the fire in her eyes burned brighter.

"Don't laugh at me," she said with a pout.

I reached around to grab her hands, covering them with my own, and then I squeezed, giving her a good handful of my ass. I watched her mouth tug into a grin.

"Trust me, I ain't laughin', darlin'. Laughin' is just about the last thing on my mind right now," I said, letting go of her hands now that she seemed to have the confidence to take what she wanted herself. I placed my hands on her hips and stroked up and down her body, barely able to take my gaze away from her in that dress.

"So," she said.

I cocked my head, wondering what was going to come out of that mouth of hers that time. Woman never failed to surprise me.

"So," I retorted.

"Are we going to do this or what?"

A slow grin crept up my face, and I wrapped my hand in her hair and dragged her body against mine again. She yelped and her eyes sparked with need. I had wanted us to do it in a bed, or at least inside somewhere for our first time, make it real special and shit for her, but the time was now, and that wasn't the sort of shit you could plan.

"Fuck yeah, we are," I said, slamming my mouth against hers once more. My jeans were too tight, squeezing painfully against my junk, and I ground against her, thin pieces of material the only thing stopping me from being inside of her.

I needed in *now*, before I had a fuckin' heart attack or some shit like that, because her whole body was trembling with need, her nails digging into my ass and her hips moving in sync with mine. And every moan and sigh coming from that dirty mouth of hers was like an electric current going straight to my dick.

Fuck me if that woman wasn't going to be the fuckin' death of me.

CHAPTER SEVENTEEN:
1994 / New Year's Day
Laney

How...how could this man have this effect on me?

That's all I wanted to know as Jesse ground against my body, every thrust of his hips making his cock tease my clit and push me one step closer to the orgasm that was building in me.

This had never happened to me before. Like ever. I'd had an orgasm before, obviously; it wasn't like I was a virgin—but it had never happened without me taking my clothes off and actually having sex. And definitely never without the man touching me. Yet there I was, on the brink of an orgasm from Jesse, again, and I was still fully dressed.

What. The. Fuck?

Seriously.

My eyelashes fluttered closed as he reached down between us and lifted the hem of my dress so he could shove his hand down the front of my panties—panties which were now soaked.

"Look at me," he growled against my throat, his tongue trailing across my skin. I couldn't even hear him, or think about the fact that someone could walk around the corner at any moment and see us. No, all I could think about was his fingers, which were playing with my clit and bringing me closer and closer to the explosion that was building in me.

"Laney, I said open your fuckin' eyes and look at me, woman," he growled again, nipping at my neck.

I yelped and my eyes shot open, and with one hand buried in my hair, holding my face captive and tilted up to him, his gaze bored into mine, the depths of his blue eyes everlasting and swallowing me whole as he suddenly plunged a finger inside of me and made me cry out, loudly.

"There it is," he mumbled, leaning in and placing kisses against my lips, a second finger sliding in next to the first one and moving rhythmically in and out over and over until I reached my peak and fell over the other side with a throaty moan, my body shattering and going limp in his arms. "I got you, darlin', I got you," he said as he pulled me against him, his woody scent washing over me.

When the stars had vanished and I could catch my breath, I tried to form words—not that I knew what to say to him at that point, but I had to say something, because that was incredible. A *thank you* seemed ridiculous, but it didn't matter because Jesse leaned in and covered my mouth with his, his tongue diving in to slide along mine and making me moan.

He gently lay me down on the ground, one hand shoving my panties down and the other caressing my breast. I reached down to him, feeling his hard length beneath the material of his jeans, and regardless of the fact that I had just had the best orgasm of my life, I wanted him inside of me, right then.

I squeezed him until he gasped, his chest rumbling in pleasure, and he looked down at me with a wolfish smile that sent tremors through my over-sensitized body. I started to unbuckle his belt and pull down his zipper, and his hands left me for a moment to reach for his wallet and pull out a condom, and then I was lying back, watching him roll the condom down himself while my eyes went wide and I worried how he was going to fit that inside of me. Because the man was big. Not just long, but wide too. The sight of it made my body flush and goose bumps prickle against my skin.

Jesse touched the bottom of my chin and lifted my gaze to meet his. He sucked in his bottom lip while he nudged my legs apart with his knee and settled between them, the tip of his cock nudging against my opening and the heat from his body cloaking me protectively.

His body covered mine, trapping me in a bubble where there was only me and Jesse, and none of the other shit in the world mattered. Because this was it.

We weren't in the woods. And we weren't at a dumb Highwaymen party. Gauge wasn't inside bitching about me, and my mom wasn't dead.

It was just Jesse, me, and the hum of lust throbbing between us.

And that was all that mattered.

Jesse leaned down and placed a rough kiss against my mouth, and then before I could say another word he slammed into me, bottoming out in one long, delicious thrust. He didn't go easy, sliding in slowly, he just demanded that he be there, penetrating me roughly, and I loved it. I gasped against his mouth and he stole the air from my lungs as he lay still, letting my body adjust to his size. My nipples peaked until they felt painful, and all I could think about was his mouth covering them, his warmth soothing the painful ache in my body.

And then he fucked me.

Jesse wasn't gentle or slow with me. He was rough and hard. He dominated me both body and mind, parts of him reaching down further and touching my soul. He took from my body while equally giving me everything I desired and then some of what I didn't even know I needed. And we came together in a flurry of sweat, pawing hands, and screams of pleasure and pain. I bit his shoulder, my legs crossed at the ankles as he pounded me, and he nipped at my nipple, sucking it hard and dragging another orgasm from me as he grunted out his own release, his fingers digging into my hips almost painfully as he held my body still so he could slam into me over and over again until I thought I would pass out.

When it was over Jesse dragged his jeans back on and lay down next to me, grabbing my body and pulling it in against his side like he had done at the lake. His large hand reached down to smooth out my skirt so I wasn't on show, and I draped a leg across his. My head was on his chest, listening to the heavy pounding of his heart against his ribs, his fingers trailing down my back and threading through my hair.

At some point I must have drifted off, because when I woke it was starting to get light, the sunlight filtering in through the trees above us. I blinked and yawned, and when I tried to move, Jesse grunted and held me harder. I smiled and looked up at him. His eyes were closed, his face looking nothing like usual. Gone was the hardness around his eyes and mouth, and instead he looked almost peaceful. He was beautiful, I realized. Not just handsome like so many people could see, but beautiful.

Jesse James Hardy was fucking beautiful, and he was all mine.

I reached up to touch his cheek, the palm of my hand cupping his face. His eyelids fluttered and he opened his eyes, and he gazed down at me, a smile crinkling at the corners of his mouth.

"Morning," I whispered, a small smile on my mouth. "I think you missed your own party."

"I had the only party I gave a shit about right here," he replied. He reached down and grabbed me with both hands, and before I could stop him I was straddling his body. Not that I would have stopped him. In fact, I couldn't imagine a better place to be right then.

Jesse was hard already and I rocked back and forth against him, feeling him growing bigger beneath me. I reached between us, using my fingers to play with my clit.

"Jesus, fucking, Christ," Jesse hissed out, his hands holding my hips and grinding me against him. His eyes were on my fingers, playing with the small nub between my legs. "Aaah, fuck this," he said, flipping me off him so that I was lying on the ground, "I need in there, right the fuck now." I giggled as he unzipped his jeans and shoved them down and then he was nudging my opening with his cock, the heated tip circling my entrance and making me gasp. He dipped inside of me and then swiveled his hips to rub my juices against my entrance.

"Condom," I breathed out.

"Want you bareback, babe," he grunted, sliding in a little bit more. "You on the pill? Because I'm clean, I swear to you, babe, and this is mine now," he said, giving a short thrust against my entrance again. "You clean? You good?" he asked.

"Yeah, I'm clean, and I'm very good," I whispered, my eyes fluttering closed.

"Gonna fuck you now, Laney."

"Okay."

"Need to see your eyes, babe," he muttered, placing a kiss on my lips.

"Okay," I replied, my eyes opening.

He slid into my warmth and I trembled around him as he sank in deep. I was sore from the night before, yet his body soothed mine and I gasped as he slid back out before sliding back in. He grunted against my mouth.

"Fuck, you feel good," he muttered. "So fucking good."

"Right back at you," I gasped.

"Fuck yeah," he chuckled, swiveling his hips and making me groan. Stars danced just out of reach, and I knew I was close. I must have tightened around him, too, because he practically growled in satisfaction.

Jesse took my body in every which way, dragging the pleasure from me until I was a weak, throbbing mess beneath him, and then he came so hard he almost shoved me out from under him. He held my face, his hands wrapped in my hair as he panted against my neck, his hard length still throbbing and pulsing inside of me, and his thumbs trailing down the sides of my face.

"All mine," he muttered.

"All yours," I agreed, enjoying the way his nostrils flared at my words. "Always."

CHAPTER EIGHTEEN:
1994 / New Year's Day
Jesse

Laney was mine now. I had claimed her, and I'd fucking brand her if I had too to. Because no one was going near my woman, and no one was keeping me from her anymore.

There'd be shit to pay for taking a brother's daughter like this, but it didn't matter. Not one fucking bit. Because I'd do it all over again without giving a second fucking thought about it.

Goddamn, she was beautiful. And she tasted and felt like fucking heaven too, just like I knew she would. Her body was tight, her hips just perfect for holding onto, her breasts not too big and not too small, just right for my mouth to cover and my tongue to play with those pink rosebud nipples of hers.

"Need to get dressed now," I said.

"No," she replied. "Let's just stay here forever. Fuck everything else."

"Can't do that, Laney."

"Why?" she whined, looking up at me.

"Because I want to fuck you again today. In a bed next time, because I've got fuckin' twigs sticking places they don't belong."

Her face cracked and she burst out laughing, her hand slapping at my chest. She sat up and I reached over and pulled some leaves from her long dark hair.

"Fine," she replied. She found her panties and started to slide them on, but I snatched them from her and shoved them in my pocket.

"You won't be needing them now," I said. I stood up and buckled my belt before reaching down to pull her up and drag her against my body. I kissed her long and hard, and I'll be damned if she wasn't ready for me again. Damn woman was insatiable. Fuck, yeah. I grinned against her mouth. I hardened beneath my jeans and her hand reached down to cup me again.

Fuck.

Yeah.

The sound of a motorcycle engine in the distance made me pull back from her, and she fucking looked up at me with a pout.

I grinned. "Gotta get back to the club, babe. Need to speak to Hardy, and Gauge, let them know how it is now." Her face paled and I reached up and cupped her face in my hand. "Don't worry, I got this."

"Gauge is going to shit a brick, Jesse," she said, looking worried.

I shrugged and grabbed her, pulling her against my side. "You worry too much," I said, and we started to walk.

"You *should* worry. Gauge is not a reasonable man."

I looked back at her with a smirk but didn't bother to reply. She was right, though: Gauge was going to shit a brick—probably kick my fuckin' ass too—but none of that mattered; it wouldn't change a damn thing. I'd claimed Laney for my own, and Gauge could eat shit for all I cared.

We came out of the woods and walked along the side of the clubhouse. We were almost at the corner when Laney pulled against me.

"Stop," she pleaded.

I turned to look at her with a frown.

"I'm not sure about this, Jesse," she said, chewing on her bottom lip.

I frowned harder, my heart hammering against my chest. She was having second thoughts? Fuck that. No fucking way was that shit happening. I'd tie her to my bed if I had to—if I couldn't convince her that this shit was right. I had waited long enough for her, and I was done waiting.

I reached over to her, dragging her against me. I reached down and pushed my hand up her skirt until I reached the apex of her thighs and the warmth that I wanted to be inside at some point that day. She yelped, her eyes going wide with need and desire. I slipped a finger inside of her, thrusting in and out and rubbing against her G-spot, buried deep inside of her.

"This is mine now, Laney. No second thoughts," I said gruffly, making it clear once and for all that I fucking owned her now. That smart mouth of hers, that tight body and that warm pussy of hers, were mine, and she needed to fucking know how it was going to be if she was going to be my old lady. "I'm not waiting any more, and I'm done being the good guy. You're mine and I need every motherfucker to know that."

Her mouth opened in a silent *O*, her eyelids desperate to flutter closed as I slid another finger inside and flicked against her, the pad of my thumb rubbing against her clit until she clamped her hand across her own mouth and shattered beneath me.

I gave her a second to catch her breath and then I slid my fingers out and drew my hand up to my mouth before sucking on my fingers, loving how her pupils dilated when she watched me tasting her juices on my fingers.

"We clear now?" I asked seriously.

She nodded.

"Good, because that's the only time you get to say no to me, you hear? From here on out it's yes, Jesse all the fucking way."

She nodded again, but still looked hesitant. "I just meant, I wasn't so sure about telling Gauge," she stammered, her cheeks still flushed from her orgasm, and goddamn, that look on her face made me want to bury myself deep inside her again. Right the fuck then, against the side of the fuckin' clubhouse. Fuck, maybe I would.

"What?" I drawled out.

"I'm sure about us, it's telling Gauge I'm not so sure about."

Oh. Well, fuck. I almost laughed. Instead I smirked and wrapped my hand in her hair.

"You owe me one then, I guess," I growled against her lips. I kissed her hard and quick and then I pulled away, taking her hand in mine, and together we walked around the side of the clubhouse.

The prospects from the night before were standing with the bikes. Fuckers looked tired, but they woke right the fuck up when they saw me and Laney holding hands. I glared at them until they looked away, and I took my woman inside my clubhouse.

Bikers and bitches were passed out all over—sitting on the floor huddled together, naked and passed out on the sofa. I looked around for Hardy or Gauge, and as if speaking of the devil, Gauge took that moment to stumble down the stairs of the clubhouse and into the main room, the woman he was with stumbling after him. He was drunk and tired, but it only took him a couple of seconds to see our hands entwined.

Gauge stopped walking, fucker even stopped swaying, as if the sight of me and his kid holding hands sobered him right the fuck up. The bitch he was with reached for him but he pushed her away, making her yelp. He glared over at me.

"Laney, get over here, now," he snarled, his gaze still on me.

"She ain't going to do that, brother. Claimed her as my own," I said.

I won't deny that a tremor of *holy shit* coursed through me as he stormed toward me, and I pushed Laney to one side to keep her safe, and then his hands were grabbing my cut and dragging me outside. Fucker caught me off balance, and I almost fell as he dragged me through the building and back into the morning air outside where the two prospects were now staring openly.

Laney was screaming at Gauge to get off me as Gauge threw me to the ground, his boot quickly following as it dug into my ribs and made me grunt in pain. Laney threw herself on the ground next to me.

"What have you done!? Stop it, Gauge!" she screamed up at him.

I pushed her away as Gauge curled his boot into my side once more, that one hurting twice as much as the first.

Laney dove up and started punching Gauge in the chest and arms, and I watched through the haze as he plowed another boot into my ribs. Brothers were coming out of the clubhouse by then, to see what the fuck was going on, and I was pretty sure Casa was placing bets on me dying—fucker that he was.

Gauge grabbed Laney by the arms as she clawed at his face, and he pushed her so hard that she fell back on her ass.

Fuck no, that shit wasn't happening. I was more than prepared to take a beating for her, but he wasn't laying a single fucking hand on her without facing my wrath. I snarled and dove up, because no one hurt my woman. I threw myself at him, knocking him onto his back and straddling the fucker while I pummeled my fists into his face. Blood exploded from his nose, and then he threw me off him so we were rolling in the dirt. At some point he caught me in the jaw and my teeth snapped together, making me see stars and blood explode as a tooth came loose.

It was a full-on fistfight as we beat the shit out of each other and our brothers formed a circle around us and cheered the fight on. Hardy pushed his way into the crowd, looking fucking furious when he saw it was Gauge and me.

"What the fuck is going on here?" he bellowed, making every one immediately shut the fuck up.

Gauge was holding me by the collar, his fist raised and ready to smash into my face for the sixth or seventh time, but he stopped and turned to look at Hardy. "Your boy claimed my girl, so I'm teaching him some fucking manners. Like how to ask before you go sticking your dick into pussy that ain't yours!"

"Well, it's mine now, so fuckin' deal with it," I bit out, spitting blood onto the ground.

Hardy looked from Gauge to me, and then he caught sight of Laney being held by Rose while she sobbed.

"This true, Jesse?" Hardy asked, his eyes narrowing on me.

I nodded and spat a mouthful of blood on the ground next to me. "Sure is. Claimed my woman and this fucker ain't happy about it. Not that I give a shit, because it is what it is."

Gauge turned to look at me again. "I'm gonna fucking kill you, Jesse! That's my little girl!"

"No, that's my fuckin' old lady, brother," I snarled out. "And I'm going to fuck her every which way for the rest of her life until she can't walk straight and has a permanent smile on that beautiful fucking face of hers. We fucking clear now?" I raged.

Gauge looked shocked, his face showing a split second of something other than hatred before morphing back. He let go of my collar, dropping me to the ground, and he stood up.

He pointed a finger at me. "I only just got her back, Jesse," he said, his nostrils flaring. "You can't hurt her and go chasing her off or I swear to God I will fucking gut you. You hear me?"

I stood up. "I hear you, and I ain't ever planning on hurting her."

Gauge was still glaring at me. "You love her?"

"Wouldn't be making her my old lady if I didn't, brother."

We stared at one another, both of us beat to hell and back, and both panting and breathless as we weighed our options. I got to my knees and then pushed up to standing, my body aching and hurting all over. I glanced over to Laney, taking in the shock written across her face—shock at me and what I'd just put myself through to have her, and shock at Gauge, finally taking some responsibility for her and making it known that he actually gave a shit about his little girl after all.

I held out a hand to Gauge. "You can beat me however much you want, but it won't change a damn thing, Gauge. She's mine now." I spat another mouthful of blood on the ground. "You hearin' me, brother? She's mine and I'm letting every brother know that she's off limits. And if anyone touches what's mine, I'll put a bullet in their brain."

Gauge turned and glared at Laney. "Couldn't fucking find yourself a nice college boy with a rich family, could you?" For once Laney didn't come back with a biting remark, and Gauge shook his head and sighed. Blood was trailing from his nose and he wiped it away with the back of his hand before finally taking my hand in his. "You do good by my girl, or I'll kill you myself, president's son or not. You hearing me?"

"Loud and clear." I nodded. "I'll fuckin' kill myself if I hurt her. That I promise you, brother."

"You better hurry up and get yourself patched, Jesse. My girl deserves that much." He pulled me in for a hug, patting my back noisily before shoving me away and making me stumble. "She deserves the fucking world," he said, taking one last sideways glance at her before walking back inside the clubhouse.

The other brothers cheered and patted me on the back as they passed me—all but Hardy. My old man just stared at me for a moment, looking like he wanted to say a thousand things but not saying any of them, and then he turned and walked back inside the clubhouse.

Rose smiled over at me like she'd set this whole fucking thing up and I hadn't been pining after my woman since I was a fucking teenager. She walked Laney to me and then she leaned over and kissed me on the cheek before walking away, finally leaving me and Laney alone again. She looked at me, her lashes still damp from her tears, and I used my thumb to wipe them away before leaning in to kiss her on the mouth.

"I'm your old lady now?" she asked hesitantly as she pulled away, and I couldn't decide if she looked frightened or excited by the prospect. Regardless, it was happening. Laney was my old lady, whether she fuckin' liked it or not.

"Damn straight you are," I replied, and she let out a little breathy sigh that went straight to my dick. I reached for her and she stepped away from me, and I couldn't stop a growl from rumbling in my chest. "Need to go get your stuff because you're moving in with me, today. Wanna have you in my bed and under me every night from now on, and that's not up for debate."

She swallowed and looked away from my face, stepping out of reach when I tried to touch her. Fuck, I needed a drink. Everything hurt. Everything. And now she was holding out on me too? No way. No. Fucking. Way.

"You got somethin' on your mind, then you better say it," I snapped.

"All right, well if I'm your old lady then we need to get one thing straight," she said, placing her hands on her hips defiantly.

Goddamn, I wanted to fuck her again, feisty little thing that she was, but I'd be damned if she wasn't pissing me off. Brothers had warned me what it was like to have a woman on your arm, trying to control everything you did. Thought it would take longer than thirty fucking seconds for that bullshit to kick in, though.

"What the fuck now, woman? I fucked you, I made you come—several times, I fought your dad, I'm beat up and bleeding and I just need a fucking drink and to sit down before you start bitching me out about some trivial bullshit like a boring old housewife!"

"You stupid fucker!" Laney reached back and slapped me hard, catching us both by surprise, and her eyes widened in horror right before her hand flew up to cover her mouth. "Oh shit, I'm sorry, I didn't mean that…" she mumbled beneath her fingers.

I leaned in and kissed her hard, even though my split fucking lip was burning with every move of my mouth and it felt like my lungs were on fire. I kissed my girl, because fuck me if she wasn't a smart-mouthed little bitch that I loved.

"You're not mad?" she asked, her cheeks flushed as we pulled apart.

"Of course I'm fuckin' mad, but I love your smart mouth. Just try and rein it in a little. Especially now," I said, reaching around to squeeze her ass and making her yelp. "Now what the fuck was you going to ask me?"

She looked confused for a moment while she struggled to recall what she had been about to ask me. "Oh, I um, I was going to tell you that you had to move out of the clubhouse, because I'm not living here," she said almost coyly. "Not with all the shit that goes on here—"

"Done," I replied. "What else?"

She looked surprised by my agreement, and I couldn't help the smugness from showing on my face.

"That's it," she replied.

"That's it?" I repeated, confused. I'd expected a long list of demands or something.

"That's it. I just don't want to live here."

"All right then, now can we please go inside so I can get a drink and some ice, and maybe a blowjob from you at some point today? Because I'm fucking exhausted, woman. We'll sort out getting somewhere together because there's no way in hell

I'm living with Gauge." I winked and grabbed her by the waist and started to guide her inside, loving the sound of her shocked gasp and then her little laugh.

Yeah, I was completely pussy-whipped, but at least I'd gotten some pussy.

CHAPTER NINETEEN:

3 months ago
Jesse

It was nearly done. Thank fuck.

Couple more days, max, and I'd be taking the Harley out on the road with the roar of the two-cylinder, V-twin engine, riding low, and loud as fuck. A guttural cry from the devil himself, no doubt.

Butch and I had been working on the bike for almost eighteen months now, though I would have had it finished a lot earlier if he'd have let me, but it had started out as our project and we'd kept it that way for a reason. Life had gotten pretty hectic recently, but the bike always brought us back together. The bike had been built from the ground up, almost every part original and custom made to order.

It was a one of a kind, more so than any of the bikes I'd built for anyone else.

It was a sight to behold, too. All matte black and shiny chrome, with rigid frames with springer front ends and ape hangers. She was fucking beautiful. I dreamed about riding that bike as much as I dreamed about riding my woman.

The shutter to the garage was up, Hardy & Son's MC Shop in full swing, but I'd found myself with a couple of hours to spare, and knowing Butch was on his way back after a ride out for the club, I knew he'd want to get straight to working on the Harley as soon as he could.

I'd been patched in a while back, but I was still mainly stationed at the garage, for the most part. Laney liked it that way, and though I liked being close to her, I wanted to be out on the road more, like Butch. He was going on longer and longer rides, meaning that we saw each other less and less. The club was my family, every one of them my brothers, but Butch was the only true blood I had. Hardy didn't count.

Laney had gone to some old lady meet with River and Charlie, Axle and Rider's women. It was supposed to be a meeting to discuss a party for Skinny's return after serving time in the DOC, but I had no doubt that Laney and the others would be stripped off to tiny string bikinis and sipping on margaritas by now.

I reached down and readjusted my dick, the thought of Laney in that tiny white bikini of hers, all wet from Charlie's pool, turning me as hard as a rock.

The roar of bikes had me looking up, and I watched as Butch, Dom, and Gauge pulled in and parked their bikes. I stood up and wiped my hands down my jeans and headed out to see them. Butch was hanging his helmet on his bars and talking to Dom as I approached, and Gauge was already heading inside—to speak to Hardy, no doubt.

"Decided to show your sorry ass back around here, did you?" I joked, referring to the poker game he'd lost the night before he'd headed out. He'd lost a shit load of cash and had stormed off in a foul fucking mood with only a *kiss my ass* as a goodbye to everyone.

"Couldn't have you running your mouth off now, could I?" Butch joked and pulled me into a hug, poker game forgotten.

"Too late for that. You'll never get laid again after the shit I've said about you."

"Oh yeah?" he smarted arrogantly, cocking an eyebrow at me.

"Yeah," I laughed. "I may have even brought up that picture you used to carry around of Mom."

His face fell. "You wouldn't fuckin' dare."

"Bitches thought that shit was cute—I probably did you a favor. At least until I told them the rest of the story, brother!"

"What fuckin' story is this?" Dom laughed, stepping into the conversation. "I ain't heard nothin' about a photograph of your mom." He frowned. "And here I was thinking we shared everything. I'm hurt," he joked, placing a hand on his heart, and we both started laughing.

The door to the clubhouse opened and Hardy stood in the doorway, his presence dominating the space. "Get in here! I need intel, now!" He turned and went back inside, and the door slammed closed behind him.

I looked over to Butch, who was shaking his head in annoyance.

"That's one angry motherfucker," Dom said, his smile gone. He slapped Butch on the back and made a cross over himself. "Good luck in there."

Butch tried to laugh it off, but it was obvious he didn't have good news to pass on. "I'll be over as soon as I can, Jesse. We'll work on the bike together tonight, yeah?" He started to walk away and looked back. "And keep your mouth shut about me from now on!"

I showed him my middle finger and laughed. Dom followed me over to the Harley, giving a low whistle as he ran his palm over the seat.

"She's looking good," he said. "She almost done?"

"Yeah, any day now." I picked up my wrench again and continued to screw the bolts tighter on the dressers. I'd sprayed them last week, and Casa had hand-painted the Highwaymen logo on them for me. Man was a genius with paint and was fucking wasted working at the strip club, in my opinion. But Casanova by name, Casanova by nature, I guess.

"Everything go okay out there?" I asked, turning back to Dom.

He shook his head, his nostrils flaring. "Not really. Shit is fucked up."

One of the clubs lead drivers—Skinny—had just got caught with a van full of our cargo and was being sent down for the pleasure of it. We were trying to piece together how the fuck he'd been caught in the first place since we'd got people on the payroll that had promised us his safe passage.

"The intel no good?" I asked, watching him with concern.

"Nah, by the time we got there, the crew the Highwaymen had paid were long gone." He sighed heavily and ran a hand through his hair. "So what's this story about Butch then?" he asked, changing the subject.

I laughed and stopped working. "Butch used to carry this picture of our 'mom' in his wallet around with him. Showed all the kids in school and had them all jealous as fuck that our mom was so hot. Told them she baked cookies and took us hiking on the weekends and shit."

"That's just sad," Dom said, not smiling. "And kinda pathetic since I know what your mom was really like. How the fuck have I never heard this story before?"

And he was right, it was sad. In reality our mom had been a junkie crackhead and had died from an overdose. But I knew why he had done it. He wanted more, for both of us. And he was hoping that I was young enough to forget what she had put us through. That maybe, just maybe, he could wipe away those tragic memories with something fucking good and pure.

It didn't work, though.

The memory of me pulling the needle from her arm and lying next to her while her body went cold and stiff still haunted my dreams, her blotchy pale face and sunken cheekbones a constant reminder of the irreparable damage the drugs had done to her body.

"It was when we had to move schools cus' we moved up here with Hardy. But this is where it gets funny. Butch was staying over at his friend's house one night and the kid's mom walked in on him giving himself a hand job in the bathroom, all while staring at the picture of our *mom*." I cracked up laughing, the memory of Hardy almost killing Butch for embarrassing him was still hilarious.

"I don't get it," Dom said, his deep voice tinged with confusion. "I mean, that's just fucking gross. I know you two were fucked up, but—"

I grinned. "Nah, the picture wasn't really of our mom, it was some model he'd cut out of a magazine years before."

Dom started to laugh. "Well shit."

"Yeah, exactly. Story went around school, though, that he was jacking off to a picture of his mom and it took three months of constant ass-kicking for the story to stop." I picked up my wrench and went on working, the memory making me smile.

"Surprised he took three months of ass-kicking. Don't seem like his way," Dom replied.

I looked back at him. "Nah, brother, it was three months of Butch kicking everyone else's asses." I shook my head and laughed. "Story still comes back to haunt him though."

Dom lit a cigarette and chuckled. "Thought I knew everything there was to know about your brother. Guess some people have skeletons hidden no matter how hard you look, huh?"

Butch chose that moment to walk into the garage. He looked from me to Dom and back again before shaking his head. "You fucking told him, didn't you?" He dragged a hand through his beard. "Why can't you just keep that shit to yourself?" he asked.

"You know me, brother." I saluted. "I'm all about honesty, integrity, and the good ole' American truth."

"Yeah, you're a real fucking saint, Jesse," he smarted. He turned to Dom and jutted his head toward the door and both of them walked out. When he walked back in a minute later, he was alone. "Gotta meet Dom for a beer later on." He grabbed a hairband and tied his hair back from his face. "Got a couple of hours before then, though." He smiled and crouched down to see what I was working on. "She's a fucking beauty, ain't she?"

"Sure is," I agreed. "You know we're gonna be arguing over who gets to ride her the most. A motherfucking custody battle over our baby," I laughed.

Butch went silent and I turned to look at him, my laugh dying.

"What is it?"

He frowned and smiled at the same time. "This bike is yours, brother."

It was my turn to frown then. "No, it's ours—we built her together."

Butch shook his head and patted me on the shoulder. "Jesse, I've spent my entire life looking after you, but the truth is, this life is hard—harder than I thought it would be. I might not always be here for you. But this," he said, running his hand along the shiny chrome, "this will always be a reminder of me. It means I'll always be with you, even when I'm not."

I stood up. "Has something happened?" I asked seriously, watching him for clues as to why he was being so morbid. "I'm serious, has something happened that I should know about?"

He smiled, though it didn't reach his eyes. "I'm fine, brother. I just realized that I'm not fucking immortal and the world don't run around me, even though it fucking should do," he chuckled. "I want you to have the bike, Jesse. You're not a little kid anymore. You're a man, with your own woman and a life apart from mine. We might end up going in different directions—fuck, I hope so because I want something more for you—but this bike will always bring us back together."

He stopped talking and stared at me, and I could tell that he wanted to say more, but had stopped himself.

"Butch—" I started to speak but he cut me off.

"All right, let's stop with the sweet talking before I grow a fucking pussy, all right? Let's get this bitch up and running. I wanna see my kid brother riding this beast before I fucking die," he laughed and I laughed with him, though his words were more haunting than humorous.

"Kid brother? Really?" I joked trying to lighten the mood. Shit had gotten serious real fucking fast, and he obviously didn't want to talk about it right now.

"You know, you may be a hard-ass motherfucker—probably tougher than even me now—but you'll always be my kid brother, so shut the fuck up and pass me the wrench," he laughed.

I didn't like his tone, or the way his mind was working, but I was also really fucking glad to have the bike for myself. I didn't have much in life; my world consisted of very few things and very few people, but what I did have I looked after and I loved hard.

Laney, Butch, Casa, and that bike were everything to me. More than everything: they were a part of me. Each one of them had somehow saved me in some small way. Sometimes from myself, sometimes from other people, sometimes from my own dark fate that was constantly trying to catch up and pull me under. But either way they had saved me.

Building that bike with Butch had meant the world to me that past year or so, and no matter what life had thrown our way, it had continued to bring us together time after time.

Little did I know that pretty soon, it would be the only thing I had left of Butch.

CHAPTER TWENTY:

3 months ago
Laney

I stood in the doorway watching Jesse and the rest of the Devil's Highwaymen start unloading our furniture from the back of the truck. Nerves fluttered in my stomach every time I looked around our new home.

It was ours. Not his, not mine, but ours.

Hardy and Silvie had helped get us a good deal on the house, and Butch, Dom, and Cutter had worked on the repairs for us—of which a lot were needed. Charlie, River, and Rose had surprised me by painting the entire place from top to bottom after the repairs were completed, and Gauge had helped us out with money for new furniture because neither of us really had anything to our name.

It had been a real family affair, and one I was entirely grateful for. I had never really had a family before coming to live with Gauge. It had always been Mom and I and whatever "friend" was living with us at the time. I couldn't say I had a bad upbringing, though—Mom had given me everything a little girl could ask for. She went to all my parents' evenings, she helped me with homework, and she always made sure my clothes were clean, as was I. But nothing ever washed away the fact that everyone knew she was a whore. And as I got older, I had learned exactly how cruel both kids and their jealous moms could be.

But now there I was, with a group of people who treated me like I was their family—a daughter, a sister, a cousin, an aunt, and of course an old lady. I had it all for the first time in my life, and more than anything I was happy.

I watched Jesse and Gauge grab the new sofa from the bed of the truck and start carrying it across the lawn toward the house. Jesse had a hard look on his face, and sweat was glistening across his skin. God, he was gorgeous—even more so when he was sweaty and working hard like that.

I turned and walked inside as they reached the door. "Over here, please."

"You sure you don't want it by the back wall?" Gauge asked, nodding his head to the wall in question. "TV will look better over there, and you won't get as much glare on the screen."

"No, Gauge, I want it there. It's not all about the TV, you know."

"Maybe not for you, but a man wants to come home at the end of the day, drink a cold beer, watch some TV, and then fuck his old lady," he replied bluntly.

"Oh, and your old lady likes getting fucked by you, does she?" I smarted.

"Might not have laid claim to a woman, but damn straight I fuck every night, you little bitch," Gauge yelled back, his temper getting the better of him.

Jesse dropped his end of the sofa down. "Will you two shut the fuck up arguing already?"

"Fuck off!" both Gauge and I shouted at the same time.

Jesse stared at us, and I wondered whether he and Gauge were going to start a huge fight in my freshly decorated living room. There had been a time that I had worried Gauge could kick Jesse's ass, but after seeing them fight previously, it was pretty obvious that they were evenly matched, despite Gauge's experience and age. Now I worried more that they would beat each other to death rather than just senseless.

Men are idiots.

Jesse saw my pleading look and dragged a hand down his beard. He gave one last glare to Gauge and then stormed back out of the house, muttering something about crazy-ass family genes and hoping that our kids didn't get them, and I couldn't help but laugh. I looked over at Gauge as he put down his end of the sofa and sighed. He looked from me to the sofa and then pushed the small sofa against the wall like I had wanted. When he turned around I threw myself at him, my arms wrapping around his neck like a little spider monkey, and I buried my face into the crook of his neck. His body froze, his muscles stiffening as he tried to work out what to do, and I half thought he was going to throw me off him—because hugging wasn't exactly our thing—but then all at once he softened and I felt his arms go around me as he hugged me back.

I was hugging Gauge—my father—for probably one of the first times ever, and it felt good.

We didn't say anything to each other, probably because the usual bullshit would only come from both of us if we did, so instead we hugged in silence and I reveled in the scent of my father's leather cut and his sweat wrapping around me comfortingly.

Jesse came back inside with Casa, both of them carrying the new mattress. He took one look at us and smiled and shook his head.

"Goddamn crazy running through their blood, that's for damn sure," he said to Casa as they carried the mattress upstairs.

"Can you imagine the fucked-up DNA you two will pass on to your brats?" Casa laughed, and I think Jesse told him to go fuck a goat and stop talking about kids.

I pulled out of the hug first and Gauge looked down at me. I had thought I'd gotten all of my coloring from my mom, but looking at him now, I could see that I got his looks too. Though his gray eyes were ghostly where mine were dark pools, our skin was a light brown and his hair was dark like mine. Gauge reached up and touched my cheek, his eyes capturing me and holding me hostage. My body trembled under his touch, because this wasn't him, or us. We were hard and rough, we fought and we hated. We were never kind or gentle to one another. And that was okay, because at least I knew what to expect with that. I couldn't be let down if I never hoped for anything more. I couldn't hurt if I never let him get close. But this was different, now.

"You look so much like her sometimes it scares me," he said, his voice thick with emotion. "She'd be proud of you, kid," he said, and then he lowered his hand and walked away.

I stared after him, a trembling feeling in the pit of my stomach and tears blurring my eyes. I wrapped my arms around myself and squeezed my eyes closed to stop myself from crying.

"See, Mom? Not all bikers are bad," I whispered to her, hoping she could hear me, and hoping that Gauge was right and she would be proud of me.

"You okay?" Jesse asked.

Casa walked out the door, giving a wolf whistle as he did, and I laughed and opened my eyes. Jesse reached around me, wrapping his arms around my waist before pulling me closer.

"Yeah, baby," I said. "I'm fine."

He kissed my mouth. "Good." He kissed me again, his hands going lower to cup my ass and hoist my body closer to him, making sure I could feel how hard he was in his jeans. "Gonna make you feel real good when everyone fucks off out of my house."

"You mean *our* house," I mumbled, grinning against his mouth. I opened to let him slide his tongue inside. His hand fisted in my hair and I groaned.

"Keep your pants on, we're coming in," River laughed, coming inside loaded down with bags of food, closely followed by Charlie and Silvie. They all laughed and went on through to the kitchen and I pulled away from Jesse, though it took some force since he made it clear that he really didn't want to let me go.

"You smell good," he said, running his nose along my throat and sending shivers running through my body.

"You, on the other hand, don't smell too good," I said, batting him away.

"Aah, you fuckin' love it," he said, making a grab for me again. "Gonna take you on this sofa later," he said, backing me up against the new sofa. It was still covered in plastic wrap and crinkled noisily when we bumped against it. "Gonna take you on this floor with you on all fours, gonna take you every which way until you don't know which way is up or down." His mouth vibrated against my throat as he spoke, and my toes curled at the images that swelled in my head.

I thought the way he made me feel would eventually wear down and become something less…intense and more normal, but in the past few months it had only gotten stronger. My attraction to Jesse James Hardy was devouring me. I moaned as his rough hands grabbed my hips and pulled me down onto the sofa.

"Want you now, babe," he muttered, dotting my throat and chest with kisses.

Gauge walked in and glared over at us. "I'll never get used to this shit," he grumbled before slamming the small wooden coffee table down and heading into the kitchen.

I giggled against Jesse's neck. "We need to keep going," I said.

"I agree," he rumbled against my neck, his hands still pawing at me.

I laughed again and shoved at him and he practically snarled before relenting. "There'll be plenty of time for that as soon as we get everything moved in and get rid of our friends."

"Fuckkkk," Jesse growled before sitting up and rearranging himself. "The second that door closes, this is mine," he said, thrusting a hand between my legs and palming me with the heel of his hand hard enough to make me sigh and almost reconsider.

Or I would have if Casa hadn't walked in with Pipes, one of the newer prospects, and they didn't both just stop and star at me and Jesse with huge grins on their faces like they'd never seen a woman on her back before.

"Move along!" I yelled at them both, and they put down the boxes they were carrying and walked back out the front door laughing.

"We need to hurry this shit up," Jesse grumbled.

"Agreed!" I said. "I'll go see what the girls are up to. You keep going with the boxes and furniture."

It shouldn't have taken that long, really. My own things fitted into one large box and suitcase, though my school stuff took up a little more space. And I'd refused to let Jesse bring half of his stuff into our home since it was either old as hell, broken to hell, or crude as hell. But everyone had been so generous, giving us furniture and buying us housewarming gifts. It made me appreciate how lucky we really were, and understand more why this life was so appealing. These people weren't just criminals, they were family—the kind of family that everyone should have. They would live and die for one another, no matter what.

Jesse slapped my ass and walked out the front door, and I headed to the kitchen only to be met with

Gauge being pushed out of it. Right behind him was Charlie, her black hair tied up high on her head and her face covered with a mischievous grin.

Gauge looked between us both. "What the fuck, Charlie?"

"No men allowed," she replied drolly. "Now get out."

"I'm hungry," he snapped back.

"You're always hungry," I said with a laugh.

"This is why I've never claimed a woman. Bitches are annoying as fuck!" he said as he pushed past me.

"Yeah, because *that's* the reason that you're single!" I called after him with a laugh, feeling much more comfortable now that we were back to our usual dialogue.

"Bitch!"

"Go fuck a horse!" I yelled, giving him the middle finger.

Gauge almost walked right into Jesse, who was coming back in with yet another box in his arms. "You need to sort out that filthy mouth of hers, brother," he snarled and continued outside.

"I like her dirty mouth," Jesse said, looking at me.

Charlie laughed and stuck her finger down her throat. "Get a room."

"Don't need to," I said, turning back to her with a huge grin on my face. "We got a whole house. Now let me into my kitchen."

Charlie grinned wider. "Can't do that."

"What?" I replied. "Why?"

She stood her ground in the doorway of my kitchen and wouldn't let me past when I tried to barge through. "It's a surprise, don't ruin it. Now go rearrange some potted plants or some other shit, Laney," she giggled, her hands on her hips.

I rolled my eyes at her. "Fine! But you girls better not have broken anything, or defiled anything in there. It's all new and shiny, and if anyone is going to defile it, it's going to be us!"

Charlie winked and laughed before backing into the kitchen. I tried to see past her but the woman was too sneaky for her own good. No wonder Rider liked to keep her on a short leash. I turned back around to find myself alone. Jesse had gone back outside to retrieve some more of our things, and I was left in the front room with boxes of handed-down silverware and curtains and bedding all ready for us. All of our furniture had been either new or handed down from our friends and family, but the kitchen and bathroom, bed and sofa, and of course the carpets had all been brand new.

I kicked off my boots and dragged my socks off my feet before wiggling my toes against the soft, thick carpet—a gift from Gauge. He'd said I walked all over him anyway, so I may as well be comfy while I did it. The thought made me smile. He'd been a shitty dad, but he was at least trying to make up for it. And I couldn't blame him for everything, I guess. I mean, if Mom hadn't bothered to tell him about me, it wasn't exactly his fault. He'd never wanted kids—he'd made that very clear to me when I first went to live with him—and he certainly didn't expect to get a teenage girl handed to him.

I sighed and walked around the living room, enjoying the way the thick pile squished between my toes. I'd never had nice carpet like that before. It had always been bare floorboards with Mom. And not the fancy kind, either, but old, crappy floors that would give you splinters in your feet if you didn't tread carefully enough.

Living with Gauge had been both good and bad. Bad because he was always bringing a new piece of ass home with him, and listening to him fuck was not a good sound—that and we really didn't get along. But it had been good because he had nice floors—not carpet, but wooden floors that he'd sanded himself. The sort of floors my mom would have loved. His furniture was expensive and nice, though all very masculine, of course. He was a bachelor and he'd made no effort to change his place for me. Whenever I had tried to put my stamp on anything in the house with either a throw cushion or a vase of flowers, I had found them in the trash later that day.

But this place, this was Jesse's and mine. It was our home, where we could be ourselves and find peace together. We were both broken, but together, there, we could fix each other. And maybe, one day, we would have our children there too.

I smiled as I looked out the window and watched Jesse pulling the door closed on the truck. He was talking to Casa and Butch, and they were laughing and carefree, and it made my heart swell with love and pride.

Jesse was an intense man, and there were only ever two people that could make him smile like he didn't have a care in the world. Well, now there were three, because now there was me.

Jesse looked over at the house, and I think he saw me through the window. His smile grew wider, and his brother slapped him on the back, making him laugh some more. I laughed too, wanting to freeze the moment and take a mental picture so that I could hold onto it in my mind forever.

The soft carpet between my toes.

My heart full of love.

And my home full of family.

This was it for me now.

I had everything and everyone I could ever ask for, and it was everything I had hoped it would be.

CHAPTER TWENTY-ONE:
3 months ago
Jesse

I shook my head and looked around. This was not what I'd had in mind—not at all.

Seriously, fuck this shit.

My house was full of people and I didn't give a flying fuck that they were our friends and family. And I sure as shit didn't care if they'd brought us food and beer. So fucking what if this party was supposed to be our final moving-in present?

All I wanted right then was for everyone to get the fuck out of my house so I could drag Laney down to the floor, tear her panties off with my teeth, and slam myself home. *Then* I'd be fucking happy. That was all I wanted for our moving-in present. But by the look on my brother's motherfucking smug face, he fucking knew that. Asshole.

I had been watching Laney all day long, walking around in those tight little denim cutoffs and her ankle boots, her hair tied in a long plait down her back that was just begging for me to hold like a rope while I thrust into her over and over. Her skin would be covered in a light sheen of sweat, her chest rising and falling as she panted and screamed against me, her arms wrapped tight around my body. There was only so much one man could take. Yet instead of burying myself home, I was fucking stuck having a moving-in party that I didn't even want to be at.

Butch winked at me and I flipped him off, and he and Dom laughed even harder and walked outside. Fuckers were all in it together, that was for damn certain.

"Cheer the fuck up," Casa said, handing me a beer.

I took it and drank it down in one. "Get the fuck out of my house and I'll cheer the fuck up, brother."

He laughed. "Better keep drinking, because we got three kegs and nobody is going anywhere until they're all gone."

"Fuck," I replied bitterly, my gaze still on Laney as she moved around the room speaking to people, her tight ass almost taunting me. She looked over and smiled and my dick got even harder—painfully so. I reached down and rearranged it, and I watched the blush rise to her cheeks before she looked away coyly.

"Why don't you just go take her upstairs?" Casa asked, sounding genuinely confused.

I dragged a hand through my hair. "She said some shit about it not being polite to go fuckin' upstairs while our guests party on around us."

"What? Are you serious?"

"Wish I fuckin' wasn't, but yeah, that's what she said."

"And you're listening to that shit?"

I pulled my gaze away from Laney to look over at Casa and I shook my head. "I'm trying to be all gentlemanly and shit," I grumbled, not enjoying it one bit.

"And how's that working out for you?" He laughed and pushed at my shoulder.

"Like my dick got cut off! How d'you think it's working out?" I yelled at him.

He continued to laugh, enjoying my misery. "Come on, let's go get you another. Might help cool you down." He smirked and pulled me away.

We headed outside to get some fresh air and another beer, with Casa smiling at every piece of ass that walked by us and making me hate him even more. Someone had lit a fire pit, which I already knew Laney was going to love, though the neighbors probably not so much, but whatever. Our back yard was big, though there wasn't anything but grass and weeds in it at the moment. A fence went around our entire property, and Laney had already talked about taking out one of the fence panels at the back end of the yard and putting in a gate because it backed up onto a small grove with a little stream running through it. Damn woman had already talked about getting a fucking dog to take for walks in it too.

I shook my head at the obscurity of my life. It had only been six months ago, give or take, that I'd been banging anything that moved. Of course that was mostly to take my mind away from wanting to fuck Laney. Then she'd casually strutted her shit right back into my life and turned my world upside down and twisted it sideways until I didn't know which way was which. Now there I was with a house, a woman, and a fucking dog on the way if what she was saying was anything to go by. Jesus, next thing she'd be talking about would be babies and marriage and—

"What's happening with you right now? Your face is doing some weird spasming shit, brother," Casa said, looking at me curiously.

I stuck my red cup underneath the spout and pumped some beer out, a huge shit-eating grin on my face. "Yeah?" I asked.

"Yeah. Like you looked like you were going to kill someone and then you looked like you were about to blow your load all over the fucking beer, now you're grinning like you just received the best blow job of your life. What's that all about?" He grimaced.

I barked out a laugh. "I'm fuckin' happy is what's wrong," I replied, realizing with absolute certainty that truth of my words.

I was happy.

Not that fake happy where you plastered on a pretend smile and acted like you weren't already dead inside and just waiting for life to catch up to you to send you to ground, but the sort of happy you got on those bullshit Hallmark cards.

It hit me like a punch to the gut, a weird, crazy-ass feeling coursing through my body and making my heart speed up so much I had to force myself to breathe. Goddamn, was I having a heart attack? That would just be my luck too: I finally get my shit together and then I die because of some bullshit or other because I drank too much and smoked even more.

I swallowed some of my beer and tried to calm myself down because my blood felt like it was running through my veins at a hundred miles an hour and was about to blast itself free from my chest, sending splinters of bone and muscle in all directions.

I looked around, feeling panicked and anxious. And fuck me, I needed Laney. I needed Laney right the fuck now! Because when all the rage and the panic built up inside me like this, she was the only one to bring me back down, to bring me to my senses.

Just as I thought it, she came out of the house and started walking over to me. Goddamn, she was a sight for sore eyes. Like a goddess she pulled me in, the warm glow of the fire pit dancing across her golden skin, her long legs, running for miles, and those tits that were just the perfect size for my hands.

But it was her smile and those deep dark eyes that hooked me the most. They lit up my dark world so I could see again, so all the anger and rage I normally felt melted away and left behind only the good—her.

She smiled as she got closer, sidling up to me and wrapping an arm around my waist. She looked up at me with concern, her smile faltering while she examined my features. And all I could do was stare like a teenage boy having a wet fucking dream, because this was my woman.

"Jesse?" she asked, a frown puckering between her eyebrows. She turned and looked at Casa. "What's wrong with him? Did you give him something?" she accused.

I pulled her against me, one arm holding her tight, the other reaching up to wipe away the sweat from my forehead. "I'm fine, Lane'." And I was fine. Now that she was there, my heart had started to slow back down to something more normal and my chest had stopped hurting.

"You don't look fine."

"Thanks a fuckin' lot," I replied with heavy sarcasm.

She batted at my chest. "You know what I mean. Why are you so sweaty?" she said, running a hand over my bare chest. Earlier I had taken off my tee and put my cut back on. Felt more naked without my cut on than if I was butt fucking naked.

"I was thinking about you, naked, spread-eagled across the kitchen counter with me between those beautiful thighs of yours," I said, leaning down and taking her mouth.

She relaxed into me, her body softening and molding to mine. I kissed her hard, I kissed her soft, I kissed her any which way I damn pleased, because she was mine and no one could take that away from me.

After long minutes wrapped around one another, our mouths exploring each other's, she pulled out of the kiss and looked up at me. Casa had fucked off at some point, and we were alone with each other. The party was in full swing all around us, but with my arms trapping her to me, we could have been on a different fucking planet for all either of us noticed. The fire danced in her eyes and I got lost in them.

Jesus Christ, I was turning into a pussy, but there was no way of stopping it.

"Are you okay?" she asked, her voice softer that time.

I nodded, sucking in my bottom lip and letting it out again. "Damn straight I am," I replied. "Gonna need to go kick someone's ass in a minute, though."

Her eyes widened. "What? Why?"

"'Cause my dick is gonna turn into a pussy if I don't. My brain's thinking all rainbows and unicorns and shit instead of tits and ass. Fuckin' weird shit going on in here," I said, tapping the side of my head. "So if I can't fuck you right now, then I need to spend this energy elsewhere!"

She burst out laughing and I looked at her seriously, because I was being fucking serious. It was no fucking joke. I rolled my shoulders and pulled away from her, though it pained me to do so, and then I looked around us to see who was outside, letting my mouth settle into a grim smile when I saw that Axle had just arrived. Brother was always looking for a fight.

"Axle," I called loudly, my tone suggesting menace and making everyone stop what they were doing and turn to stare at me. Axle was facing the opposite direction but he turned slowly, already guessing what was on my mind. We'd been doing that for the past couple of years. What started out as him teaching me to contain my anger and use it more productively had ended with us now being an even match, which only made fighting with him that much better because we had no clue who was going to win.

Lord knows I was one angry motherfucker most of the time, but between Axle's teaching and Laney's pussy, I was softening and letting go of that anger. Wasn't sure if it was a good thing, but when I looked at Hardy and saw how full of rage he was all the time, I knew it couldn't be a bad thing to learn to at least control my temper.

"What up?" Axle called back, throwing his cigarette to the ground and stamping it out. Sick fuck was already cracking his knuckles in anticipation.

I leaned down and kissed my girl hard on the mouth and then I stepped away from her, needing to grow my balls back, even if they were blue right now. I rolled my shoulders as I stepped toward him, and he laughed and did the same.

"You sure you're ready for this, Jesse?" he mocked, a wild gleam in his eyes. "Looks to me like you're setting up home and turning pussy."

"It's you who should be worried, brother," I said with a grin.

"You sure? I don't want to go upsetting that old lady of yours when I rearrange your face. We all fucking know what bitches are like when they're unhappy. Make everyone's lives hell. I'm just trying to help you out some," he joked while grabbing his long hair and tying it back from his face.

"You're such an asshole, Axle!" River yelled and slapped his arm, but she might as well have been using a feather duster to tickle him, for all the difference it made.

"Why don't you get your weak ass over here and find out how much of a pussy I am, brother?" I laughed, cracking my neck from side to side.

Around us people formed a circle and started taking bets, but I zoned them out in favor of the rush of adrenaline pumping through me. Axle and I circled each other, smirks on our faces and a gleam in our eyes.

"First one to get the other out of the circle or to get them to tap out is the winner," Gauge called, and I knew that bastard was betting against me.

"I'm not sure that you're—" Axle didn't finish his sentence as I plowed into him, football tackling him at the waist and sending him to the ground.

I punched him, hard, my knuckles making contact with his jaw and making both of us grunt out. He flipped me off him and sent me rolling to the side, and I was staggering up to my feet before he could send a punch to my stomach. I looked across to him; fucker was rubbing his jaw and sneering at me.

"That all you got?" he said, and then he swung for me, his fist connecting with my ribs and making me groan in pain.

I stumbled sideways, and Casa and Butch pushed me back into the circle before I fell out. Axle grinned and spat blood onto the ground at my feet.

"I'm just warming up," I said seriously. Because there was no fucking way I was letting him win. It was my night. It was my house. And it was my fucking fight. He just didn't know that last part yet, but he would soon enough.

I spotted Laney from the other side of the circle. She was watching my every move, a hunger in her eyes that told me exactly what my prize would be when I won the fight.

Yeah, that fucker was mine and it was time to shut that shit down and go take my woman to bed, no matter that there were people in our house. I was done waiting.

Axle dove for me, his arms wrapping around my waist as he pushed all his weight against me in the hopes of getting me out of the ring. My fists pummeled his back and I pushed against him, sending him back a few steps. I leaned further over and gripped my arms around him before lifting him off the ground and then slamming him back down. He grunted out loudly and let go of me, and then I spun him around and shoved him hard until his weight pushed through the crowd and he fell back, landing hard on his ass.

The crowd cheered and I walked over to him, panting as I held out my arm to him. Everyone went back to doing what they had been doing before and Axle took my hand, letting me pull him back up to his feet. He slapped me on the back.

"Won't be so lucky next time," he laughed and stalked back over to a very-pissed-off-looking River.

I turned around and found Laney right behind me. Her tongue darted out to wet her lips, and that was all it took for me to lose my shit and take what was mine, regardless of the other people there.

I reached out and grabbed her, swinging her up and over my shoulder.

"Jesse!" she shouted and laughed at the same time. "I said no, not while we have guests over."

"What did I say about you telling me no, woman? No isn't in your vocabulary now, so shut up and get ready to put up." And with that, I slapped her ass.

I stalked back into our home, the sound of cheers and wolf whistles sounding out behind me. I passed through the living room, ignoring Hardy's hard glare, because fuck him, that's why. I slapped my hand across Laney's backside again, harder this time, eliciting a nice little scream from her as I carried her up the stairs and into our bedroom, where I dropped her unceremoniously onto the bed.

She looked up at me, her gaze hooded and intense, and I reached down and unbuckled my jeans, loving how she never looked away from me. I let my jeans and boxers slide down my legs and hit the floor, and then I stepped out of them both. I pulled off my cut and placed it carefully over a chair by the window and then I returned to Laney, enjoying the way her gaze followed my every move.

I grasped her ankles and pulled her to the edge of the bed so her legs dangled off the edge, and then I reached up and unbuttoned her shorts before dragging both her shorts and her panties down her legs. I threw them across the room and I stared down at my woman, my dick hardening with every passing second. Her chest was rising and falling, her tits pushing up against the thin cotton vest that she was wearing and I reached over, gripped either side of it, and tore it right down the middle, enjoying the way her eyes widened at the sound of her clothing tearing.

Her flesh was hot and damp, a light sheen of sweat covering her almost naked body, and I leaned down and licked across her stomach all the way up to her right breast, where I reached under her and unclipped her bra, freeing her tits, and then taking her nipple into my mouth in one swift move.

She moaned as I sucked harder, my hand reaching between us to stroke against her folds, my fingers slipping inside of her and making her hips buck against my hand. I stroked along her, the pad of my thumb rubbing against her clit while I flicked my tongue across her nipple and made her cry out.

Her hands clawed at me, desperate for me, and I used my thigh to push her legs apart as I lay between her legs, replacing my hand with my dick as I slid into her, bottoming out in one hard, swift move. She gasped and wrapped her legs around me and I grabbed her wrists, holding them against the bed above her head as I swiveled my hips over and over.

"Jesse—" she hissed as my mouth covered hers, my tongue sliding along hers as I slid myself into her, my balls slapping against her ass.

Her tits were pressed up against my chest, rising and falling with every thrust of my hips. I sat up, letting go of her wrists to grab her hips so I could hold her still while I fucked her senseless.

Now this was exactly how I had wanted to celebrate moving into our own home: Laney naked and writhing underneath me. I slammed into her again, feeling close, and I rubbed the pad of my thumb against her clit until she blew up around me, tightening that little bit more as her muscles contracted and I couldn't take it anymore. I thrust into her a final time, riding the wave as I came, staring down at the most beautiful woman in the world and knowing that life couldn't get much better than this.

CHAPTER TWENTY-TWO:
Present day
Jesse

We hit the road, aiming to get back to the clubhouse around noon. I already knew that Hardy was going to lose his shit with me, but I was past the point of caring by then. Too much else was going on to worry about his wrath.

Besides, what was the worst he could do? I'd already ripped my own heart out.

We pulled up to a gas station as we came back into town, most of us needing to fuel up. The day was already heating up, as it always did at that time of year in Georgia. I'd be surprised if they didn't impose the water ban at some point. I finished filling up my bike and headed inside to pay, stopping to grab a bottle of water as I did. I closed the door on the tall fridge and looked over to see Charlie standing there glaring at me, her arms folded across her ample chest.

"You have a nerve," she bit out.

"Not in the mood for your shit today, Charlie."

That was a fucking understatement.

She took a step forward, uncrossing her arms so she could point a long-nailed finger at me. "Do you have idea what you've done to her?"

I rolled my eyes in reply and she narrowed her eyes at me.

"Jesse fucking James, you're killing her, you prick! And I'm done trying to convince her that you're not a total asshole, when all I see you doing are asshole things."

I gripped my bottle of water so tightly that I could hear the plastic cracking under my palm. "I never asked you to say anything to her. And I never said I was the good guy," I replied grimly. "In fact, I've been real fucking honest with her from day one and always told her that I was a bad guy and she could do better. Looks like I finally lived up to the reputation." I pushed past her, feeling fury burning through my veins.

"She's been crying nonstop for you, Jesse!" Charlie shouted to my back.

I stopped and tried to count to ten before I replied, but I barely made it to three before I turned back around to face her. "Yeah?"

"Yeah!"

"Didn't see her doing much crying for me when she snuck out in the middle of the night and fuckin' left me. Didn't see her crying then!"

Her face softened. "Jesse, I know you're hurting, but you're not the only one," Charlie said, her voice softening. "We're all hurting because we all miss him. Don't push us all away. It doesn't have to be like this."

I shook my head and laughed. "What? So now you're going to tell me that you understand?"

She nodded and I laughed again.

"You don't understand shit, and neither does she. He was my brother, my family, and now he's dead and I've got fuckin' no one!" I yelled, a tsunami of rage sweeping through my body ready to destroy anything and everything in its path.

Charlie stamped her foot, anger radiating from her small frame. She was a beautiful woman—thick, dark hair, dark eyes and heavy makeup—but she was also one tough bitch. "You're alone because you've pushed everyone away, Jesse! She's tried being there for you, but how can you help someone who's already hit the self-destruct button?" Her voice had risen too high and I swore that any moment the glass in the fridges was going to smash.

If she wasn't a woman, I would have kicked her ass by then for speaking to me like that. Because what did she know about me, or Laney or Butch? Nothing. She only knew what we told her. She didn't live with the pain. Or see the pity in Laney's eyes every time she looked at me. Poor fuckin' Jesse

James. Dead mom, dead brother, and a father who hated him. Poor fucking man. That was what she thought every time she looked at me. And she was right. I had to get her out of my life before I ruined her like I ruined everything else.

"You should speak to her," she continued, her voice softening. "Despite everything you've done, she still loves you."

I shook my head at her. "Are you not hearing me, woman? She finally saw sense and left me!"

"Will you stop feeling sorry for yourself and just listen to me! She's staying with Rider and me. Go and see her—right now. Just drive over there and take back what's yours. Sort it out before it's too late, Jesse. There's still time! Rider's out of town and I'll keep out the way for a bit."

I thought about what she said, seriously considered it. But what was the fucking point? I missed my woman like crazy. Fucking needed her more than I needed my own heart and lungs and motherfucking brain to live. But I couldn't destroy her, not if I loved her. And if she stayed with me, that's exactly what would happen. I'd take everything beautiful from her and tear it down until there was no semblance of my girl left.

Because that's what I did.

"I'm done listening to you, Charlie. Now fuck off before I do something we both regret." I turned and walked away from her, heading back out of the door without paying for my fuel. Casa was standing in the doorway and he tapped me on the shoulder as I passed him.

"I'll pay," he muttered, but I wasn't listening anymore. I just needed to get away right the fuck then. Because if not I was going to hurt someone, and I really didn't want to do that—at least not while all so much other shit was going down with the club.

I slammed my helmet on and straddled my bike before starting it. Casa came out of the gas station at the same time as I sped away, leaving my brothers and Charlie behind. Fuck them, and fuck that shit. And fuck Hardy too, I thought as I felt my cell phone vibrate in my pocket. Fuck them all.

I drove straight, riding through red stoplights and ignoring every other thing on the road. Deep down, I felt like part of me was almost intent on causing an accident so I wouldn't have to deal with this shit anymore, but the other part stopped me at the very last moment each time.

I passed straight through town and out the other side, not really aiming to go anywhere, but needing to move no matter what. I drove and drove, but the anger wouldn't dissipate like it normally did. Instead it built up inside me until I felt like a human fucking bomb that was waiting to explode.

I needed to vent.

I needed to fight.

I needed to fucking kill, if I had to.

And I knew that there was ever only one cure for the way I was feeling right then, only one thing that ever calmed me down, and that was Laney.

I pulled over to the side of the road and got off my bike before tearing my helmet off and throwing it to the ground. My chest felt tight, and my lungs burned like they were on fire. I was suffocating in my own anger. I leaned over and placed my hands on my knees. Every breath in felt restricted and painful.

The highway was pretty empty, but what little cars there were all made sure to get a good look at me as they drove by. I gave them all the finger, and screamed at them as they passed until they sped up and looked away.

I was losing my fucking mind.

That was the only explanation for any of this. I pulled out my gun and thought about sticking it in my mouth and then pulling the trigger, but I knew I wouldn't. I couldn't. I wasn't a pussy and that was a pussy's way out. No, I would go out in a blaze of fucking glory—the same way Butch should have gone.

Not drunk and driving our bike off the road like an asshole. Stupid fucker got what he deserved for drinking and driving; he knew the risks, yet he still got on that bike—the bike that we built together.

I kicked at the ground, my hands shaking from the anger coursing through my veins, and then I looked up at the sky and screamed Butch's name. The single word tore me apart, splitting me open down the center and reducing me to nothing but dust.

I'd barely been able to say his name since he'd died. Because every time I said it, it was a knife wound twisting I my gut, and with every twist my insides tore up some more. Butch was all I had left.

He wasn't just my brother, he was my only true family.

He was my fucking world.

He was both my mother and my father, my brother and my best friend.

I thought of his face the last time I'd seen him, and I wished I could go back in time and have that last moment with him again. He'd taken my place on a job for the club—nothing serious, just checking out our new warehouse. He promised me he'd be back to finish off the party and have a beer with me and Dom.

But he never made it back.

Apparently he stopped off to buy beer and got to drinking it before he even got back to the party. And then he'd ridden his bike off the road and crashed it into a ditch. His life blinked out in a split second.

My final words to him had been the nail in the coffin, and one of the reasons I hated myself so much.

3 MONTHS AGO

The party was in full swing—bitches hanging off any available man, and brothers drinking and fucking as much as they wanted. We'd had some shipments go missing the last couple of months, but todays had been business as usual. Put Hardy in a fuckin' great mood, too—hence the party, though you wouldn't have thought it from Dom's expression. Fucker was in a bad mood and had stormed out earlier on. That fucker was never happy, even when he had a woman on his dick and a beer in his hand.

I walked with Butch toward the door. "You sure you're cool with going?" I asked.

"Fuck yeah, Laney is drunk off her ass, you need to get her home," he replied. "Besides, I need some fresh air anyway."

"Rider gave me the order to head out to the new warehouse, though," I said, patting Pipes on the shoulder as he passed me, his arms laden down with beer.

"It's cool. It don't matter who goes, only that someone does. Just need to make sure it's secured for the night and we can get it checked over properly tomorrow. Besides, I could do with getting some space." He turned to watch Pipes cross the room. "Keep an eye on him," he said.

I followed his gaze, watching as Pipes put the beer down with the rest and turned to leave. Rider stopped him and grabbed a beer before handing it to Pipes and patting him on the back.

"You not feeling him?" I asked. Pipes had felt like a good fit to me. Few more months and I reckoned he'd be patched in if he kept up the work he was doing.

"Something about him I'm not feeling." Butch finally looked away and we headed outside. "Save me a beer too," he laughed.

"I think you're worrying about nothing. Pipes seems right to me, and you know my instincts are always good," I joked and drank the rest of my beer.

"Yeah, it's just your moral standards that are piss poor, right, brother?" He laughed back and straddled his bike. "Save me a beer."

"You think I'm saving all the beer until you get back?" I laughed. "Not a chance. I'm celebrating finishing our bike."

"You fucking better. I've worked my ass off building that bike and I expect a fucking cold beer waiting for me when I get home as thanks."

"Thanks? I would have finished that shit off long ago if it wasn't for your slow ass!"

He laughed. "Fuck you then, little brother! I'll bring my own beer, just be sure to save me a seat on the sofa, at least." He turned and walked to his bike.

"I'll try, but you better hurry and you better bring more beer back with you!" I laughed. I put my hand in my pocket and fished out the keys to our bike before handing them over to Butch.

He looked down at them and then back up to me quizzically.

"She could do with a ride out. Only had her on short bursts so far. Seems only fair since you're riding out for me."

Butch smiled. "Well all right, if you insist, little brother. I'll see you back here soon enough."

I nodded to our bike, jealous that he was going to get to ride it that night. "I expect you to ride like the fuckin' wind, brother," I replied and walked back inside laughing.

He said something else but I didn't hear it, and I never knew what it was because I never saw him alive again.

Pipes was on his way out as I got inside. "Everything okay?" he asked.

"Yeah," I replied.

"Butch need any help?"

"Help?" I frowned. "Why the fuck would he need help?"

"Just saw him arguing with Dom about going somewhere is all. Just making sure he didn't need me to ride out with him instead."

"Nah, he's good, he won't be long. You wanna help out, then make sure some beer gets saved for him." I laughed and patted him on the shoulder.

"I've got his back," Pipes replied with a laugh as I walked away to find Laney. Party was getting out of control, and it was time she left.

All I knew was that he had taken my place that night. But worse, I had told him to speed, and I had told him to bring beer. And it was a combination of those things that had gotten him killed.

I had gotten my brother killed. And on the bike we built together, no less.

*

No matter how many times I tried to ignore it, the twisted metal of the broken barrier always called me back to it. Like death to the Grim Reaper the place where Butch died always dragged me to it.

I let out a heavy sigh and picked up my helmet before getting back on my bike, still feeling full of anger and grief, and wishing that I had never walked into the gas station earlier. I had been doing pretty good at keeping everything bottled up, or so I thought. But my argument with Charlie had brought it all to the surface. Goddamn meddling bitch that she was. Always thought she knew so much better than everyone else, when really she knew jack shit about anything at all. The only thing Charlie knew was that Laney and I loved each other and I was burning our love to the ground.

She still loved me.

Despite everything that I had done already; she still fucking loved me.

I sat on my bike, contemplating my next move. I cracked my knuckles, feeling pissed off because I couldn't just walk away from my woman—from Laney. I had done the unimaginable to her, but when I needed to leave her the fuck alone to hate me all I could do was go crawling back. I was a selfish asshole, and no doubt I'd break her heart again. But like a crack head to their dealer, I just needed one last taste of Laney before I could let her go.

Just one last touch and I would walk away, I lied to myself.

I started my bike and began to ride again, that time heading toward Charlie's house, because there was no time like the present for this shit.

I pulled up in front of Charlie and Rider's house twenty minutes later and stormed up to the front door, not really sure what I was going to say to her, or even if she would listen, but I needed to see her at least one last time. I was angry with myself, angry with the world, and angry with Butch. None of this shit would be happening if he wouldn't have died.

My fist slammed against the front door over and over until Charlie threw it open, her eyes going wide with just the right amount of fear in them when she saw me.

"You said I should come and see her, so here I am!" I growled out.

"Now's not a good time," she stammered and tried to shut the door on me.

Was this bitch fucking kidding me?

I thrust my foot in the doorway, stopping her. "Now's the best fuckin' time, now get out of my way." I started to push inside and she put a hand against my chest.

"Jesse, I said no! Get the fuck away from here before I call Rider!"

I laughed in her face. "Your old man's out of town, Charlie. Now I'm coming in to see Laney, so get out of my way before you get hurt."

Fear and anger took ahold of her features, her gaze darting behind me. I turned and looked at the driveway, finally noticing the black truck that was parked there next to Charlie's little red Jeep.

"Who the fuck is here?" I snapped, pushing my way inside, and hoping that Charlie was fucking around on Rider because if not then whoever was here, was here for Laney, and that shit was not going to end well.

Charlie grabbed hold of my cut and tried to stop me from walking further inside, but despite her ferociousness I easily shrugged out of her grip and stormed toward the living room. The door was closed and I pushed it open and walked inside, and my heart stopped in my chest.

It wasn't my finest moment in history, but no one can say it was entirely unprovoked either. Any man would have done the same if they had found their woman in the arms of another man.

Laney untangled herself from the asshole that currently had his arms around my property, and she glared at me in fear and anger.

"Get out of here, Jesse!" she said calmly, though I knew she was anything but calm by the tremble of her chin.

"Who the fuck are you?" I snarled at the man that was about to go to ground. "And what the fuck are you doing touching my woman?"

I sized him up with one quick, scathing look. He was as big as I was, and just as built, but he had a pussy-boy softness about him that meant he'd never had to have a real fight in his whole goddamned life. Looked like Laney had finally got herself a god's honest college boy to treat her right. The thought brought an ugly sneer to my face.

He looked nervously toward Laney. "Thought you said you were single."

I took a step towards him. "Hey, fuckface, you don't talk to her, you talk to me. You feel me?"

I felt Charlie come into the room and move to stand with Laney, putting her arm across her shoulder. Laney shrugged out from under her grip, her tits jiggling in her low-cut top and grabbing pussy-boy's attention immediately.

"Don't you even fuckin' look in her direction again or I will fuckin' kill you!" I yelled, and he had the sense to look away from her though he refused to back down from me. Asshole was clearly still hoping that his size would make me rethink my current plan of ripping him to pieces and setting him on fire before pissing on the flames. He thought wrong.

"Jesse! This is not what it looks like, but even if it was, we're through and I will see anyone I want," Laney screeched, taking a step toward him.

"You touch him and I'll kill him, Laney." I glowered at her, my dick was hard despite the rage I felt burning through me, because goddamn, she looked fucking beautiful right then. Her hands curled into little fists by her sides, her eyes alight with anger and stubbornness. Wanted to take her upstairs and drag her panties off before shoving my way deep inside of her and claiming her all over again. Fuck it, after this, I was branding the bitch!

But first I needed to deal with this little pissant.

"You got two choices," I said to him. "You walk away now, and I don't see your face again, or you stay and I put you to ground."

Laney looked between us both. "Do not listen to him! We're separated! What I do has nothing to do with him anymore." She reached out to touch his arm and he shrank back from her, which was good because I meant every word I'd said.

She may have decided that we were over, but seeing her with another man…nah, fuck that shit. She was mine until *I* said we were over. I thought I was ready to let us go, that she would be better off without me—hell, that part was still true, but regardless she was still fucking mine. Call me a selfish dick all you want, but I wasn't done with Laney Williams yet. Not by a long shot.

Fuck, Butch would be turning over in his grave if he saw the fucking mess I'd made of this shit.

"I think I better get going," college boy said, though he refused to look at her.

"Think that might be a good idea if you still wanna be breathing in five minutes' time," I sneered.

He started to walk away, carefully sidestepping me and my radiating circle of hate for him. Laney stared after him, tears welling in her eyes, and Charlie, that bitch, was smiling like the cat that swallowed the canary, and I had a feeling that she'd set this shit up.

"I hate you!" Laney screamed in my face before barging past me.

I grabbed her arm and she flipped out on me, acting like a damn crazed cat, hissing and spitting, scratching and kicking until I let her go again.

I followed her as she ran outside and toward his truck and started talking to college boy again, begging him to ignore me, but that wasn't going to happen anytime soon. He looked over at me and I gave him a grim smile, my warning to move the fuck on because my offer to let him live was quickly expiring.

Laney grabbed at his arm when he tried to open the truck door, and he pushed her away. Unfortunately for him, too hard, and Laney fell sideways, landing on her side with a yelp.

Oh fuck no, he wasn't getting away with that.

I stormed toward him, reveling in the fear that came from him as he climbed into his truck and tried to shut the door, but I got there before he could. I gripped the handle and ripped the door back open, and then my hands were dragging him from the truck and slamming him to the ground.

"No, Jesse! Don't!" Laney screamed from next to me, but I ignored her in favor of my throbbing fists begging for blood.

It all turned into a blur as I pounded fist after fist into his face and chest, and the blood began to flow. He fought back, but his strength was nothing compared to my experience and my raging fury, and I lost count of how many times I smashed my knuckles into him.

All I know is that when the veil of red lifted, he was unconscious, I was covered in his blood, and there were two police officers aiming their guns at me.

I stopped hitting him and sagged back on my haunches, breathless and exhausted, my anger finally spent. Laney was hysterical and being held back by Charlie, both of them looking fucking petrified.

"Put your hands behind your head and get down on your front!" one of the officers yelled, while the other one got down on his knees and checked college boy's pulse. He stood back up and spoke quickly into the walkie talkie at his shoulder.

"We need medics here ASAP—"

I zoned him out as I lay down on my front with my hands behind my head and my cheek pressed against the hot blacktop of the driveway, and I stared at Laney, wishing, for not the first time, that I was dead. Because in her eyes, I was dead now anyway.

She looked over at the man I had probably just beaten to death, one hand covering her mouth to stop the noises she was making from escaping. Charlie was holding her, her own gaze wide-eyed and in shock at what had just happened.

Sure, in this life, it wasn't a surprising occurrence, but if, like I believed, Charlie had orchestrated the whole thing as a way to get Laney and I back together…well, shit, then it was just as much her fault as it was mine. Because you don't set a trap for the devil and expect someone to live through it.

The sound of bikes pulling up drew my attention away from Charlie and Laney, just as one of the officers put his knee between my shoulder blades and grabbed my hands so he could cuff me. I grunted in pain as he pushed all of his weight onto the one spot.

"Jesse?" Casa yelled my name and started toward me, and I watched as Dom held him back.

The other cop had his gun aimed at Casa and the rest of my brothers that had turned up. Poor cop looked like he was about to crap himself, too. In the distance I could hear the sound of an ambulance, the distinct wails echoing through the neighborhood.

I looked back at Laney, watching the trail of tears streaming down her face. "What have you done, Jesse?" she sobbed, breaking what little piece of me there was left. "What the fuck have you done!?"

CHAPTER TWENTY-THREE:
Present day
Jesse

The loud clank of the cell door closing vibrated through my bones. Always hated being locked up, but right then I knew it was the safest place for me and everyone else I loved.

I had fucking lost it, that was for damn sure. And I was almost certain that I had completely lost Laney. The worst part of everything had been seeing the fear in her eyes. Sure, she knew I did shit like that for the club, she wasn't stupid, but to see it happening right in front of you is very different.

God, I was an idiot. Yet every time I thought about the asshole touching her and shoving her so hard she fell down, I felt the rage clawing its way back up my throat.

Yeah, being locked up was definitely the best place for me at the moment. Because I'd likely go on a killing spree if I were anywhere else.

The light was fading, and no one had come to turn on any lights, which was good. I wanted to sink into the blackness of my cell and pretend none of it had ever fucking happened. What would happen next? I had no clue, but it sure as shit wasn't going to be a slap on the wrist, that was for damn certain.

I was lying back on my bed, the cold metal underneath me. The sound of footsteps coming closer made me look up, and I watched as a guard dragged a chair over to my cell and sat down on it. He cleared his throat and then slid a bottle of water through the bars of my cell, placing it on the ground.

"Thought you might be thirsty," he said.

I didn't bother to reply. Instead I turned to stare back up at the ceiling.

"You don't remember me, do you?" he asked.

"Why the fuck should I?" I replied darkly.

"We went to school together."

"So?" I snapped, already tired of the conversation.

"Drink your water, Jesse."

I sat up in one movement and glared over at him. "Get the fuck out of here!" I stood up and walked toward the bottle of water and picked it up, ready to launch it across the cell, but the light from the window caught his face and I realized I did recognize him.

"I've only got a few minutes, so sit the fuck down and listen to me," he snapped in a whisper.

"You sure you wanna be speaking to the guy that just beat someone to death with his bare hands like that?" I growled out.

"Looks like there are bars separating us," he replied.

"Won't always be."

He sighed and stood back up. "You know what? Fuck this. I was trying to help, but I can see you got your shit handled, right?"

I laughed darkly. "Wouldn't be stuck in here if I had my shit handled." I sat back down on my bed. "Besides, ain't no one who can help me."

"I have information—information you'll want."

I looked down at my hands, still covered in college boy's blood. I flexed them feeling the split skin stretching. "What kind of information?" I asked, thinking of the club.

Because that was what it always came back to, didn't it? The club and Laney. That was all I had left. Not that I had Laney anymore, of course. But I still had the club, and they'd make sure I was looked after if I got sent down. At least, I hoped so.

"It's about your brother," the guard replied after a long silence.

I stopped flexing my hands and looked over to him. "Ain't nothing you can tell me about him that I don't already know."

He stalked forward until he was directly in front of me, his hands reaching out to grip the bars. It took me a moment to place his face, but yeah, I remembered him. He'd grown since last time I saw him, though. Of course, the last time I'd seen him he was getting his ass handed to him by the college quarterback for being gay. Don't know what had made me do it, maybe it was that I was so full of rage at the time that I couldn't think straight, or maybe I just liked spilling blood. Either way, I'd stepped in and beat the shit out of that quarterback and hadn't bothered to stick around for this kid's thanks afterwards. Little punk had turned up at my house later that day to speak to me, though. Of course I didn't give a shit what he had to say, but Butch had spoken to him and accepted the thanks for me.

Funny thing was that he was in Butch's year, not mine. Yet I was one angry little shit that was looking for any way to vent my fury on the world.

"What's your name?" I asked, standing back up.

"Parker," he replied.

I stalked forward. "You need me to kick someone's ass again for you, Parker?" I sneered. "Gonna need to start charging if this becomes a regular thing."

He shook his head at me. "Your brother was a much better man than you."

I snorted out a laugh. "Tell me something I don't know."

"How about I tell you how Butch really died?"

Time stopped, the air stilled, and even the dust motes froze as his words settled over us both.

I scowled. "You better think really careful about what you say next, Parker."

He didn't look away from me, though he sure as shit should have if he wanted to live. "It wasn't an accident, Jesse."

"Fuck you! Fucking pussy, you don't know shit," I snapped, my jaw clenching. "He was drunk, and speeding, and the dumb motherfucker couldn't handle the beast of a bike we just built together. Idiot had a lapse in fucking judgment—" I couldn't finish my sentence without choking on my words.

"He wasn't drunk, Jesse, but he *was* speeding, and then he was rammed off the road."

I stepped toward the cell bars and gripped them, trapping his hands underneath mine. "I'm going to crush your hands now, and you're not going to make a fuckin' peep, you hear me?" I gritted out between my teeth, my grip tightening. "And then when I get out of here, I'm going to carve out your fuckin' tongue and then make you eat it. You hear me?"

"Do what you have to. I don't need to tell you this—I want to. Butch was good to me, and I want to do right by him."

"Yeah?"

"Yeah! And any moment now I'm going to get told to get out of here, and you'll get sent down and probably killed before you reach trial. Then I might not ever get to tell you the rest, so back the fuck off, Jesse!" Sweat glistened off his forehead as I continued to glare at him, but he didn't pull away or fight me. Instead he gritted his teeth while I continued to squeeze his hands under mine.

"So tell me, now," I growled.

Parker glanced over his shoulder to the doorway, where we could both hear voices. "He was driven off the road because of what he found out."

I thought about his words, and what it would mean if they were true. The guilt. The pain. The misery we had been through. And what the fuck would it mean for the club? I let go of his hands and Parker had the good sense to wait a second before he pulled his hands off the bars.

"What did he know?" I asked, suddenly more serious than I'd been in all my life.

Parker nodded, and looked relieved that I was finally listening to him. "You ever heard of the Razorbacks?"

An alarm bell rang in my head, sparks flying in all directions. Because damn straight I'd fucking heard of them. And if they'd had something to do with it, I would kill every last one of them before I died.

I started pacing my cell, realizing what an idiot I was because I was fucking trapped in that damn cell. "What about them?"

"So you have, that's good. That makes it easier. That night, a large shipment of ice had just come in for your club. Butch got wind of a deal going down between the Razorbacks and another MC club that were looking to steal it."

"Highwaymen don't deal in that shit," I growled out. We might have dealt drugs, but ice was something we had always stayed away from. It was off-limits. Always had been because of the shit that had gone down with my mom.

"Looks like your club is changing," Parker replied bluntly.

I glared at him for a moment, thinking about all the ways I was going to hurt him when I got out of here. "Who was the other club?" I asked tightly, because now he had my fucking undivided attention and I wanted to know every piece of information he had, and I wanted it right the fuck then.

"That's not the most important part," Parker said with a shake of his head, like I was wasting his time with dumb questions.

"Who the fuck was it?" I asked again, my temper rising.

"I told you—," he started but I cut him off.

"Of course it is!" I yelled, pacing my cell. "Stupid fucker should have told someone what he saw—should have told me. I would have gone with him, I could have helped him."

"He did," Parker replied calmly.

"What?" I snapped, turning to stare at him.

"He did tell someone."

"Who? Who the fuck knows about this? Because any brother of mine who knows about it would have said something, and whoever rammed him off the road—the Razorbacks or whichever dumb fucker it was—they would be in the ground now." I was raising my voice when I needed to be calm. I knew it but I couldn't keep calm. I was angry and wanting to break something, but I was stuck inside that fucking cell with no way out.

"Keep your noise down! They don't know I'm in here!" Parker hissed at me.

"Who gives a fuck?" I yelled. "This is club business. This is family business. And I want to know now so I can destroy everyone who had a hand in Butch's death."

The sound of footsteps coming closer had him backing up. "Keep your mouth shut," he mumbled to me as another guard walked into the room.

"What's going on, Parker?" the new guard said. Fat son of a bitch too—looked like he'd been greased up like a fat hog ready to be spit-roasted.

I glared in his direction, warning him away from me.

"Heard him shouting and thought I best come check it out," Parker replied, completely blanking me like he hadn't just told me news that would tear my world in half.

The other guard stepped forward, pulling out his baton, and I stepped toward him, gripping the bars. "The fuck you looking at?" I asked, my voice tinged with unhinged rage.

"Looks like he'll live," he replied with a sneer. "The man you almost beat to death. Good for you, too, or it would be a murder charge you'd be on. Though I think we should line men like you up and just shoot you down. That'll teach you people who's in charge."

I laughed in his face and spat on the ground at his feet, not giving two fucks right then whether the man who had pushed my woman to the ground lived or died.

"You bikers, you're all the same—none of you give a damn about the lives you ruin!" He shook his head and swung his baton at my hands clasping the bars and I let go quickly, the baton just barely missing my fingers. "I'll be making sure he presses charges against you and you get sent down for it, don't you worry." He took a step back from me. "Come on, Parker. Let's leave him to sweat alone in the dark."

He turned and walked out of the room and Parker watched after him.

I stepped forward again. "Who did he tell?" I whispered angrily.

Parker looked back at me. "I don't know. What I do know is that it was someone in your MC. And whoever it was, it was the wrong man, because less than three hours later your brother was dead."

My body was humming with anger and restlessness, but with no outlet for it, all I could do was try and breathe through it. The possibility that Butch hadn't died for something like drinking and riding, but because of club business, that somehow made me feel both better and worse.

"How do you know he told someone?" I asked. "Unless you were there, there's no way for you to know that shit," I said, the cogs turning as I tried to piece everything together.

"Because he told me," Parker said almost bluntly. "He was at my house, and he said he needed to make a phone call—asked me to leave the room since we always promised to keep our work out of everything else." He smiled. "Our jobs didn't exactly make us compatible."

"Why the fuck would he be with you—a cop, of all people? Now I know you're bullshitting me, and I swear to God, Parker, I won't always be in here so you better be fucking careful what you say next, because my brother ain't a rat."

"It's not my place to tell you Butch's secrets, but I promised him I'd watch his back, and when the time came I couldn't, so now I'm passing my promise on to you." Parker paused and I stared at him. "I have to tell you, because I need your help."

"What the fuck are you going on about?" I snarled at him, wishing that there wasn't bars between us because I was ready to destroy him for tearing my world apart. His words were going to rip my club in half, and my club was the only thing I had left. But he had to be telling me the truth, didn't he? What reason would he have to make that shit up?

Parker took a deep breath and dragged a hand down his face. "Butch was a good man. After the day when I came to your house, we met up more and more and became friends."

I laughed. "Butch wouldn't be friends with some fuckin' cop, asshole!"

"I wasn't a cop then," he bit out, his temper flaring to life.

"But you are now, fuckwad! He wouldn't have put you out if you were on fire! Yet you expect me to believe that you and he were best buds? Get fuckin' real."

Parker glowered at me. "We were more than friends," Parker said, and the words sank into the pit of my stomach as guilt washed over his features. "I shouldn't have said that."

"Why? Because you're a piece of shit liar?"

"No, because it wasn't my secret to tell." He took a deep breath and looked away from me. "I had no right to tell you that."

I stared at him for a long moment, trying to understand what he was saying to me. None of it made any sense, and yet it did. Everything made more sense. Despite the huge questions hanging over everything, things were much clearer.

Parker shifted uncomfortably and looked back to me. He swallowed noisily before speaking. "Butch and I were seeing each other, Jesse. We had been on and off for some years. He was in love with someone else, though—but they weren't ready to come out, so whenever they fought, he'd come to me. They fought that night, and after the meet he came to my house to talk about it. I loved him. Had ever since that day I met him." Parker shook his head sadly.

I staggered backwards. "Fuck off, Butch wasn't gay," I whispered, confused as to what he was saying, though in my heart I knew it made sense.

"He would have told me if he was gay. We told each other everything."

"Not everything," Parker replied, almost smugly.

"I'll fucking kill you for saying shit like that about him!" I snarled, ready to rip his throat out with my bare hands. What I'd done to that other pussy was nothing compared to what I would do to Parker. "You think you can say shit like that about my brother and get away with it? You filthy motherfucker, I will rip your throat out and shove it up your ass. Do you hear me? Your days are numbered!"

Parker shook his head. "You sound just like your father now," he replied grimly.

And there it was, the ultimate punch to the gut.

I was just like my fucking father.

CHAPTER TWENTY-FOUR:
Present day
Jesse

I stared at Parker quietly, my body almost collapsing under me.

"What did you just say to me?" I hissed out through gritted teeth, my body burning with anger.

"That's pretty much what your dad said to Butch when he found out. Told him he was going to kill him. That he refused to live with the shame of it." Parker shook his head. "Clyde Hardy might be the feared and revered president of the Devil's Highwaymen MC, but he's a fucking homophobe who turned on his own son, and it looks like you're just as bad as he is."

I staggered back to my bed and sat down, because my legs couldn't take my weight any longer. If I'd had a gun, I'd have put it to my head right then. I might as well just die if I was anything like my father. And the fact that Butch had kept that from me proved that I must have been—or that he at least thought I was. Everything was fucked.

"I loved my brother, and I ain't nothin' like Hardy," I said, talking to no one in particular. And I meant every word of it. I didn't care if Butch was gay or not; shit like that didn't bother me—shouldn't bother anyone else, either—but Butch obviously thought I would reject him just like Hardy had. The thought was almost too much to bear.

"He loved you too," Parker said.

"Parker? Where are you?" the fat fucking guard from before called, and Parker took a step away.

"I need to go."

"So go," I replied. "This has nothing to do with you anymore. This is club business now."

"I have more to tell you," he replied. "Besides, I told you I promised him I'd always have his back."

I laughed, the noise having more to do with hate than happiness. "He's fucking dead, and I'm a grown-ass man—I can take care of myself, now get the fuck out of here, Parker."

"I promised him!" Parker hissed impatiently, his voice tight with emotion. "I can't let him down, not again."

"I don't need help from some dirty cop. Now get out of here." I lay back on my bed, everything swirling around in my head.

"I'm not dirty! I'm probably the only clean cop in this place!" he snapped. "Just don't mention to anyone that we talked, okay? Butch said you would always have his back, and that if you knew I was important to him you'd have mine too."

But I wasn't listening anymore. Instead I was thinking about Butch keeping that secret from me for so long and why he felt that he had too. Was I more like Hardy than I realized? My thoughts switched to wondering about who Butch had called—which of my brothers knew about Butch, and did they help toward his death.

I dragged a hand down my face, a million questions swimming through my mind. When I looked over, Parker had gone.

The whole thing was a mess. I had more questions than answers, and no one to talk to about it. But the one good thing about being arrested was uninterrupted free time. I had all night to think about everything I'd just been told, and to think of a solution.

I stared up at the ceiling, glad for the dark around me. My knuckles still hurt from earlier, but it was nothing compared to my heart right then. One thing was for certain, though: I was going to sort out this mess and fix this shit. No way was I being sent down for beating up some little pussy and letting my brother's killer get off. No fucking way.

No, the club would get me out of there and then I was going to find out what really happened to Butch, who those fucking Razorbacks were, and then I was going to make everyone involved pay for his death in blood.

3 MONTHS AGO

I walked back inside the clubhouse, a smile on my face. The party was getting a little too wild and I needed Laney out of there. She knew what went down, but she didn't need to see it. Rider and Axle looked like they were rounding up their women and sending them packing too, but I couldn't see Silvie so I made a guess that she'd already left for the night. Either that or she was in Hardy's office on her hands and knees before she went.

I liked Silvie; she was a good woman. If things had been different, she would have made a great mom and a great old lady. As it turned out, it was obvious by then that Hardy didn't intend on making her his property. Real shame, too, 'cause it was clear that she fucking loved him, hard. Despite all the bullshit he threw at her, she was strong and took it all—probably believing that deep down inside of him, there was still a good man somewhere. Butch and I both knew differently.

Laney came out of the bathroom, half stumbling in tiny heels that she'd decided to wear. Woman always wore those little black ankle boots, laces always undone like she was ready to kick 'em off and sprint away at a moment's notice. But that night she'd gone out with her girls and they'd made her up like she was their pet project. Turned up looking beautiful, dressed in a tight little black dress and heels, her hair all piled up on top of her head, and her lips painted a vibrant red. Couldn't deny that she looked fucking stunning, of course, she never looked more beautiful than when she'd just woken up—her face clear of all that crap, her hair loose and trailing over her bare shoulders. And she always looked her best when she was naked. Charlie and River were great friends to her, but she was a class above them and she didn't need all that shit.

Laney stopped by the wall and leaned back against it. I watched her lips moving like she was talking to herself and I cocked my head to one side, wondering what the fuck she was doing. I stalked over to her, wondering if I could take her back to my old room and fuck her brains out before I sent her home with a prospect.

By the time I got to her, her eyes were closed and her head tilted up to the ceiling. She was still whispering something and I leaned in closer, desperate to know what it was. I couldn't stop the laugh from escaping when I realized that she was singing "Ninety-Nine Bottles of Beer on the Wall."

Her eyes opened abruptly, her head tilting to look at me, and I watched as she struggled to focus her eyes on me, a slow, sexy smile crawling up her face once she did.

"Hey, baby," she mumbled.

I put my hands on her waist and gave a little squeeze before sucking my bottom lip into my mouth and letting it go.

Her eyes sparked when she focused in on me. "Had a little too much to drink. Charlie is a whore. Bitch gave me tequila, and I told her no tequila," she slurred. "I told her twice!" she said, hiccupping. "No fucking tequila."

Fuck, she was too drunk to…well, fuck.

I dragged her body tight against mine, loving the feel of her tits pushed up against my chest. The material of her dress was tight and clingy, showing every fucking curve that God had graced her with, and as I held her to me I got a hard-on that I thought might punch out of my jeans if I didn't blow my load soon. Her pupils dilated as she felt me press against her stomach.

"You want me to take care of that, baby?" She grinned, her arms wrapping around my waist and moving lower to squeeze my ass.

Yes, my dick screamed out. I dragged one of my hands through my hair and let out a frustrated breath.

"Nah, babe, I'm all good. Let's get you home," I said instead, pressing a quick kiss on her mouth. She tried to force the kiss deeper but I pulled away. Not that I wanted to pull away. Fuck no. What I wanted to do was pull up that dress, turn her around, bend her over with her palms against the wall, and slam my dick home.

But I wouldn't—not like this.

She deserved more than that.

My blue balls were crying at my chivalrousness.

I took Laney's hand in mine and started to lead her across the clubhouse, looking back to see her eyes wide as she watched Cutter, Dexter, and Casa all groping the same club bitch. Laney's tongue flicked out to wet her lips and my dick laughed in my face, because yeah, there was no fucking way I wasn't getting in that tonight, no fucking way. Drunk or not, my woman wanted it.

I nodded to Dom as he came back inside, but the man was a moody motherfucker that night. Had been for weeks. Definitely some beef going down with him and Butch. They were usually inseparable, yet they'd been avoiding each other for weeks. Not sure anyone else had noticed much, with all the other club drama going on, but I sure as shit had.

Rider had ordered me to go check on our new warehouse earlier, but Butch had offered to go instead. Said he'd needed some space, whatever the fuck that meant. I'd let him take our bike since it was the least I could do for taking the job for me.

I walked Laney outside, wanting her on the back of my bike but knowing she was too drunk to stay on it, so I headed to one of the trucks instead. Hated driving those things, always felt so trapped, like the air was being sucked from my body. No, I much preferred the freedom of my bike. Couldn't fucking wait to ride the bike Butch and I had built. It had been our project for over a year; every piece was custom built, and she was fucking beautiful—almost as beautiful as Laney. We'd finished her earlier that day, but I'd barely had time to ride her round the block. The next day I'd ride that bike into submission, though, and tonight Butch would get to ride her and test her power out.

A prospect was standing with the trucks, and I called for the keys as we got close.

"You want me to take her home?" he asked. "You can head back in and party."

Fuck, it would be so much easier to do that. Just let the prospect take her home and make sure she didn't choke on her own vomit. That was their job, and I could trust him, too. He'd only been prospecting for a month or so and was barely eighteen, but he was a good kid, and it was already looking obvious—to anyone that bothered to look—that he was going to be a great fit for the club.

But I couldn't let him take my woman home. That shit wasn't right by me. What would I do? Head back inside, get drunk, and find some pussy that was available to fuck? Fuck that. No pussy would ever match Laney's. She was it for me. Hadn't looked at another woman since I'd been inside of her, and there was no way I would until the day I died. Plenty of brothers fucked around on their old ladies, and most of the women just turned a blind eye to it, but I couldn't do it to her. I knew I'd kill any man that put his dick anywhere near her, so why should it have been any different for me?

Besides, unless their pussy was made of gold, ain't nothing that any woman could do for me better than Laney already did.

"I've got it," I called back to the prospect, and he nodded before reaching into his pocket and throwing the keys across to me. I caught them in one hand, not even missing a stride as I continued to walk toward the truck. I unlocked it and opened the door and then reached around and grabbed Laney by the waist, hoisting her up into the truck in one swift movement, loving the way she let out a little squeal as I did.

"I love you," she slurred in my ear. "So so much."

"Yeah?" I asked, pulling back to look at her.

She nodded and gave me a drunken smile. "You know, Jesse, I never thought I'd have this."

I put my hand on her legs and pushed them inside the truck, though really I wanted to slide my hand up that skirt and tear her panties off. I slammed the truck door closed before heading round to the driver's side and climbing in. Laney sat back against the seat, her head turned toward me.

"Never thought you'd have what?" I asked as I started the truck, desperate to get home.

"This, baby," she slurred. "This thing that we have. Always felt like there was something wrong with me, like I wasn't worthy of love, and then you came in, all big and butch and bikerish, and you loved me." She gave a little giggle and hiccupped.

"Think you'll find that it was you who came into my club, and I'm pretty sure I wasn't big and butch then. Also pretty certain that there ain't no such word as '*bikerish*,'" I laughed back.

She slapped at my thigh playfully, but then her playfulness gave out to something else and she dug her nails in and gripped my muscle before sliding her hand up.

"You know what I mean," she whispered, her tongue darting out to lick her lips. Her hand reached my cock in my jeans and gripped it, and I groaned. Pretty sure my dick was about to explode in her hand.

"Time to get home," I said between groans as her hand simultaneously rubbed and squeezed me. "Right the fuck now."

She giggled again and I started to back the truck out of the clubhouse grounds. Yeah, fuck being chivalrous. I'd take her home, fuck her, put her to bed with a bottle of water and some aspirin, and then head back to the party. Fuck, this day was going good.

The streets were pretty quiet since it was after ten on a Tuesday night; not much ever happened around there during the week. It was a small town, with even smaller-minded people in it. While the world developed and changed, that town seemed to be standing still; the only thing moving in it was the club. Business was booming for the Highwaymen, and it didn't look like it was going to tail off any time soon, either. We'd had a couple of shipments go missing, but we were pretty certain we'd plugged that leak now.

Laney kicked off her shoes and slid down, resting her cheek on my thigh muscle. Her hand had stopped rubbing on my cock, and I hoped that was because she was about to give me a drunken blowjob while I drove.

As I pulled the truck to a stop outside our house, the sound of Laney's soft snores broke through the quiet of the truck. I looked down at her and shook my head. I wanted to be pissed that I hadn't gotten any action, but I couldn't stay mad at her—woman was too damn beautiful to be mad at for long. Besides, she looked after me good every night, so no doubt she'd be making it up to me the next day. Definitely something to look forward to.

Make-up sex was one thing, but guilt sex was even better.

I stroked the side of her face until she began to stir, her body stretching out like a cat's across the seats, but she didn't wake up.

"We're home," I said quietly, and she mumbled something in response but didn't move. I smiled down at her, wondering how I got so fucking lucky. My life had been fucked up since the day I was born, with no one other than Butch giving two shits about me. I was born into a world of anger and fighting and death and lying. I had been beginning to wonder if I was cursed, given that everyone I loved either died or hated me, but then Laney had loved me back and the rest was history.

I clicked open the truck door and slid Laney's head off my lap so it was easier to reach in and take her in my arms, and then I jumped out before reaching in and grabbing her. I kicked the truck's door shut behind me as I carried her to the house, her head resting against my chest and her breath fanning against my skin and sending shivers through me every step of the way

I unlocked our front door with one hand, grateful that Laney weighed barely a hundred pounds, and kicked it behind me before carrying her up to bed.

She hardly stirred the entire time, even as I laid her on top of the bed and peeled off her dress. She was dressed in matching black bra and panties underneath that tiny dress, and my dick throbbed painfully as a reminder that it was there and still hadn't been taken care of yet. I reached down and adjusted it before sliding a hand up her thigh, all the way up until I cupped her ass cheek.

Her eyes fluttered open and she smiled lazily, her hands reaching for me and tugging my mouth to hers. I kissed her long and hard and then I pulled away and dragged the duvet over her body. Because if I didn't cover her up I wasn't going to be able to control myself much longer. My dick wanted inside and it did not like being told no.

"It's okay," she mumbled.

I shook my head and smiled down at her, my hair trailing into my line of sight until I tucked it behind my ears. It had been getting longer and longer and I kept on meaning to get it cut, but now it was chin length I was debating leaving it to grow some more.

"I want you to show me that you love me," she slurred, her left hand reaching up to pull the covers away from her breast.

"You know I do, I don't need to fuck you to show you that," I replied.

Her eyes filled with tears and I panicked that she was going to start crying. Fucking hated it when anyone cried—and not in a sympathetic way, either. More in a shut-the-fuck-up-because-that's-annoying way. Yeah, I was a real-life saint, I know.

"I miss my mom," she said quietly, rolling onto her side.

I hadn't turned a light on, so the only light shining in was from the streetlights outside the window, but I saw enough to know that she was definitely crying then—even if she was only doing it quietly. Strange thing was, it didn't annoy me; instead it angered me. I hated that she was sad and I couldn't do shit about it. I couldn't stop her from missing her mom, I couldn't bring her back. All I had was me.

"I wish you could have met her, Jesse," she said, her face still turned away from me.

I sat down next to her and reached out to pull her onto my lap, and she wrapped her arms around my waist and buried her face against my stomach and cried harder. I rubbed her hair back and stared into the dark, hating hearing her cry.

"I wish I could have, too," I replied. "If she was anything like you, I bet she was fucking great."

Laney fell silent and I wondered if I'd said the wrong thing. I was no good at this shit. I could fuck her and make her feel good, but I wasn't used to giving out advice and shit like that. She needed one of her girlfriends there to talk to, not me. I debated if it was too late to call River or Charlie—fuck, Silvie would have been good too. But not me.

"I'm nothing like her, but I wish I was," she finally whispered, her breath fanning across my stomach. "She was loveable, everyone loved her."

I frowned and looked down at her before putting my hands on the sides of her face and making her look up at me. "You're loveable, Laney."

Her bottom lip was trembling. "I am?" she asked.

I laughed lightly. Not a bitter, mean laugh, but one full of disbelief. "Well *I* fuckin' love you. Your friends love you—fuck, even Gauge loves you, though he doesn't know how to show it."

"Thank you," she whispered back.

"For what?"

"For loving me."

"Don't thank me, it ain't a good thing," I replied.

"Of course it is!"

I shook my head. "Nah, it really isn't. I'm not a good man, Laney, I don't do nothin' good, and I sure as shit don't know how to keep somethin' good. One of these days I'm going to wake up and you'll have left me, and then I'll be back on my own. And this, this'll be like a dream—like it never fuckin' happened."

I looked away, embarrassed by my own honesty. I hadn't meant to say those things to her, but now that I had, I realized the honesty I felt behind them.

"I don't deserve you," I said, swallowing loudly.

"Of course you do!" she yelled. "Why would you say that? And I'll never leave you. It's me and you forever, Jesse, no matter what."

I smiled sadly. "It's never forever," I replied.

"Why would you say that?"

I pushed back her hair. "Because it's the truth, baby. Everyone I love dies, and everything I touch turns bad. If I wasn't such a selfish fucker, I would have let you go by now. But I am selfish, and I don't want to let you go. I'm a bad man, Laney, and one day soon you're going to realize that and run as far and as fast away from me as you can."

She stared at me in silence, her expression sad. A single tear trailed out of her left eye and her hand gripped my waist tightly. "Don't say things like that," she whispered.

"It's the truth."

"I can't lose you."

"I told you: I'm a selfish asshole, I ain't going anywhere. You'll have to push me away—and I have no doubt that one day you will," I replied.

Her forehead scrunched up and I used my thumb to rub the little creases away.

"Until then, though, you got me, babe. You got all of me."

"I'll never push you away," she said, defiance in her tone.

"What if you hate me? What about then?" I was only joking, but a deep-down part of me, the sick part, needed to know. How far would I have to push her to stop her from loving me? How long would it take before she came to her senses and realized I was no good for her? A month? A year? Two? It'd happen, I knew that like I knew my own hands. Because a woman like Laney—no matter what she thought about herself—a woman like Laney was far too fucking good for me.

"I could never hate you," she said, sitting up and staring into my face, her mouth puckered into a little frown.

Goddamn, she was sexy, even when she was drunk off her face and pissed off at me. And that's exactly what she was—drunk and pissed off.

"Never!" she repeated, pushing my hands away.

I smiled. "What if I fucked someone else?"

She swallowed, and I knew I'd touched a nerve. Sex for her was something sacred, and she knew I knew that. It had something to do with her mom being a hooker, and the fact that she'd slept with someone new every night for almost twenty years.

"You wouldn't ever do that." Laney moved back from me, like if she put some distance between us the words couldn't touch her.

"But what if I did? What then? Would you still hold me in such high regard then? Or would I be just as bad as every other asshole out there?" I gritted my teeth and forced a smile. I didn't know why I was pushing the issue, or why it was so important to me to know, but it was, and now that I had started I knew I couldn't stop until I knew.

I wanted to know what it was that would make her stop loving me—maybe because if I knew, maybe I would know why my mom hadn't loved me enough to quit drugs, or why my dad didn't love me enough to treat me like his son. I wanted to know what it was that would make her hate me so that I could use it against her one day to send her somewhere far far away from me. Somewhere better. Somewhere without me in it to fuck everything up for her.

"Go on, tell me the truth, Laney: if I fucked someone else, would you hate me then?" I sneered.

She nodded, her eyes glistening with unshed tears. She opened her mouth to say something and then closed it again and I grabbed her and pulled her to me. She clung to me desperately, like I was her lifeline, and I felt like the piece of shit I was for talking to her like that and making her cry.

"I'm sorry," I hushed against her head, kissing the top of it. "I'm sorry, I'm an asshole. I don't know why I did that."

My dick was soft, and nothing was going to rouse it again that night so I leaned over and dragged the comforter over us both and she pushed herself in against me. As her sobs died down and her breathing evened out, I thought about heading back to the party, but eventually I decided against it. That night, the only place I wanted to be was in her arms.

CHAPTER TWENTY-FIVE:

3 months ago
Jesse

I woke to my cell vibrating against my thigh, and Laney groaning and trying to roll away from me. Instead I took my cell from my pocket and threw it across the room before grabbing Laney and pulling her backside tight against my dick.

I was hard and ready for her, and she writhed against me with a sigh.

I reached between us, sliding my hand over her body and then dragging her panties down her thighs. I unzipped my jeans and pulled my dick out, and I used my thigh to nudge her legs apart before I placed my dick at her entrance and slowly slid myself inside. She sighed and moaned as I sunk balls-deep, pushing back on me and giving a little grunt.

My cell continued to ring from across the room, and it was important that I answered it because, from the sound of the ringtone, it was the club and you always answered when the club called. But my dick was tucked deep inside of her and my hand was cupping one of her breasts while my hips rolled over and over. She moaned as I sped up, and I rolled her nipple between my fingers as I slid all the way out and then slammed myself back home, making her gasp and cry out, her hand reaching around to claw at my thigh muscles.

I pushed her onto her front and dragged her up to all fours so I could settle myself behind her, my hands on her hips as she dipped her head low and raised her ass high, and then I was pounding into her over and over until I felt my balls tighten and then release and make us both call out. I laid myself over her back, letting the final throes of my orgasm wash over me while I massaged her breasts and kissed her shoulder.

My cell rang again and I growled in annoyance. I was more than ready to blow someone's fucking head off for continuously calling me.

"You better get that," Laney said with a little laugh. "I need to go shower. And get some aspirin. And eat. And get some coffee," she grumbled.

I pulled out of her and she lay back down.

"But first I need to sleep some more." She dragged the covers over her head and I laughed and slid out of bed.

I found my cell on the floor by the chest of drawers that Butch had gotten us from a yard sale. It was solid oak and looked like brand new. I picked up my cell and opened it and pressed it to my ear.

"Who is it?" I snapped into the phone. "And what the fuck do you want?"

"It's Casa."

"Great—anything else you got to tell me or were you just calling to hear the sound of my voice while you jacked off into your hand?"

"It's about your brother," he replied. His voice sounded grim, like he'd just been dragged from sleep himself, and I paused to give myself a moment before saying anything else. He sounded like shit; his tone deep and hesitant, not like his usual; upbeat and fast-paced.

"What about him?" I asked. I backed up to the bed, suddenly needing to sit down. I didn't know what Casa was going to say next, but my body was bracing myself for bad news all the same.

"He's gone," he replied.

"Gone? Gone the fuck where?"

"Jesse?" Laney said, sitting up behind me and clearly sensing that something wasn't okay.

"Casa? Where the fuck is Butch?" I asked, this time the words barely making it out of my mouth. My chest felt tight and heavy, like something was pressing against it, and I put a hand to it, wondering why the fuck it felt so constricted.

"He's dead, brother, I'm sorry," Casa said, his final word a whisper.

"Fuck you, Casa, that shit ain't funny. Now what do you want?" I stood up but then immediately sat back down again.

Laney sat up next to me and I could feel her worried gaze on the side of my face. I stared into the air in front of me, my own gaze unfocused as I let Casa's words sink in. It couldn't be true; Butch couldn't be dead. Not Butch.

"I'm serious, Jesse, and I'm sorry. Real fucking sorry, brother."

"Go fuck yourself!" I snarled out and hung up.

I continued to stare into the air in front of me, trying to process what kind of fucked-up person would say something like that to his friend. What kind of sick motherfucker would tell someone that their brother was dead? I was struggling to think of reasons for not going to Casa's house and blowing his brains out right that fucking minute, because that was what he deserved.

The shit he was spewing, well that shit wasn't funny.

Laney put her hands on the side of my face and turned my head so I would look at her. "Jesse?" she whispered out. "What is it?" her eyes were glassy, tears already brimming.

Her cell was ringing from somewhere in the house, but it sounded distant. She looked away from, her eyes scanning the room until she eventually saw it, and she reached over to pick it up. Panic slammed in my gut and I gripped her wrist tightly and pulled her back to me.

"Don't answer it," I pleaded, my voice harsh and threatening.

A tear slipped from one of her eyes and she nodded quickly. "Okay, okay. Just come here." She pulled me back up the bed and I lay down next to her, putting my head onto her stomach.

My whole body was tense, through anger and grief and realization. Because Casa wouldn't have made that shit up. There was just no way he'd do that. I clutched onto her body tighter, feeling the tremors running through her as she tried to conceal that she was crying, and I buried my face against her stomach as she wrapped her arms around me.

"I'm here, I've got you," she whispered, her fingers stroking my hair. "I've got you, Jesse, always."

Always, I thought bitterly. I had never believed in always, because always didn't exist in my world. Always was merely a fleeting moment, or a splash in time. That was the longest that *always* was in my world.

Always was just like forever: a vicious lie upon an angel's lips.

Because always died just like everything and everyone else.

Always was never forever.

I don't know how long we lay there for, but neither of us wanted to move because we knew that once we did, we'd let the nightmare truly in. At the moment it lingered on the peripheral, scratching against the doors and begging to come in. But we fought it for as long as we could.

We fucked six times that morning, until my dick was sore and Laney winced with every thrust of my hips. We fucked away the pain that we knew was coming. And we fucked in the hopes that we could keep our world together. We fucked, we didn't make love. It was raw and rough and dark, and more to do with pain than pleasure, especially toward the end.

Our bodies were covered in slick sweat, the sheets crumpled underneath us, as I lay back on the pillow and stared up at the ceiling, my dick flaccid against my thigh. We lay naked, side by side, both of us too scared to speak in case we let the world in, pushing it away with every beat of our hearts and every thrust of our hips.

But nightmares, just like dreams, eventually seep into the blood.

And there they find you, no matter how much you hope and pray they won't.

The sound of bikes outside, roaring in a chorus of throaty metal and anger, woke me up from my daze. I reached over to Laney and grabbed her hips, my dick already hard at the thought of having her again, even as it burned from the constant fucking. The day had seeped into night, and shadows clung to the walls. Laney opened her thighs to me without question and I pushed myself between them, watching as she bit her lip when I entered her, sliding in deep. I didn't want to hurt her, but fucking her was the only thing keeping me sane at the moment. She knew it and I knew it. So we fucked and we clung to each other, knowing that our world was about to be blown apart.

A heavy thumping came at the door, my name being called out as I slid in and out of her, and tears trailed out of her eyes. She held my face in her hands and wrapped her legs around my waist, pulling me closer to her whispering that it was going to be okay. I leaned over her body, burying my face in the crook of her neck and I thrust fast and deep, needing the release of pleasure before I let the world in. Before I let the pain destroy me.

I came, suddenly and unexpectedly, and she held me while I squeezed at her ass cheeks and kissed her neck. The thumping downstairs continued, both of our cells illuminating the room.

"Jesse, you need to go now," she whispered in my ear sadly. "It's time."

I nodded, hating her in that moment for making me do that. Hating her for making me face the unfaceable. I kissed her, sucking her bottom lip into my mouth as I slid my flaccid dick out of her. She was crying and I wiped her tears away with my thumb,

"Don't cry," I murmured.

She blinked back her tears. "He's gone, isn't he?"

"Jesse!" Dom yelled from outside, his fist hitting the front door again. "Open the door, brother."

I nodded, finally accepting it. Destiny, fate, whatever the fuck you wanted to call it. It had caught up to us, finally. "Yeah, baby, Butch's gone," I said.

Something broke inside of me once the words left my mouth. Something I didn't know I had until it broke away and turned to dust.

"I'll get the door," Laney said, but I shook my head and pressed a kiss to her bruised lips.

"I've got this." I slid off the bed and pulled on my jeans. When I turned to look back, Laney had wrapped the bedsheet around herself and tears were trailing down her cheeks. I gritted my teeth and vowed to be strong.

I wouldn't cry. Not ever. Butch wouldn't want me to.

I headed down the stairs, my jeans hanging at my hips, and I opened the front door. Outside Casa, Dom, Gauge, and Rider stood, their faces painting the look of horror that I had dreaded.

"What happened?" I asked, feeling numb, the anger merely a spark in my gut for the moment.

"We should come in," Rider said, and I nodded before walking back inside.

I faced the window, looking out on the street and remembering Butch unloading the van with mine and Laney's things in it.

"Last night, after he left," Rider started. "He crashed his bike."

I nodded. "Okay."

"They say he was drunk," Dom said angrily. "But he knew better than that. Butch wasn't some dumb fuck."

I turned to look at him, the anger burning brighter. "Who's 'they?'"

"The cops," he replied, darkly.

I shook my head. "Butch would never ride drunk. The man lived to ride, no fucking way he'd do that. He knew the risks and he wouldn't take those chances."

I was certain of it. One hundred percent fucking certain.

Dom shrugged and let out a long breath like he was relieved that someone else thought the same thing as him. "That's what I said to them."

"Cops said there was beer all over the road. They're checking his blood now, but that's what it's looking like. Between riding his bike too fast and drinking…I'm sorry, brother," Rider said. "He was a good man. The best." He dragged his hands through his silver hair, holding my gaze steady, unsure of what to say to make this okay, and already knowing that there was nothing. He grabbed me and pulled me into a hug, before patting my back and letting me go. "The club won't be the same without him."

"Nothing will," I replied.

"I hear that." Rider looked down but didn't say anything else.

"Laney upstairs?" Gauge asked and I nodded. "Mind if I go up?"

I shook my head. "I'd knock first if I were you, but go on up."

He nodded and made his way up the stairs. I sat down on the sofa and put my head in my hands, listening to the mumble of voices coming from our bedroom, and then her cry as the reality forced its way in and destroyed the final part of our bubble.

Casa sat down next to me. "I'm real sorry, Jesse."

I listened to Laney crying, and I heard Casa speaking, but his words didn't make any sense. Nothing made any sense anymore. Butch would never drink and ride. Never. Not unless someone told him to. Not unless someone told him to bring more beer and hurry back.

And that someone was me.

CHAPTER TWENTY-SIX:

3 months ago
Jesse

The air was thick and heavy, the Georgian heat hanging heavy in the sky. The past week had felt just like that—like we were waiting for something, but none of us knew what.

Butch's death had been signed off as misadventure—riding under the influence. His blood sugar and alcohol levels were too high, and by the skid marks on the road where he'd gone off, not to mention the mangled mess his bike had been in, he'd been speeding. Took a sharp corner and slid off the road.

It didn't make sense to anyone, but it did to me.

I had done this.

I wasn't arrogant enough to think it was all my fault—after all, he was a grown man and had made that call himself, but it should have been me on that job. I was supposed to have been checking on the warehouse, not him. Worse still was that I was the one that had put the thought in his head to drink that night. I'd told him to bring more beer, to have one for the road, and I'd told him to speed and get back quickly.

And I had given him the keys to our bike. I had built her to ride faster than anything I'd ever built before. I knew the bike was dangerously fast.

The shame I felt made me feel sick and clawed at my skull every time I closed my eyes, but I couldn't bring myself to tell anyone. Laney kept telling me I was strong and brave and she was there for me, but I wondered what she'd think if she knew the truth. If she realized what I coward I was. What a killer I was.

We stood by the graveside while the priest said some words that were supposed to comfort. I couldn't speak for anyone else, but I felt nothing from them. I was empty, numb, and barren of anything. Laney was next to me, her hand clinging to mine while mine limply held hers.

We took turns in walking forward and throwing dirt on the coffin, but when it came to my turn I couldn't do it, so I stood there, staring at the dirt hole that contained my brother's body. Hardy hadn't spoken to me since Butch's death, and it felt like he knew what I had done and was punishing me for it. But of course there was no way he could have known.

He came and stood by my side, and we stood silently for a moment as the crowd of bikers and women began to disperse.

"That should have been you in there," he said, so quietly I wondered for a moment if I had imagined it. "He was always better than you. You, you were always trouble. Killed your mom and now you've killed your brother."

I heard the words, but it took a moment to understand what he was saying, to grasp the full atrocity of his accusation. I swallowed and slowly turned to look at him. His eyes were dead. His expression blank. The man was made of stone, his heart and soul nonexistent.

"What the fuck did you just say to me?" I growled out.

"I said this, this is all your fault, Jesse." He waved his arms at the hole in the ground. "You were always worthless, but your mother, she saw something in you and wouldn't let you go, even when I told her you were no good."

"I was a baby—a fucking child," I said, my body shaking, trembling from head to toe. The anger that had been flickering in the pits of my stomach since finding out Butch was dead flared to life and became its own entity.

"You were poison," he said, his voice hushed. "Always were and always will be."

Laney came to stand next to me, her hand taking mine. "You okay, baby?" she asked, her tone suggesting she was at breaking point and was going to cry at any moment.

"Yeah," I replied. I looked over to where Gauge stood, and caught his eye and he nodded and came over to us. He wrapped his arms around Laney's shoulder and gently guided her away, and I let her go.

"You'll kill her too, you know. Everything and everyone you touch turns bad or dies. You should let her go if you really love her. Walk away from her and all of this before it's too late, because I'd rather die than hand the gavel down to you." Hardy turned and walked away, done with talking to me.

It was the most he'd ever said to me in weeks. Maybe even ever. The deepest thing he'd ever said to me in years. I wanted to hate him for saying those things, deep down knowing he was just fucked up and evil. Knowing that I couldn't possibly have had anything to do with my mom's death. She was a drug addict—and that was all on her. She didn't love any of us enough to stop, to stay with us so we could be a family. The call of drugs was more important to her than family.

Everyone had gone, and I finally had my moment alone with Butch. I walked to his graveside and crouched down, grabbing a handful of the dirt, but instead of throwing it, I held onto it and then I spoke to him. Laying it all out on the line for him to hear. Baring my soul to him.

"Not sure why it's you down there and not me, Butch." My words came out choked, and I cleared my throat and continued. "Because you're a better man than I'll ever be. Everyone is thinking it, so it seems sort of twisted that it's happened this way, you feel me, brother?" I stared at the dirt in my hand, at the small grains of soil and minerals, wondering how long it would take before Butch was a part of the earth too.

"I don't know what to do now that you're not here," I said with a shake of my head. "I don't know who I am without you, brother. Or how I'll carry on without you. You were my whole family and now I'm alone. Hardy is right—I'll kill her if I stay with her, so I have to walk away."

I threw the dirt onto his coffin and stood up, and I shoved my hands in my jeans pockets and pulled out a scratched key. Laney would never let me go though, not unless I made her. Unless I made her hate me.

It was the only way to keep her safe—to keep her alive.

"You said this bike was for me," I continued. "That you wanted me to have something that always reminded me of you if anything ever happened to you. That it would show me the way to carry on and always pull me back when I started fucking up. But I don't want it, Butch. You keep it. It's what killed you in the end—I'm what killed you. And if it was so important to you—if *I* was so important to you—you wouldn't be dead."

I threw the key into the grave, listening to the sound of the metal hitting the wood of the coffin lid, and then I walked away. The anger burned brightly inside of me, the hate and the guilt for what I had done, and who I had become making it almost impossible to see straight. Voices whispered in my ears and I tried to catch my breath.

When I got to my bike, Laney reached for me but I pushed her away. "Go home, Laney."

"Jesse," she sobbed, still reaching for me, wanting to comfort me.

Wanting me to comfort her.

But I couldn't.

How could I?

She had a chance without me. She had a future.

But with me…I'd destroy her like I destroyed everything else in my life.

I looked over to see Hardy straddling his bike. He glanced up at me, watching me with those cold, dead eyes of his. He was right about one thing: I had to do the right thing by Laney. I had to cut her loose before it was too late. What kind of man would I be to keep her? What kind of father would I be if she got pregnant? My father was Clyde Hardy, a monster of a man who cared for no one—not even his own son—and I would turn out to be just like him.

"Jesse!" Laney cried my name again, the sound of her tears scorching my heart.

I looked back over my shoulder, seeing that Gauge had her, his arms wrapped around her, dragging her to his body, keeping her from me. He was giving me space, and he was protecting her from me. Because right then, I was a dangerous man indeed, and he could see that.

I climbed onto my bike, started it, and drove out of the cemetery, still hearing Laney calling my name long after I had gone. Every fiber of my body wanted me to turn around and go back to her. To be with her. But I could no more be loved by that woman than I could be by anyone else.

I was unlovable, I was a murderer, and Laney deserved someone so much better.

That was the start of the end for Jesse James Hardy.

CHAPTER TWENTY-SEVEN:
Present day
Jesse

I breathed in the humid, early morning air and walked toward my bike. My head felt like it had been hit by a sixty-foot truck and now my brain was just rolling around inside my skull.

Casa and Dom sat on their bikes next to mine as a prospect waved and then took off in a truck. I reached them and Casa stood up and pulled me into a hug, slapping my back harshly. When I pulled away he was smiling, a large, shit-eating grin covering his face, though it didn't quite reach his eyes today.

"You ready to bounce?" he asked.

"Fuck yeah," I replied, taking my helmet and sitting on the seat of my bike. I looked over at Dom, his expression blank and his gaze faraway. "You okay, brother?"

"Yeah, just tired after being up all night with your attorney." He lit a cigarette. "Man knows his stuff. Not sure how he turned you attacking an innocent man and almost killing him into you defending yourself, but he pulled it off. Gonna have to keep your ass clean until your hearing in a couple of weeks, though, but you should be okay. I hope."

I nodded. "Laney okay?"

"Nah, brother, she's a fucking mess," he replied with a heavy sigh, like it was him that would have to sort out this whole fucking thing and not me. "And I'd keep clear of Charlie for a while if I was you—she's out for blood after what you did. You really fucked things up this time."

"Nice of you to break that down gently for me," I said and he shrugged. "I can trust you, can't I?" I asked, and from the corner of my eye I saw Casa watching us both intently.

Dom turned to glare at me. "What are you fucking getting at?"

"Just making sure you ain't got shit that you're keeping from me is all. I trust you, like I trusted Butch, and I'd hate for that trust to be misplaced." I felt shitty speaking out of turn to him, but I had to. Those things had to be said, and I had to gauge his reaction.

Dom scowled darkly at me, his eyes finding a little fire. "You got something to say, you say it. Don't be creeping around that shit like a peeping fucking Tom. Just spit it the fuck out."

I knew as he spoke, in the way his shoulders sagged and his eyes held the same pain as mine, that

I could trust him, and that my guess was going to be correct.

"Now's not the time, but when this shit is over, we need to talk," I said, slipping my helmet on and turning away from him.

"About?" he dared me.

"Butch," I replied, looking across at him.

Dom fell silent before swallowing and looking away.

I looked over at Casa, who looked confused as fuck as to what was going on, but I wasn't going to tell him, despite how much I needed someone to talk to. Butch had kept certain things a secret for a reason, and for some reason Parker had told me. I wasn't going to let either man down. Because if Butch said I would look out for Parker, then that's what I would do.

"Go back to the clubhouse, brothers, I've got shit to do," I said to both men as I started my bike.

Casa's eyes widened and then he barked out a laugh. "We're coming with you, Jesse. Who knows what you'll do next you crazy motherfucker!" He laughed again, but I could tell he was nervous because my behavior was becoming more and more irrational. What he didn't know, though, was that that shit was over. I was thinking clearer than I had in months now.

I shook my head. "I don't want either of you a part of what I'm about to do. It's safer for you both back at the clubhouse," I replied.

"I'm going with you," Casa pressed. "It's not up for debate, Jesse." For once all his humor had gone, and instead he stared at me straight-faced and serious as fuck. "Whatever it is, I've got your back. You want to get Laney back? I'll help. You want to go finish that other guy off? I'm packing. You got shit to blow up? Let me make a call so we can pick up supplies along the way. I've got a shovel in the bed of my truck and a map that'll direct us to the perfect spot to bury a body that'll never be found. Whatever it is, I'm down for it—always have and always will be." His forehead was pulled into a heavy frown, his words clipped and to the point, and I knew he meant every damn word of it.

"Brothers for life," I said.

"And my life for my brothers," he returned and held out his hand.

I took it in mine and nodded. I looked at Dom, who started his bike as his only reply.

"You sure?" I asked him.

"Promised Butch I'd watch your back." He shrugged. "But you mind filling me in on what's going down?"

"Seems like my brother made a lot of people promise things," I said with a shake of my head.

Dom looked over to the doors of police station, watching, as did I, as Parker and another officer walked outside. Parker ignored me, like he hadn't exploded my world to pieces the night before, but the other officer glared at me like I was the devil himself. Who knows? I might have been. Dom had spotted Parker, though, and it was as obvious as the pope is Catholic that he recognized Parker.

Parker got in his car—a beat-up silver Toyota Corolla—and pulled out of the parking lot, and I waited a beat before I gave my orders.

"All right, if you're in then you should know that shit's about to go down in a big way. Found out some shit last night, and I think there's more to come, but right now isn't the time to talk. Right now we need to follow him," I said, nodding toward the Toyota driving away. "Now let's get a move on before I lose him."

I watched Dom carefully while I spoke, but the man was a blank canvas, as always. I pulled away from the sidewalk and my brothers followed me. And in turn, we followed Parker, making sure to keep our distance at all times, though I had no doubt in my mind that he knew I was following him—in fact I hoped he knew, but I didn't want anyone else to know I was.

After thirty minutes, Parker pulled down a side street, taking a left into a dead end, and several moments later we pulled up at a small storage facility. He got out of his car and walked inside, and after parking, we followed him inside too.

Casa pulled out his gun and Dom did the same, because regardless of everything Parker had told me earlier, he was still a cop. I grabbed my gun from the secret compartment underneath my saddlebags, more than ready to use it if I had to. A friend of my brother or not, I didn't trust cops. Shit had gone too far, and I needed to know the truth like I needed to breathe. I had a feeling that instead of setting me free, the truth would poison me. But fuck it, I was dead in the water anyway. My club and my brothers were all I had left. But that wasn't enough. Not anymore.

With Laney I had tasted what life could be. I'd had something I didn't even know was missing, and I couldn't bear the thought that I would never have that again. My life had derailed the night Butch had died, my own guilt and Hardy's words destroying me, and in turn letting me destroy the only woman that could ever save me from myself.

Laney was gone now, no way would she forgive me after yesterday. So now all I had to hold onto was getting to the bottom of this nightmare, even if it killed me.

I pushed open the main door and we stepped inside. It was quiet with no one around, the hallways painted a dull gray color. Shutters were down on the storage spaces, large locks preventing anyone from getting to whatever shit lay inside. After walking for several minutes I worried that we'd lost Parker in the maze of corridors, but then I saw the back of him turn another corner and we rushed to catch up.

When we turned the corner, Parker was waiting in the doorway of one of the storage rooms. He nodded for us to go inside and we did, his gaze zeroing in on the guns. He closed the door and flicked a switch, and then he turned to stare at Dom, not me, with anger and hurt in his eyes, confirming exactly what I had suspected since around three that morning.

Dom was the man my brother had been in love with.

Always knew there was something different about Dom—never suspected he and my brother had a thing, though. Didn't bother me much, other than that Butch had never felt that he could tell me. The rest, well, it wasn't any of my fucking business who my brother fucked or didn't fuck. Or who he loved or didn't love. In fact, it wasn't anyone's business, and I'd kill anyone who thought it was theirs.

Parker and Dom glared at each other for long minutes, with Casa looked utterly confused by the obvious connection between them.

"Something I should know about?" Casa said eventually, breaking the silence. His gaze flicked across to me and I shrugged.

"Dom? We gotta problem, brother?" I asked.

Seconds passed before Dom finally put away his gun and looked across at me. "Let's just get this shit over with and get out of here."

I nodded and glanced at Parker, who finally tore his gaze away from Dom. "You told me you had more information," I said, slipping on the safety and putting my own gun away. Parker was armed, but he hadn't once tried to reach for his gun. I took that to mean we wouldn't need to spill each other's blood. At least not that day.

"I do," Parker replied tensely. "But I'm putting my neck on the line for you—for your club, Jesse." He eyed Dom nervously. "For Butch."

The air shifted, turning deathly cold in seconds, and I wondered whether Dom was going to blow Parker's brains out just for mentioning my brother's name. Fuck knows that if the look on his face was anything to go by, he sure as shit wanted to.

"So the fuck what? What do you want from us? Cash? Fucking dirty cops always after something," Casa growled out.

Parker gritted his teeth and glared at Casa, and fuck me if he didn't look like one mean motherfucker just then. Course, he was outnumbered three to one, so it wouldn't mean shit for him. But still, I had to give a little respect to someone who still stood their ground when faced with three angry bikers. Parker had clearly come a long way since high school.

"I'm not dirty," Parker snapped at Casa. "And you'd do well to fucking show some respect to the man who knows shit that could save your club."

Casa stepped forward and pressed the barrel of his gun to Parker's head. "Let me blow this fucker's brains out, Jesse." He laughed cruelly. "I'll fucking deliver them piece by piece to your wife and kids, dirty cop."

I put a hand on Casa's arm, because shit was about to go south and Parker had information I needed.

Casa turned to stare at me. "It's like that, huh?" he asked, sounding furious.

"He has information I need. Now go take a walk or chill the fuck out," I said, hating the hurt and anger that crossed his face. "But either way, you need to back the fuck off so I can talk to him."

He turned back to Parker. "Another time, pig."

"I'll be waiting for it," Parker replied darkly. His gaze moved across to me. "You got my back?" he asked, and I heard Casa suck in a breath.

"I ain't got shit for you until I know what you know. So you better make sure your Intel is solid or

Casa there has got free rein on you. Now," I asked, already tired of this bullshit, "who the fuck killed my brother? And where the fuck can I find them?"

I felt both Dom and Casa staring at me, probably wondering what the hell I was talking about. —in fact, definitely wondering what the hell I was talking about. Up last night, the whole club and everyone connected to it had believed that Butch had ridden drunk and crashed his bike. Including me. But now I knew differently and I was about to blow this shit wide open.

Now I had a new purpose in life. And my purpose was to find who had harmed Butch and send them to ground in the most painful fucking way possible. No matter what or who the costs were. Someone had to pay.

"The Razorbacks," Parker replied, and his tone didn't just hold sadness and grief, it was filled with the same regret and anger that matched my own.

Both Casa and Dom looked way ore alert after hearing that name.

"And who are the Razorbacks?" Dom asked, finally pushing his personal shit to one side to join in the discussion. Thank fuck for that.

Parker's gaze shifted across all three of us, and I could tell he wasn't happy about what he was about to say. "Cops," he finally said, the words lying heavy between us. "The Razorbacks are cops."

CHAPTER TWENTY-EIGHT:
Present day
Jesse

"Fucking pigs!" Casa growled out. "Knew you dirty fuckers were just as twisted as us."

I dragged a hand down my face before looking over at Casa and Dom, understanding the shock that covered their faces. For me this wasn't new news, not really—more like a confirmation. Around three a.m. I had finally realized what the name Razorbacks meant. And it was so obvious I wanted to shoot myself in the fucking head for missing it to start off with.

Razorbacks are pigs—dangerous pigs, to be exact. Ain't that the fucking truth. But Casa and Dom were new to this loop, and they looked irritated as fuck that pigs were the ones trying to move in on our territory. Pretty sure Parker didn't know that part, but I could have been wrong. I'd been wrong about a lot of things recently.

"How the fuck are they operating under your noses? Don't you cops have bureaus to sniff out shit like this?" I shook my head. "I mean, fuck, how are they operating under *our* noses, for that matter?

Barring the run-in the other night, this is the first we've really heard of them."

Parker took a long breath. "From what I know, it started out by pure good luck—bad luck for the Highwaymen, though. We busted a guy of yours a few months back, goes by the name of Skinny, right?"

"What about it?" I asked, already not liking where this was leading.

Skinny had gotten caught by the ATF a few months back and was now looking at serious fucking time in the DOC for his services. Poor bastard had a wife and two kids, too. Of course the club would look after them, but that wasn't the point. It wasn't like he hadn't known the risks, but I still couldn't help but feel sorry for him.

Parker looked regretful as he continued. "Well, a security guard named Robert Brady used to work the night shift over at the evidence lockup in Atlanta. Stupid fucker had a gambling problem and somehow got the bright idea that he could steal a kilo or two of blow from the evidence lockup that he's supposed to be watching—the blow that your guy had been caught with when he was arrested. He traded it in with his debtors as a way to clear some of the money he owed. But then he got greedy because he's making easy money, right? And good money, too. The stuff in lockup is pure and uncut. Dumb bastard is rolling in it before long." Parker paced the room and shook his head. "Man thinks he's some kind of hotshot and starts stealing more and trying to sell it on. But all good things must come to an end, and eventually the Reverend got wind of it and had a few words with him—of the violent type, if you get me. Well, Roberts's body showed up a day or so ago, down by Kenilworth Lake. Turns out, the Reverend switched out Robert for one of his own guys on the payroll, and now the Reverend is taking the drugs. *Your* drugs."

"And the whole thing's going unnoticed?" Dom scoffed and looked across at me.

"No, it was noticed, but only by people who didn't care to look too closely since they were being paid off by the Reverend." Parker stopped pacing and waited for me to say something, but it took me a moment to gather my thoughts.

"Well, let's give Hardy a call and get the Reverend taken care of. Never good when clubs go to war, but if the Rev knows those are our drugs he's selling, then fuck him, right, Jesse?" Casa looked at me and I nodded.

"Fuck yeah, man needs to go to ground," I reply. "I got another question though, before we speak to Hardy and settle this shit up. How did Butch get involved in this? I know my brother well enough to know he wouldn't have turned his back on his brothers and gone over to the Reverend. Money just wasn't important to him—family was. And drugs were never his thing."

I didn't doubt Butch for one moment. He'd always been loyal and fiercely protective of those he loved—same as all my MC brothers—but for Butch it was more than that. I was his blood, and there was no way he'd do that to me. I glanced at Dom and knew he wouldn't do it to him, either.

"The night Butch was killed, he stumbled upon a meet between the Razorbacks and someone else. He said he saw things he wasn't supposed to see," Parker said regretfully. "He turned up at my place afterwards, but he wasn't himself—he was acting erratically, told me he thought he was being followed and he didn't know who to trust anymore. I told him to call you, Dom, but he said he didn't want to involve you, especially since you'd argued earlier on. But he did make a phone call to someone, Jesse, someone in your club, and then he left, saying that he was going to meet them and blow this whole thing wide open." Parker went silent, his head bowed slightly, and when he looked up at me, the pain on his face was almost too hard to look at. "The next time I saw him he was in the morgue."

The room fell silent, and for a moment I felt numb to everything. Only for a moment, though, and then the familiar pang of rage began to blossom in my chest and surge through me. My mind strayed back to the night that Butch died, and my stomach sank. He had been going to check on our new warehouse. Rider had sent me to check it out, but Butch had taken my place because Laney had been drunk and he'd wanted to clear his head or some shit.

Once again, Butch's death fell back on me, landing heavily on my doorstep. I should have been the one that stumbled on that meet, not him.

But worse still was that someone in our club had betrayed him. Names popped up in my head, familiar faces flashing before my eyes, but my heart wouldn't let me pin Butch's death on any of those men. They were my brothers, my family, and I couldn't believe that one of them would turn on another. I had thought for a while that morning that it had been Dom that had turned on Butch. They'd been arguing that night. But then I remembered the pain in his eyes at the funeral. The way he'd gone into himself after Butch's death. His pain was too raw, and too much like my own for it to have been him. Besides, I might have been blind once and not seen the depth of the feelings he had for my brother, but I could see it now.

"Wait, so the Reverend is behind all of this? Behind Butch's death?" Casa asked, breaking the silence. "And he's been ripping off our club?"

I looked up sharply, my stare finding Parker, who shook his head. "Not all of it. The Razorbacks and the Reverend are in bed together for sure, but it gets deeper."

"This shit gets any deeper we're gonna be sitting side by side with the devil," Casa replied darkly.

"Funny you should say that," Parker said sounding hesitant. "The other club that's involved, it's your club—the Devil's Highwaymen. I know that there's at least one of you that's turned on your club."

Casa pulled out his gun at the same time that Parker did, and both men stood glaring at each other with their guns aimed at one another's heads. I was in too much disbelief to do jack shit about it, despite the fact that there was going to be a river of blood running through that lockup any second.

"You're fuckin' lying," Casa growled out. "Jesse, say the fuckin' word, brother, and let me end this lying sack of shit! None of our brothers would do that, and this sorry fuck needs to die for saying it."

"He made a call to someone in your club, asshole! Whoever took that call is the one that set him up," Parker yelled. "Dumb fuck can't see what's right under your nose."

"And how do we know that you're telling the truth, huh? You could be making this shit up, for all we know," Casa yelled back.

"Why? Why would I do that?"

"Dirty cops don't need reasons." Casa spat on the floor at Parker's feet. "But who knows, two clubs taking each other out would make your job a hell of a lot easier. Maybe that's the reason: we go to war and you get a badge of fucking honor!"

"Butch was important to me," Parker said, his gaze still on Casa. "I want vengeance for his death, I don't give two shits about your war or your drugs or your fucking clubs. None of that matters to me. What I care about is Butch, finding his killer, and making them pay. What I care about is finding out who he made that call to…" Parker's words died off as we all stared at him.

For once Dom didn't look like he was going to kill Parker; instead he just looked wounded by his words, as if they had cut him deep.

Casa looked at me, his aim still steady but the anxious look in his eyes showing me that he wasn't so sure on what to believe anymore, but that he'd kill Parker either way if he felt like it.

"What do you think?" I asked Dom, because the whole thing was getting deeper by the minute, and if we got part of it wrong, someone was going to end up dead who didn't deserve it.

"I think he's right," Dom said with a shake of his head. "And I think I know who it is."

Both Casa and I stared at him in surprise.

Dom pulled out his cigarettes and lit one up, his face thoughtful as he struggled to word what he needed to say. Eventually he looked up at me, his eyes full of pity. "I've suspected something for a while, Jesse, but I didn't have any proof. Still don't, not really, but my gut says he's telling the truth." He nodded toward Parker.

"Who is it?" I asked, my brain buzzing from all the information.

When I think back to that day, I think I already knew who he was going to say. I think, deep down, if I would have been able to see past my own self-pity, I would have seen the man's face that had sentenced my brother to death. Goddamn, the air in there was too thick and hot, fucking choking me with every breath I took. Because with the realization came the guilt.

The man who hated me had gotten the wrong brother killed.

Dom's shoulders sagged, his face taking on lines of pain as he spoke. "Butch taught me to trust my instincts, and my instincts tell me that Hardy is dirty and has been for some time. The name the Razorbacks—that night down in Atlanta when we read the note—I'd seen it once before, I just couldn't place where. It wasn't until last night that I remembered where." Dom dragged a hand down his face and went on. "Rose had been emptying the trash from Hardy's office a couple of weeks ago—you know how he is with shit like that. When Pops had the stroke she had been coming out with the bag of trash, and had dropped it when she ran to him. We'd both gone with him to the hospital, though I left her there once Pops got the all clear and a couple of prospects turned up to watch over him. I headed back to the clubhouse. When I got back, the trash was still all over the floor—so I cleared it up, and on one of the pieces of paper I saw the name Razorbacks. Didn't think anything of it, because it was just a name and none of my fucking business, and then I forgot about it."

"That doesn't prove anything," Casa said angrily, but behind the anger I could hear the doubt in his voice. "It's just a name on a piece of paper."

"He's right, that could mean anything," Parker said.

"Shut the fuck up," Casa yelled at him. "This is club business—you shouldn't even be here."

To me, it all made sense, right down to the fact that Hardy hadn't seemed even a little bit surprised when I mentioned the name to him. But why would he send me to the meet if he knew they were going to be there?

It was obvious now that Hardy had turned on his club.

On his brothers.

But would he really turn on his own sons?

Because if he had, I was going to make him pay for it even if it was the last thing I did. Because if I thought I had felt rage before that day, it was nothing compared to what I felt as the pieces began to fit together, and the desire to walk right out of there and blow Hardy's fucking brains out was instinctual.

"Easy, Jesse, we need to do this right," Dom said, sensing my next move.

But I could barely hear him through the rage ringing in my ears. Dom reached out and put his hand on my shoulder, but I shrugged him off and glared up at him as another thought dawned on me.

"How long have you suspected?" I asked, slowly.

Dom shook his head and threw his cigarette to the ground. "Couple of weeks," he replied. "Rider had let slip that Hardy had gone on a couple of meets on his own—not wanting any club support, extra money in the safe when I put the books away, that sort of shit. Nothing huge, but enough to make me wary of him."

"But did you suspect he had something to do with Butch's death?" I gritted out, needing to know for my own selfish reasons.

Dom nodded, his gaze slipping from mine as guilt crossed his features. "That night we found out about Butch, he didn't seem surprised—like, not at all. He seemed pissed off more than anything else. Thought it was weird when he stalked off to take a phone call in his office instead of dealing with the fact his eldest boy was dead, but people deal with pain in their own ways, right?"

"It was supposed to be me," I said. "Rider had asked me to go check it out, but Laney had been drunk as shit so Butch told me to go because he said he needed some air anyway, and I let him go even though it was my job."

All those months I had blamed myself, when it had been Hardy's doing, not mine. The pain I had put Laney through as I tried to push her away from me to avoid the fallout from my crazy, fucked-up life. I had ruined everything in my self-pitying. And Hardy had let me—likely watching from the sidelines and enjoying every minute of it since it was him that had burned his words into my mind…

'It should have been you…'

Yet Dom's betrayal felt worse somehow. I hated Hardy, always had, and I knew the feeling was more than fucking mutual, but I had thought Dom was my friend, yet he had let me live on in agony, blaming myself for something I had nothing to do with.

I didn't think when I punched Dom in the jaw; I reacted. His words cut me deep and hard, like a blade to the heart as they tore through me, destroying muscle and bone and organs as they created a great chasm in the center of my chest, like a bomb had exploded. I hit him over and over, reopening the healing wounds on my knuckles from the day before. And Dom didn't fight back once.

Casa and Parker grabbed me and began to drag me off of Dom, but not before I managed to get in another hit to his face and make a large cut right above his eye. Blood began to ooze out of the cut and trickle down his face, and the sight somehow brought me to my senses.

I pointed at Dom, aiming my rage at him because Hardy wasn't there, my nostrils flaring and my teeth bared to him. "You're dead to me."

Dom slowly got up to his knees, wiping the blood away from his with his sleeve. "I hear ya, brother."

"You're no brother of mine," I gritted out.

He nodded and swallowed, reminding me so much of Butch in that moment with his broken expression. I shrugged out of Casa and Parker's grip and glared at Dom.

I paced the room like a tiger in a cage, my body trembling with untampered rage. "How could you continue to let that piece of shit fuckin' breathe after what he's done!?"

"I had to be sure, Jesse." He spoke in a broken whisper, his words coming out choked and starved of life. The oxygen sucked from his very lungs. "I had to be sure before I made my move or I'd get us both killed, and I couldn't let that happen. He'd get away with it, and I promised Butch I'd always look out for you, and him. I was trying to keep that promise to him." He dragged a hand across his face. "I thought it was all my fault. We'd argued and he'd walked out, taken your place on the ride, and then he was gone—and it was my fault."

"He had him killed!" I roared in anger. "And you did nothing, Dom, nothing! You self-pitying motherfucker!"

"I just wanted to do right by him and keep his little brother alive. Never thought it would come to this—to you and me and this whole fucking explosion of shit. Hardy fucked us all. He fucked Butch over, and despite how much you hate me right now for not telling you, we have to take him out and make him pay now. You can hate on me later. I'll leave the club, walk away from fucking everything, but right now we need to work together to end Hardy!"

Casa and I glared at Dom. I had lost the inability to form words so Casa took over.

"How can we still trust you, motherfucker? You kept this shit from all of us. How many times have you put another brother in danger by not saying something?" Casa yelled, his fury matching my own, because he had seen the toll that Butch's death had taken on me—hell, he'd been there trying to help me through it every step of the way. But nothing had tempered it because my rage and anger were built on guilt and poisoned lies—but it was all bullshit. Not one single thing was true.

I hadn't done it, Hardy had.

Hardy—my father—had tried to have me killed, but instead he'd killed my brother.

I swallowed and took a long breath, Casa's anger somehow caging mine as it simultaneously set me free. "What makes you so certain now?" I asked.

Dom looked up, his gaze straying to Casa's gun before moving to me. "I heard him talking about another deal." He dragged his hands down his face. "I didn't know who I could trust—how deep the fucking poison seeped. I didn't want to risk anyone else before I could figure it out. I was going to go myself, alone, finally find out exactly what the fuck was going on before I came to you, but now…" He looked at me and I nodded, agreeing with him

Butch had tried to do it on his own, and look where it had gotten him. No, this time we were doing it together. We'd kill Hardy together or we'd die together trying to honor Butch.

"What about Rider?" Casa asked. "Do you think he's in on it too?"

"Good question," I replied. "Real good fuckin' question. I guess we'll find out when we turn up and surprise the traitorous motherfuckers. He's the one who sent me over to the warehouse that night, so he must be a part of it, right?"

My thoughts strayed to Laney who was staying with Charlie and Rider and I had a fleeting moment of worry for her safety. But Old ladies and family were untouchables, and Charlie was best friends with Laney. Unless that was bullshit too? The hate Charlie had directed at me in the gas station had been real though; the pain and anger she felt for Laney—her friend, that was real too. No way was that bitch that good of an actress. At least that's what I hoped.

I looked down at Dom and finally felt some pity for him. I hated the fact that he hadn't said anything to me about any of it, that he'd continued to be Hardy's bitch and errand boy for the past few months despite suspecting that he'd had a hand in Butch's death. But Butch had always trusted him, and I knew I had to too. Dom didn't know my final words to Butch, so he didn't know my guilt. He only knew that I had lost my brother and best friend. He only saw the misery I had been in—the same misery he had been in himself. More so because of their relationship.

It dawned on me then that he had been holding a guilt of his own inside for all that time, but worse still was the fact that he'd known Hardy was involved somehow but had had no one to talk to about it.

Butch was in my head, begging that I listen to him and trust Dom, and I knew I had to. Because somehow I had to get past the betrayal so we could move forward. If I didn't, we'd never get our revenge. And that was the most important thing of all now. The Reverend was going to pay for it, and so were the Razorbacks. But more important to me was that Hardy pay, too—and I couldn't do that without brothers at my back.

Dom was right about one thing: there was no way to know how deep Hardy's reach in our club was, or how many brothers—if any—he had on the inside. And until we knew that, the only people we could trust were there in that room.

I reached a hand down to Dom, and he stared at it for a long second before taking it firmly and letting me pull him up. The blood was still oozing from the cut above his now swollen eye, and his lip was split. He spat the blood on the ground, his eyes holding me and begging me to forgive him.

I couldn't though, at least not yet. But we could move past it until there was a time to clear the air more. I pulled him to me and held him, both of us sharing our guilt and misery with one another without saying a damn word.

We had both loved Butch, and it was our love for him that fueled our hate for everyone that had a hand in his death.

They would all fucking pay.

CHAPTER TWENTY-NINE:
Present day
Jesse

The three of us rode toward the supposed meet between the Reverend, the Razorbacks, Hardy and whoever else it was in our club that had betrayed Butch and the rest of their brothers.

My anger fueled me in a way it hadn't before, and I thought of all the ways I would make my supposed prez and brothers suffer. I would burn the Devil's Highwaymen tattoo off the traitor's backs before killing them slowly.

We left Parker to head home, deciding it was best if he kept a low profile in case shit went south when we got to the meet. No point in all four of us dying. Besides, the fact that Parker was important to my brother hadn't gone completely unnoticed to me, and if he was important to Butch, it mattered that he stayed alive. Therefore I'd do my best to keep him living and fucking breathing if I could. I didn't know what would happen when we got where we were going; I only knew that I was going to put as many of them in the ground as possible.

This club, these men, they were my entire family now.

My life.

My. Fucking. World.

I had stewed in my own self-misery for the past couple of months and they'd had my back, and now it was my time to have theirs. The veil of guilt and shame that had clouded my judgment since Butch's death had lifted, and I was wide awake and ready to do what needed to be done.

I had a fire in my belly and I was ready to unleash hell on any motherfucker who stood in my way.

Hardy hadn't just betrayed me, or Butch; he'd betrayed us all. He'd made our club look weak, corrupted us from the inside out, and there was no way was I going to let that go. My only thought at the moment was how many of my brothers he'd turned against the club. How bad had the poison seeped into the Highwaymen's blood to make them turn on their brothers so easily?

As we rode toward the meet, I thought about Rider. He was our VP. Man had a kid and an old lady—Charlie; bitch already hated my guts, but she'd be hating them a fuck of a lot more if I had to kill her old man. I'd always thought he was a good man and a good brother. He was quiet, unassuming. Basically he was the fucking opposite of Charlie. But the man got shit done when it needed to get done. I would take no pleasure in killing him, but I'd do it all the same if it got vengeance for Butch. I prayed I wouldn't need to, though. Yet every road I drove down led me back to him, because he'd given me the orders to go check out the warehouse that night. And Gauge...how the fuck had he missed all of this happening? He was our Sergeant-at-arms, and the only way I could see this going was with me putting a bullet in his head, effectively killing him and my relationship with Laney. Because there was no way he couldn't have known. The thought sickened me.

The meet was supposed to take place in the old granite quarry, so we drove the bikes as close as we dared before parking them and walking the rest of the way. Up ahead, several bikes and a police car came into view, and I knew we'd all be thinking the same thing: the Razorbacks were getting fucking arrogant, turning up to a meet with their true colors on show like that. Fuckers wouldn't be arrogant for much longer, that was for sure.

Hills of old granite were piled all around, giving us decent cover, so we headed in the direction of voices, cresting the hill closest to them. I leaned with my back against it and pulled my gun out, and looked across at Casa and Dom. They nodded, both of them ready to do what needed to be done, but all of us dreading who we'd see on the other side.

Shouting broke out behind us and Dom frowned. Shit was going down. When I looked over at Casa, the crazy bastard was grinning.

"Maybe they'll kill each other off," he said, still grinning.

"And take all the fun away?" I sneered back. "Fuck that."

I stood up to head over the hill and end that shit and so did my brothers when a gun went off and we all dropped back down. I started to slide down the quarry, almost sliding to the bottom of it in surprise, but I managed to get a grip and stop myself around half way. More shouting ensued and we started to scramble back up. An engine started, and when we looked round, two men were getting in the police cruiser and driving away.

Dom started to make a move on them, but I grabbed his arm and stopped him, shaking my head no. "They'll get theirs. Today we deal with Hardy," I gritted out and he nodded.

We stood up and started toward the top of the hill again, because it was now or never, and never wasn't a possibility in this lifetime. Hardy was facing away from us, shouting at Rider, who was on his knees, blood trailing from the top of his arm. Pipes was there, a gun aimed at our VP while he bounced from foot to foot eager to spill more blood.

Another body lay cold on the ground, but I couldn't tell who it was from that distance.

We piled down the other side and started to run and slide almost equally, not giving a shit how much noise we made anymore. Rider saw us first, his head turning in our direction and a look of relief washing over him as Pipes and Hardy both turned to look in our direction. Dom wasted no time and fired his gun at Pipes as we slid down the other side of the granite hill, and Hardy pulled out his gun and fired at me. Of course he fucking did—wouldn't expect any less from him. Lucky for me that I had a good aim and I shot out Hardy's left kneecap before he could get a decent shot in.

Shots flew out over my head as I tucked and rolled the rest of the way down, before coming to a sliding stop at the bottom and getting right back up and aiming my gun at him. Casa shot at Hardy's arm, and our president dropped his gun as the bullet when through his bicep in a spray of blood. I stalked over, keeping my gun level with his head. Hardy was on the ground reaching for his gun as he groaned into the dirt. He looked up as I got closer and quashed his pain in favor of scrambling for his gun. But I was quicker and I kicked it far out of his reach.

The man that was supposed to be my father glared up at me, his face contorted in hatred for his youngest son.

Dom had Pipes by the back of his jacket and was dragging him toward me, and Casa was helping Rider up. The man's face was bruised and swollen and his arm was shot to hell and back.

I looked back down at Hardy and sneered. "Looks like you had a visit from the local cops. Thought we'd come and give you a hand, Prez," I said, disgust in my tone.

"Get on with it, you stupid bastard. I ain't got time for you or anything you have to say," Hardy said darkly.

I crouched down, my gun still aimed at him and his eyes flitting to it before coming back to mine. Dom had Pipes on his knees next to us, holding him upright. Poor fucker was bleeding out by the second; wouldn't last for much longer. Not that I gave a shit about his death, but I needed words with him first.

I looked across at Pipes, watching as his eyes began to roll back into his head. Casa grabbed him and slapped him around the face, bringing him back around before he could pass out. Pipes focused in on me.

"What did he promise you?" I asked. "He promise you VP status? Money? Or are you just a traitorous fuck for no good reason?"

"I follow my prez, that's what," Pipes said breathlessly, blood spilling out over his chin. "His orders are the only orders."

"Nah, that's not how it works, not in my club," I spat the words at him. "Brothers for life," I started.

"And my life for my brothers," Casa, Dom and Rider finished for me.

Hardy laughed bitterly in the background and I swung the butt of my gun at his head opening up a wound that started to pump blood straight away. "Shut the fuck up!"

I nodded to Casa and Dom stepped back, letting Pipes fall backwards. Casa aimed at Pipe's forehead and fired, and Pipe's blood pooled under him, spilling out and tainting the quarry ground red with blood.

I looked back at Hardy and let out a heavy sigh before standing upright again. Casa, Dom, and Rider were waiting for me to do something, anything, but the moment felt like it was more than just me. Bigger somehow. Like my whole life had been leading up to that moment.

"Want me to do it?" Rider asked as he came to stand by my side. "Be my fuckin' pleasure, too, Jesse."

I turned and looked at him, my gaze going to his arm. "Fucked you up real bad, brother."

"Ain't nothin' that a couple of beers won't fix," he growled out, but both of us knew that weren't true. His arm was hanging limply by his side. Casa had tied some material around the top of it to stop the blood, but if there was nerve damage he'd never ride again.

I patted him on the opposite shoulder. "I got this one." I turned back to Hardy, his glare burning holes in my skull. "Now now, Prez, no point looking like you just got wrongly shot the fuck up. This is all your own doing. But don't worry, I'll make sure it's over and done with quick enough."

Dom lit up a cigarette, and fuck me if I didn't wish I still smoked. Laney had asked me to quit, so I had, but fuck it, if there was ever a time to start up again, it was now.

I nodded to Dom. "Gimme one of those."

He nodded and handed me his before lighting another for himself, and I took a long drag on it, feeling light-headed as the nicotine hit me. Goddamn, that was good—not as good as other shit, but I'd missed smoking. Probably the only good thing about being single again.

"What the fuck are you waiting for, son? You waiting for me to beg? You think I'm gonna break down and plead you for my life? Fuck you, that ain't never gonna happen. If I was on fire I wouldn't beg you to piss on me and put out the flames," Hardy snarled out.

I barked out a laugh, a calm settling over me that scared me more than it should have. I wasn't a believer in God, or any other higher power, but it felt to me like Butch was right there with me—standing by my side and aiming his own gun at our father.

'Son? That's a joke,' he laughed with me.

I smiled. "Firstly, don't call me son. You've never treated me like one, so let's not go throwing names around that we don't mean," I said, staring down at him, a strength I'd never felt before alive in my muscles. In every fiber of my body.

"You're right, you ain't never been a son of mine. Bastard boy of a crack-whore. Never a truer word spoken there, Jesse." He laughed without humor, but fuck me if he didn't have my attention now.

"Secondly," I continued, because fuck him; I wouldn't give him that power over me. Not anymore. "If you was on fire, I wouldn't piss on you anyway, not even if you begged me, so you don't need to worry about that," I said, using his own words against him.

We glared at one another, and I threw my cigarette on the ground and put it out under my boot. Then I aimed my gun at his head.

"And thirdly, don't ever call my mom a whore!" I bellowed.

Butch clicked off the safety on his gun and looked at me with a smirk. 'You ready, little brother?'

I nodded in response, knowing I was either going insane or I had one foot in the grave already because I could feel the heat from Butch right next to me. The anger pouring from him in waves.

"All right, enough fucking around." I flicked off the safety on my gun.

Hardy lifted his chin. "You don't even care, do you?"

"Care?" I snapped. "Why the fuck should I care? After everything you've done, everything you've put your club through, your own sons. No, I don't care. I don't care at all."

"I meant, you dumb fucking bastard, you don't even care that you got him killed."

Dom was too quick for me to stop as he dove at Hardy, slamming his fist into his face over and over until Casa managed to drag him back off. And the whole time Butch laughed from next to me.

Casa let go of Dom and dragged Hardy back up to his knees. Hardy spat blood on the ground in front of him. "Always had a good right hook. Would have made a good sergeant at arms one day." Hardy rubbed his jaw, and Dom looked like he was about to dive at him again and punch a hole right through his fucking face. "Shame you're too weak to stand as one."

"*You* got him killed! No one else, just you," Dom roared in anger. "And I would never stand under you, so go fuck yourself!" Dom kicked out, slamming his boot into Hardy's ribs repeatedly, and I could have sworn I heard the snapping of bones. But I got it. I did—that same anger had been my driving force since Butch died, fucking up my life on every level. But not anymore. I saw all too clearly now exactly what I needed to do.

Butch continued to laugh by my side, but his laugh had turned bitter and hungry for violence and more of Hardy's blood. With every kick Dom gave to Hardy, Butch watched with satisfaction. His gaze never leaving Dom as he stared in adoration at his long-term friend and lover.

Dom finally stopped, his chest heaving, and Casa once again dragged Hardy up to his knees.

"He's right," I said, looking down at Hardy. "You did this. Not me. And now I'm done being your scapegoat."

"It was supposed to be you that went, not him. Though I can't say I was overly disappointed anyway. Your brother turned out to be just as big a disappointment as you in the end." Hardy spoke with so much rage that I could practically feel his anger vibrating in the air between us. "Fucking weak, all of you!"

"A disappointment? He couldn't have been a better man if he'd tried."

"I blame your mom. Something bad in her genes that she passed on to all of you boys. Every one of you had something wrong. Billy died before his first breath, Butch liked to take it in the ass, and you were the bastard son of a crack whore." Hardy saw the look on my face and he smiled. The blood on his teeth was bright as he spoke. "Yeah, that's right. You're a bastard. Never knew who your fucking daddy was, but it sure as shit weren't me."

My breath caught in my throat, his words burning a hole in my chest.

I felt Butch's hand on my shoulder. 'Now,' Butch whispered in my ear. 'It's time now.' He squeezed my shoulder and then aimed his own gun at Hardy's head.

"Yeah, now, brother," I replied before squeezing the trigger and catching Hardy between the eyes. I saw the flash of confusion in his eyes right before the life went out of them, and then he fell backwards, his body slamming onto the dusty ground, and I let go of the breath I had been holding since Butch's death.

We all stared in silence as his blood pooled and mingled with Pipes', and none of us felt a damn thing about it. Gone were the hate and the anger, the pain and the suffering.

It all died with Hardy.

It all ended now.

Butch patted me on the shoulder and when I turned to look he smiled at me. 'You did good,' he said. 'You did real good, brother.'

I stared at my brother in silence. Wanting to say a million things, but not having the words for any of them.

"What now?" Rider asked.

I turned away from Hardy's body and looked toward our VP. "That's up to you. You're the president now. We follow you."

Rider smiled and dragged a hand through his silver hair. "We need to make some calls. Get some men up here to help clear this mess up, and then we need to go to church. Shit needs to be spoken about. Too many secrets and too much being left unsaid. Brothers need to know what's going on."

"No doubt," Dom agreed. "You think they'll understand?"

Rider held his arm tightly, the blood seeping slowly through his fingers. "Fucking hope so, or we're all dead men walking."

"It's gonna' be alright," I said and all three men turned to look at me.

"Yeah? And what makes you so fucking positive all of a sudden?" Casa mocked me.

I looked back to where Butch had been, but he was gone. "I just know it," I replied.

CHAPTER THIRTY:
Present day
Jesse

The chapel was standing room only. A room full of pissed-off bikers stared back at me, waiting for me to say something. The room was tense, and I looked around the table, my gaze straying across the faces of my brothers, my family, and wondering what they thought about the proposition. It had been a long fucking day. Make that a long fucking three months. But today was the start of something new, and I was starting to realize that new didn't always mean bad. New could be a good thing.

It was a start, but I had a long way to go.

We had the club's national president—Marbles—on speaker phone, and after talking to him about our suggestion, he'd agreed. Surprisingly easily. Fucker caught me right off guard, because I thought it would have taken way more convincing than it had. But after a quick check of Hardy's accounts, it was obvious that he'd been scamming our club out of thousands of dollars for a long fucking time. No clue where that money was, but I had no doubt that we'd would find it.

"So, we're going to vote on it now. I know it's been a lot of information to take in, but you've all seen the proof, you've heard from Marbles, but we won't move forward without every one of you on board." Rider looked across the table, his expression grim. "It's time for us to clean house, and we're going to need a strong leader for the job. One we can trust." He turned to look at me and I nodded approvingly.

The blinds were turned, stopping anyone from looking in, but the clubhouse was full. The day's events had far-reaching repercussions, but ones I think a lot of us were ready for.

"A show of hands, please, brothers," Rider said.

"Not even a damn question," Pops yelled from the end of the table, raising his hand. Dumb fucker had come on over just for the meeting, even though he should have been resting up at home after his stroke.

Slowly, the room filled with *ayes* and raised hands. Dom was the last to raise his hand, giving me a slow grin as he pretended to look thoughtful for a second before doing so.

"Fucking aye," he said with a chuckle.

Brother just chuckled! I shook my head. Day was fucking crazy, all right.

Rider looked across at me. "It's unanimous, brother." He slid the gavel across to me and stood up, and we swapped seats before we both looked across the table. "Brothers, meet your new president, Jesse James Hardy—one of the youngest fucking presidents on record." He patted my shoulder. "But he's gonna be one of the best."

The room was filled with cheers and claps and then everyone began to filter round to shake my hand and give me their thanks. When it was Gauge's turn, his expression was grim. He'd just got in from a fucking goose chase errand that Hardy had sent him on. Turns out, he'd been doing that a lot. And Gauge had fallen for it. Rider started to clear the room, and Gauge and I stepped to one side to garner a little more privacy.

"It ain't no secret that I ain't never been a fan of yours, Jesse." His hard look bored into mine. "And after the shit you pulled on my little girl these past few months, I should probably put you in the ground myself—you broke her fucking heart so I'd have every right to, no doubt."

I nodded in agreement. Because how could I not? Fuck me, if that was my daughter I would have already ripped my dick off and shoved it down my own throat.

"But we all fucked up recently, that much is true." Gauge sighed and dragged a hand through his hair. He shook his head and his gaze softened from a glare to a hard stare. "This is your one chance,

Prez." He said my title with disdain. "After this, you ain't got no more. You feel me?"

I nodded. "I do."

"She's been alive longer than I've known her, and fuck me if she isn't fucking amazing. I ain't gonna let you go chasing her away now that I've finally got to know her. She's too important to me. You sort this shit out, if you can, and if you can't, you find a way to make it okay for her to stick around either way. If she's done with you, you fucking accept that. That shit ain't up for debate." He patted me on the shoulder and walked away, and I breathed a sigh of relief.

When I turned around, Rider was standing there waiting to talk to me. He came forward with a smile and we shook hands.

"Went well?" he asked.

"Sort of," I replied. "I mean, I'm still breathin', so there's that." We laughed together and then he frowned.

"Your brothers and I thought of your road name, finally," he said, and I grinned.

"Yeah?" I asked, having no clue what it could be. Some brothers went their whole lives without getting one, but a road name was a badge of honor.

"Shooter," Rider replied. "You got skills, mad skills, Shooter—the sort that's in your blood. Whoever your father was, the man knew his way around a gun. The way I saw you shooting today, it's obvious that he passed those genes on to you."

"Shooter," I said, letting the name settle on me. It sounded strange, being given the name Shooter for the way I had killed Hardy, but it also felt right. "Shooter it is, then."

Rider smiled, but it fell quickly. "I'm sorry about Butch," he said.

"I'm sorry about a lot of things, but sorry don't change the way they are." I shrugged.

He scratched the back of his neck with his one good arm. The other was covered in plaster, and we were waiting to get the results back on if there had been any permanent nerve damage. At the moment he could barely grasp the handlebars of his bike, but it was still early days yet. For his sake I hoped everything healed up okay. A brother needed three things in his life: his bike, his brothers, and his old lady. Take away a man's bike and you broke him, permanently. I'd seen it happen before.

"I should have known," he growled out, his gaze holding mine. "I should have fucking known, Shooter. I'm the motherfuckin' VP, it's my job to know. I put the club and my brothers in danger. I got Butch killed."

He sank into the chair behind him, the air leaving his body in one gust.

I pulled out a chair and sat down opposite him. "It wasn't your fault—Butch's death, that's all on Hardy. He turned his back on his brothers, his club, and his sons." I paused before continuing. "His son," I corrected.

No one had a fucking clue who my real dad was. Hardy had called my mom a crack whore, and me a bastard, and well, he was right. She'd been a beautiful storm, my mom. But she'd had her problems. A chemical imbalance, a dark turn of fates, who the fuck really knew. The only thing we knew for certain was that Hardy had loved her despite the drug addictions, and the cheating. He'd moved out after my birth—apparently couldn't stand looking at me and knowing I wasn't his, but not wanting the shame of anyone else knowing.

The only man who had known was Rider. He'd helped set me and my brother up at the clubhouse and made sure we had everything we needed. He'd spent a long time trying to find out who my dad was—Hardy had wanted to drop me off on his doorstep when he eventually did find out—but it had never happened.

Now Mom was dead, and so was Hardy, and the truth had died with them. I'd never know who my real father was, but I was okay with that. I could live with the Hardy legacy. My mom was a Hardy and so was Butch, and I wouldn't want to be anything less or more than them.

"He kept you out of the way," I said to Rider, and he looked up at me, the guilt evident on his face. "I mean it when I say that it wasn't your fault."

A knock on the door sounded out and we looked up, seeing Charlie standing there, hands on her hips, eyes scorching through my soul.

Rider looked at me apologetically. "Sorry, brother, I ain't got no control of that crazy bitch." He stood up and walked toward her.

"Don't," she warned as he got closer. "Don't even try that injured hero bullshit with me, Rider, not if you ever want your dick sucked again."

Rider turned back to me with a wince and I nodded. He left the room and Charlie stormed over to me, sashaying those hips of hers with every determined step.

"You," she said, pointing a finger right into my chest, so close her nail dug through my tee and into my skin. "You better go see my girl, you piece of shit, because if you don't make love hearts and bunnies bounce around her like some dumb fucking cartoon then I'm going to make you suffer more than you've ever suffered before, Jesse fucking James!"

I took a deep breath, not happy with the way that crazy bitch was talking to me, but also knowing I damn well deserved every word of it. Still, I couldn't have a woman talking to me like that.

"Firstly, you don't talk to me like that again. Secondly—" I held up my hand when she tried to interrupt me. "—secondly, I'm going to make her see fucking unicorns and kittens by the time I'm done groveling to her and tearing so many orgasms out of her body that she can't walk straight for a month. And if that don't work, I'll spend the rest of my life making sure she's happy, with or without me."

That last part was a lie and told purely for Charlie's benefit. Because there was no way in hell that Laney was ever going to be with anyone but me. Every time she got with someone new, I'd put them in the ground, right up until she realized she had no choice but to be with me and she gave up.

Laney was mine, and I would spend the rest of my life making her see that, if that's what it took.

Charlie's scowl fell away and she threw her arms around my neck. When she pulled away she was grinning. "Now that's what I'm talking about." She turned and left the room, leaving me alone finally.

We still didn't know who was running the Razorbacks, and they would have to be dealt with, sooner rather than later. A war was on the horizon between us and the Reverend, and that shit was not going to be pretty. But Hardy had gone to Hades, we knew the truth about Butch's death, and I was president of the Devil's Highwaymen.

The day was fucked up.

But fucked up in a real good fucking way.

I pulled out my cigarettes and lit one, taking a deep pull on it. But shit didn't taste as good as it did before. Laney hated me smoking; if I was going to win her back, that was the first thing that had to stop again. I leaned over and stubbed it out into the ashtray, and then I turned and walked out of the chapel.

Brothers stopped me as I walked through the clubhouse, patting me on the back and congratulating me on my presidency, and I thanked them right back. There'd be a party that night, no doubt—men drowning their sorrows, and cheering to the future. It would be fucked up for sure. But before anything else, I needed to go get my girl.

Casa stood by the door, leaning against the wall and waiting for me. He smiled as I got closer.

"Prez," he said, tipping his head to me obnoxiously.

"Fuck off," I laughed.

"Oh, you're not too good to talk to a simple brother like me, then?"

I punched him in the stomach, hard enough to hurt but not so hard that he'd hate me, and he doubled up laughing and struggling to breathe.

"Motherfucker," he called as I walked out the door.

"That's President Motherfucker to you!" I called back with a laugh.

"Thought your name was Shooter now."

I turned and looked back, pride blossoming in my chest. "Yeah, that as well."

CHAPTER THIRTY-ONE:
Present day
Laney

I sat on the sofa in Charlie and Rider's house, my feet tucked up under me. I'd wanted to go to the clubhouse and see Jesse, make sure he was all right after what I'd overheard Rider telling Charlie. But I couldn't.

That wasn't my world now, and the sooner my heart understood that, the better.

I'd been thinking about moving back to Florida a lot since leaving Jesse. I had friends there—at least I'd had friends before Gauge had dragged me away from there kicking and screaming. Regardless, I wasn't worried. I knew I could take care of myself now. I just knew that I couldn't stay, watching Jesse go through woman after woman like they were trash. Watching him tear apart everything we'd worked for. Watching him destroy our world.

I just couldn't do it. To him, or to myself.

The roar of an engine startled me out of my thoughts, and I stood up and pulled the netting back on the window. A bike was coming down the street, but I didn't recognize it. Of course, there were plenty of bikers around there, and I couldn't know them all, yet something in my heart made me go to the front door and open it. Something in my heart told me that that biker was there for me.

I stood in the doorway as the biker pulled to a stop at the sidewalk, and whoever it was turned off the engine. I definitely didn't recognize the bike, not even from any of the club events that I had gone to.

It had a dark forest green body, with large ape handlebars and beautiful chrome pipework. And the sound: the engine roared like a caged lion, the sound trembling over my flesh and giving me goose bumps. It wasn't the sort of bike you bought from a shop. Shit, I didn't know much about bikes, but I knew it wasn't one that was just built as a custom job. That bike was special, and it had been built from the ground up with love. It was also covered in scrapes and dents along one side.

The biker shut off the engine, and the sudden silence was unnerving. He climbed off the bike and pulled off his helmet, and I swallowed as I took him in.

Jesse stood there, his cut wrapped over his shoulders and hanging from his lean and muscled body. I swallowed, because despite the fact that I'd chosen to leave him, my body couldn't deny the attraction I still held for him, nor the love I felt. I would always be in love with Jesse, no matter how many times he broke my heart.

He stalked toward me like an animal moving toward its prey, and my heart sped up. The last time I'd seen him he'd almost killed a guy with his bare hands. The cuts were still visible on his knuckles, the blood still stained on the driveway.

His hair was loose around his shoulders and the sun kissed his skin, making the light sheen of sweat on him glisten.

And then he was there, in front of me, his heated gaze bearing down on me. His beard twitched and his eyes narrowed, and I opened my mouth to say something to him but the words fell away as his large hands reached out and grabbed me, dragging me to his body.

He slammed me against his chest and I tried to push away from him, but I'm not too prudish to admit that it was a half-assed attempt. And then Jesse wrapped one hand in my hair, tipped my face up to his, and he pressed his mouth to mine. I fought him for seconds before finally surrendering myself and going limp in his arms, and opening my mouth to he could push his tongue inside. And then we were kissing.

It was a kiss of claim.

Jesse was claiming me once more.

Owning my mind and my body with that kiss.

And I was powerless to stop him.

When he finally pulled away, my lips were red and sore and I stared up at him in a daze.

"I'm telling you now that you're coming home with me," he growled out. "I fucked up real bad, I know that, but that's over now. That shit ain't ever gonna happen again, I swear to you. I lay down my life to that promise Laney."

I tried to pull away from him, needing the space to give my mind the clarity it needed to think clearly, but Jesse held on tighter, practically snarling at me, so I gave up.

"I don't know if I can forgive you," I whispered. "You broke what we had, Jesse. You turned it into something ugly, where there should only have been beauty. How do I get over that? Tell me and I'll try."

Jesse's eyes softened and he nodded, and I worried that he was going to back away from me but he didn't.

"We don't," he said. "We don't get over it. Because we never get over the bad shit that happens, we just somehow learn to live with it. You keep the good vibrant in your mind, and you hold on tight to it, and that makes the bad bearable."

I nodded, feeling tearful, and he leaned down and kissed me again.

"I will never hurt you again, Laney. I don't know what was wrong with me these past months—grief, insanity…but it's over now." He gripped me tighter.

"You are my family. You and the club. I couldn't see it before. All I could see was that Butch was gone, and I'm sorry for that, but I see it now."

I thought about the first time I met him—the kid who looked at me like I was made from the stars. I thought about the first time he'd kissed me, and the way my heart sped up and my mind spun out of control. I thought about the way he made my stomach feel like there were butterflies living inside of it. But mostly, I thought about how every time I looked at him, I couldn't help but love him, no matter how much I wanted to stop.

And so I kissed Jesse back and I thought about the good and somehow, he was right: it made the bad seem more bearable. Who knows? Maybe one day the good would be so good that the bad would be obliterated.

That time when he pulled out of the kiss I felt something other than anger and resentment toward him. I felt the love I'd always felt for him growing inside me with every breath I took.

"If you'll let me, I want to spend the rest of my life making it up to you," he said, and I couldn't stop the tears from falling. Because just when I thought he couldn't surprise me anymore, he did.

Jesse got down on one knee and pulled a small box from his pocket. The poor man looked nervous as hell and was practically shaking like a leaf. He opened the box and watched my face for a reaction before speaking. "If you'll have me back, I'd like to marry you, Laney. That way I can spend every minute of every day making you the happiest old lady there ever was."

I wiped the tears away with the back of my hand and I nodded, and he let out a sigh of relief. He stood up and grabbed me by the waist before swinging me around.

I laughed as I spoke. "What would you have done if I had said no?"

He stopped spinning me and looked at me seriously. A grin split his face. "I would have handcuffed you to my bed and kept you there until you agreed, of course."

He pulled the ring from the box and slid it onto my finger and we both stared at the beautiful green emeralds in the ring, watching as they sparkled in the fading sunlight.

I couldn't forgive him for the pain he had caused us both, but I also couldn't stop loving him, no matter how hard I tried. So maybe it was time to admit that we were meant to be together, ugly mistakes and all. We were both human, and we both made mistakes, but our mistakes were what made us and what defined us as people. Without our mistakes we were just people moving through life and never learning anything new. And that wouldn't do either of us any good.

I was Jesse's and Jesse was mine, and we were meant to be together, forever this time.

"I love you, Laney," he growled against my mouth.

"I love you too," I replied breathlessly.

He pushed me back inside the house, his arms wrapping around me.

"I have something to tell you," I said.

His hands reached out to squeeze my ass, and I giggled as he hoisted me up into his arms.

"Can it wait?" he asked carrying me down the hallway.

I nodded and laughed again. "Yeah, it can wait."

He carried me up the stairs and I thought about the life that was growing inside of me. The start of our family. The start of something good and pure. The only good that came from Butch's death. A baby created through pain and sadness, and love.

I thought about how we would do it right. How we would give that little person everything we'd never had growing up. A real family. It would still be a fucked-up little family, because Lord knows there wasn't anything about those bikers that wasn't fucked up; they loved hard and they fought even harder. But the club, those men and women, they made up a family that you could always depend on.

Family didn't have to be made from blood; it was made from love and loyalty, and those people had that in abundance.

I smiled as Jesse carried me up the stairs, one hand giving my ass a quick, sharp slap, and I thought about how happy Butch would have been for us if he would have been there to see his niece or nephew grow up. But he was there in spirit, and I knew he'd be with us every step of the way. Of that I had no doubt.

THE END... FOR NOW.

RIDE OR DIE #2

A Devil's Highwaymen MC novel

By *USA Today* Bestselling Author
Claire C. Riley

Read on for a sneak peek

PROLOGUE

I had never wanted anything more in my life.
Not a *home.*
Not a *family.*
Not even the *air I breathed.*
He was everything to me.
And that's what made his words hurt so much.

"I'm sorry, Harlow," he said, his tone more gentle than I was used to. "I just can't do it anymore. What we're doing—what I'm doing, it's not fuckin' right. You deserve more than this. More than I can give you."

He meant it too. If I would have been too ignorant to hear it in his tone, I would never be too blind to see it on his face. In his grey eyes that had always seemed to speak to my very soul, but now only seemed empty. But his apology didn't matter. It didn't stop the pain his words caused. It didn't stop my heart from shattering into a million pieces.

"But," I started to speak, but the words caught in my throat and I almost choked on them. I reached for him and he clasped my hand in his, holding me back while he tried to comfort me.

He shook his head and his hair—hair that I had ran my hands through a hundred times, moved over his left eye.

"I've tried. Believe me, I've tried," he said, his words full of regret.

"But I love you!" I pleaded.

He winced at my words. "I love you too."

"But not like that." I bit out, and he shook his head no.

His shoulders slumped and he looked away from the hurt in my eyes and let go of my hand. "I gotta go."

"So go!" I bit out angrily. The truth was though, was that I wasn't angry at him, I was angry at myself. I had done this—this was entirely my fault. I had pushed him too fast, hoping that we could somehow make it work. But in turn, I had pushed him further away from me. I took a step back and lifted my chin defiantly. "I said go."

He nodded his head and finally turned away from me. Each step he took was another dagger in my heart. I wanted to run to him and beg him, but what would be the point?

He'd decided.

He'd chosen.

And I had lost.

I watched him walk towards his bike and sit down on it with a heavy sigh, as if the weight of the world was on his shoulders. Then he dragged his helmet on his head and started the engine. We stared at each other, the throaty rumble of his bike the only thing filling the empty space between us. And when I couldn't bare it any more, I turned and started to walk away.

I listened to his bike start to ride away and I turned back, my heart in my throat. He didn't look back, not even once, and I knew I would probably never see him again.

I was suffocating on the sadness and grief I felt as I called for him, a part of me dying as the distance grew bigger between us.

"Please don't leave me," I sobbed.

But it was too late.

He had made his choice, and I would have to accept that. I wrapped my arms around my body and cried harder and I stared at the Devil's Highwaymen logo on the back of his cut until he crested the hill at the top of my road, and then he was gone.

RIDE OR DIE #2
OUT NOW!

THANK YOU

There are always so many people to thank in these things, and I always seem to forget someone, but I'll do my best and try and keep this short and sweet.

For my husband, for *always* believing in me, especially when I don't, and for teaching me how to love myself even when the self-doubt is gnawing away at me. I love you so so much. Much more than you could ever know.

Thank you to Abbi and Elizabeth for always pushing me, and encouraging me. I don't know what I'd do without you. You always know what to say to pick me back up and to keep me moving forwards. I love and respect you bitches millions!

And to Kelli, who, without her help, this book wouldn't be what it is. You gave me the insight into this world. And you gave me faith that this was going to be awesome. But mostly, you gave this book love when no one else had read it but me. Thank you, from the bottom of my heart. I feel blessed to call you a friend.

And thank you to this amazing book community—the bloggers, the readers, the authors and the organizers. We're all a cog in this crazy little machine, and each and every one of us is needed to make it work.

Finally, I would be so pleased if you could find the time to write me a review for this book on either Goodreads, Amazon or your blog. They really do help so much.

Big love

Claire xox

ABOUT THE AUTHOR

Claire C. Riley is a *USA Today* and international bestselling author.
Claire writes in the darker side of fiction, dipping her pen into genres such as post-apocalyptic-romance, dystopian, thrillers, gritty MC romance and even some horror.

Claire lives in the United Kingdom with her husband, three daughters, and naughty rescue beagle, where she can be found whiling away her days taking long walks in the rain and smiling happily… just kidding! She's normally looking after her kids, running around after her naughty beagle, and chasing her dreams!

Author of:

Odium The Dead Saga Series
Odium Origins Series
Limerence (*The Obsession Series*)
Out of the Dark
Twisted Magic
Beautiful Victim
Blood Claim
Wrath #3 in the Elite Seven Series

Co–Authored Books with Madeline Sheehan:

Thicker than Blood
Beneath Blood & Bone
& Shut Up & Kiss me

MC Romance
Ride or Die a Devil's Highwaymen MC series
Devil's Highwaymen Nomad Series:
Crank #1
Sketch #2
Battle #3
Fighter #4
Cowboy #5

CONTACT LINKS:

Website:
www.clairecriley.com
Claire C. Riley FB page:
https://www.facebook.com/ClaireCRileyAuthor/
Amazon:
http://amzn.to/1GDpF3I
Group: Riley's Rebels:
https://www.facebook.com/groups/ClaireCRileyFansGroup/
Newsletter Sign-up:

https://clairecriley.us14.list-manage.com/subscribe?u=eda86431d68098539defc1e7b&id=4e6a3dd390

Ride or Die A Devil's Highwaymen Mc Novel

Printed in Great Britain
by Amazon